SAVANNAH DRAGON

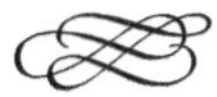

ALAN CHAPUT

ISBN: 978-1-947295-07-0

Savannah Sleuth (Book One): Patricia's darling mother, a prominent philanthropist, drops dead, and the police are baffled by her untimely death. Patricia recruits her three friends to help her investigate what she believes is murder. "Savannah Sleuth" is a page-turning journey from Savannah's Southern wealth and grace into the hidden corners of Savannah and across two continents in a deadly pursuit of justice.

Savannah Secrets (Book Two): When Patricia Falcon's husband Trey is kidnapped, she is plunged into a complex race that crosses continents and decades and will push her to her emotional and mental limits. Patricia's investigative talents are further challenged because her husband's ransom isn't money. Desperate to ensure the safe return of Trey, Patricia reaches out to a Catholic bishop, a local witch doctor, and two secret organizations hoping to piece together the clues she needs to find and deliver what the kidnappers want before it's too late.

Savannah Justice (Book Three): At the urging of a close friend, amateur sleuth Patricia Falcon investigates a massive, fast growing private investment plan and discovers serious irregularities that could shake the financial foundations of many of her friends and most of Savannah's major institutions. When things take a stunning turn, Patricia finds herself in the midst of something much more serious, and she may well be the prime suspect.

PROLOGUE

*D*r. Rebecca Cortez, dressed in hazmat gear, shuffled into the air-pressurized chamber of the Infectious Disease Laboratory in Athens, Georgia, to continue her testing of wild bird and sentinel chicken blood samples sent in from all over Georgia. Of particular concern to her was a blood sample from a Savannah Sparrow. The blood had initially tested positive for the highly lethal bird flu strain H5N1, but the H5N1 sample structure hadn't completely matched the three types of the virus normally seen. Today, she would start a more advanced test that could detect ten distinct strains of H5N1. The test was 100% accurate and would reveal results within a few hours.

Two hours later, Dr. Cortez stood in shock as she reviewed the test results for a second time. The sparrow blood didn't match any known H5N1 sequence. Had the lethal strain further mutated? Was *this* mutation the feared Disease X, a highly contagious strain that would freely spread lethal bird flu to humans? It had a hemagglutinin sequence that was already known to latch on to human trachea tissue. She called her contact at the Centers for Disease Control in Atlanta, who requested a blood sample, then set about to confirm her findings.

CHAPTER 1

It was a few minutes before sunset when Patricia Falcon exited the Hyatt Regency Savannah elevator on the sixth floor and walked to the corner suite where *Salon Li* did business.

As usual, Patricia would be Ken Li's only client tonight, so she wasn't surprised to see the hairdresser's lobby empty. Sometimes Ken would meet her at the door, but usually he would be in the salon making sure everything was perfect for her.

The lights were on in the back, and through the wall of floor-to-ceiling windows, she could see the last remnants of the orange sun on the horizon.

Patricia strode into the salon's workroom and froze.

Ken Li sat, unmoving, in a salon chair. A knife was plunged deep in his chest.

A short whimper of horror echoed in the silence, and Patricia realized it was her own. Her stomach clenched with nausea and ice-cold shock. Without thinking, she took a step toward her friend to see if she could help, even while knowing he was dead. Her survival instinct stopped her.

With shaking hands, she reached into her purse and pulled out her Kimber 45. Both hands on the weapon, she moved to Ken's side, eyes systematically scanning the room looking for movement Seeing none, she took one hand off her weapon and felt his neck for a pulse. Nothing. His skin wasn't cold. How long did that take anyway? Hours, if she remembered correctly. Had his death just happened? There was no sign of a struggle. The only wound seemed to be the knife in his chest.

Harsh mercury light from overhead glistened on the engraved golden hilt of the knife. Dragons with ruby eyes.

She grabbed her phone from her purse and called 911, then her husband. Once Trey answered, she paused to compose herself. "Ken Li has been killed. Right here in his shop."

"Are you okay?" Trey asked in a calm, authoritative voice that anchored her.

"It must have happened just before I arrived. But I'm an emotional wreck."

"Did you call 911?"

"Yes."

"Then get out of there now," Trey instructed. "I'll meet you downstairs in the hotel lobby."

She wanted to leave, but both physically and mentally, she couldn't. Fear kept her legs from cooperating, and her mind wanted to stay to protect whatever evidence remained. "I can't leave."

"If you're not getting out, what do you see?"

"Ken. In a chair. With a knife in his chest."

"Take a photo."

Patricia nodded, even though Trey couldn't see her. "I will."

"When the first responders come, move slowly and keep your hands over your head."

"Will do." She quickly took a photo of Ken, then put the phone back to her ear, looking around for somewhere to safely wait for first responders. "Okay. I have a photo."

"The first responders will get a statement from you. It could take a while."

"I know."

Trey blew out a strained breath. "Okay, Patsy. Count on your training. Please stay safe. If you even suspect someone is still there, get out. I'm going to hang up now so you can focus. I love you."

"I love you too." Patricia ended the call and slipped the phone back into her purse, getting two hands back on the gun. Then she ducked behind a workstation and waited.

Her ears prickled at every sound, causing her to flinch and look. A ping as the window glass contracted. Water passing in the pipes. A ding of a far-off elevator.

Her mind swam. She inhaled sharply. Ken's death would strike his wife, Cora, hard. Of that, Patricia was sure. Cora and Ken were so close they functioned as one. Now their precious partnership was gone, and Cora would have to face life alone. Sure, Cora had her children, but none of them could ever replace what Cora had in Ken.

Patricia brought a hand to her mouth. She so wished she could spare her good friend the heartrending pain and perpetual loneliness that was sure to come. Patricia swallowed the lump in her throat. She didn't know how to prevent Cora's pain. All Patricia knew to do was to stand by Cora through this for as long as it took for Cora's pain to become bearable.

If the killer was still in the salon, she needed to be rock steady to survive. Adrenaline pulsed through her arteries, but she couldn't let that get in the way of survival. Her training kicked in. She took a deep breath, then another, as she zeroed in on the job at hand and only that. She continued focused breathing. Though caution remained, fear diminished until her mounting curiosity overwhelmed her remaining fear.

Gun forward, she eased up and cautiously looked around for any obvious evidence of who had murdered her friend. The distinctive knife was a clue. She zoomed in her phone camera and took a closeup photo of the knife, as well as another photo of Ken slumped in the chair.

At the front door, she checked for forced entry and found nothing suspicious. She glanced at the cash drawer at the reception desk and found it intact. Careful not to disturb anything, she went into the kitchenette. All looked in order.

As she was returning to the workroom, the overhead lights went out, casting the room in dimness. A timer? Lighting system failure? Or did someone turn them off? Hyper-alert, she dropped to a crouch behind a counter. The only light came from the diminishing sunset through the wall of windows.

Was the killer still there? More adrenaline kicked in. For years, she had trained to fight and to shoot and to calm her emotions. Again, she fell back on focused breathing. She listened closely. There were no telltale sounds, but her heart continued thudding in her ears. Distant sirens sounded.

She had visited the salon countless times in the last twenty years and, despite the growing darkness, knew the layout well. There was nothing behind her but a wall. Two workstations stood to the right and one to the left, which she was tucked tight behind. The silhouette of the chair with Ken Li's body loomed large between her and the faint sunset showing through the large windows to the west.

The elevator at the end of the hall chimed. Her chest tightened. The killer leaving, or the police coming? She eased up a bit, searching the room with eyes now adjusted to the darkness. Nothing. She had cover behind the workstation and didn't want to move into the open, but sheltering in place could get her killed by a trigger-happy rookie cop charging in. If it was the police arriving, it would be better that she met them in the well-lit hall. Crouched and gun at the ready, Patricia made her way to the salon's lobby and peeked down the hall.

Patricia's close friend Chief Collin Patrick, a competent, cautious man, and two middle-aged men in civilian clothes were approaching with guns drawn. She didn't recognize the other two, but assumed they were detectives. She put her gun on the reception counter and, arms raised, eased into the hall.

"Collin," she said in a voice she didn't recognize. "Thank goodness you're here. Ken Li's been murdered, and the killer may still be here. I think he might have turned off the lights just minutes ago," Patricia jabbered, her voice loud, stressing a fearful warning.

"You can put your hands down, Patricia," Patrick said warmly.

"You don't normally respond to 911 calls," she said.

"We were meeting with the Saint Patrick's Day parade committee downstairs. Where's the body?" he asked, wariness in his eyes.

"In a chair in the back of the salon." She wrung her hands. "Through the second door. On the right."

Patrick made a call and told someone to post men at all exits of the hotel. The two detectives went in.

"What time did you discover the body?"

"No more than ten minutes ago. I called 911 immediately."

"Stay out here. We'll get a statement from you, then you can leave."

As more and more of his investigative team arrived, the

hall became her prison. But she couldn't leave until they took her statement.

After standing in the chaotic hall for a while, she was shown into an adjacent hotel room to wait to be interviewed. The suite was nicely furnished. The temperature was a bit chilly, but tolerable. The stillness was such a contrast to the chaos in the hall. It was good to get out of that depressing commotion.

But absent the many hallway distractions, latent emotional reactions to Ken's death quickly bubbled to the surface unimpeded. Sadness. Anger. Loss. Her chest tightened.

She'd never see Ken's ever-present smile again. Never hear his infectious laugh again. Gone forever were the wise discussions she so savored. Her lips quivered. She compressed her mouth to still them. Gone. What a sad, hollow word.

Patricia felt her composure slipping away again. She tried deep breathing to no avail. The far-reaching consequences of Ken's death continued to disturb her. She'd lost a close friend, but Ken's wife had lost a husband, so much more of a loss. Patricia couldn't imagine losing Trey. The pain. The chaos. The utter emptiness. Patricia had lost her mother a couple of years ago and that still hurt. A lot. But to lose Trey? Well, that was unimaginable. And yet, that terrible event was exactly what Cora was about to experience, and Patricia felt so helpless to do anything about it.

Patricia rummaged through her purse, pulled out a tissue and dabbed her eyes.

There was a knock.

She went to the door. "Who is it?"

"Detective Rodriquez, Chatham Police."

She opened the door.

Detective Rodriquez, dressed in faded jeans and a black

golf shirt, entered, hand extended. His longish black hair flopped over his face, and he brushed the hair out of his dark eyes. "Good evening, Mrs. Falcon. Nice to see you again. Though I wish it could have been under better circumstances."

She took his hand. "Nice to see you as well, Detective. And please call me Patricia."

He nodded. "Patricia."

"What can I do for you?"

"Chief Patrick assigned me to the Ken Li case. I understand you were the person who found the body."

Sadness swelled. She nodded, unable to find any words.

"I'm sorry you had to go through that. I'm sure you're eager to get home." He gestured to the sofa. "If you'd like to sit down, we can get started on your statement." As Patricia settled on the sofa, Rodriquez pulled the chair from the desk and sat in front of her. "Do you need some water or something?"

"I'm fine."

Rodriquez put a pocket recorder on the table between them and turned it on. "March 4th. Seven-thirty. Hyatt Regency. Room 644. Interview with Mrs. Falcon. Please state your full name for the recording."

"Patricia Falcon."

"Thank you." He pulled a small notebook from his pocket and put it on the table next to the recorder. "Let's get a timeline established. What time did you arrive at the salon tonight?"

"Six-fifteen. Maybe a bit later."

Rodriquez pulled out a pen and made a note. "Why were you here?"

"It was my monthly hair appointment with Ken."

"That's an unusually late appointment."

"We always did it that way. Ken is-was-a friend. Once a

month, he'd keep his salon open a bit late for me. We'd chat, have a glass of champagne, and he'd do my hair. The sunset from there is beautiful. I don't know if I'm the only client he gave a special appointment to, but I looked forward to it every month. He is-was-a special man. Very talented."

The detective made a note. "When you arrived tonight, what exactly did you see?"

Patricia stared down at her hands, momentarily unable to answer. The void Ken's death had left was just too great to face. She inhaled deeply. The sooner she answered these questions, the sooner the interview would be over. She looked up. "I saw Ken in the chair with a knife in his chest."

Rodriquez made another note. "Did you see anyone else?"

"No."

Rodriquez's black eyes narrowed. "Was that unusual?"

"Yes."

"How?"

"Ken's receptionist, Lily, is usually here."

"But not tonight."

"Correct."

"Tell me again exactly what you saw."

Patricia closed her eyes to help her concentrate. As painful as it might become, she forced her mind to the moment of discovery. She had exceptional powers of obser-vation and hoped her memory could recall something of value to the detective. "Ken. Seated upright in a salon chair. Head slumped forward. An elaborately decorated knife plunged to the hilt just left of center of his chest. Engraved gold handle. Dragons with ruby eyes. Not much blood on his short-sleeved blue shirt." She paused to further focus on the image lodged in her mind. "No visible defensive wounds on his arms or hands. No tears on his shirt. No other wounds visible. Both arms hung loose to either side." She hesitated to shift her focus. "No blood on the floor beneath Ken. Just his phone." She opened her eyes and looked at Rodriquez. "I recall wondering how Ken could bleed out with so little blood on or around him."

"Yeah. We have the same question. Did you touch or move anything? The body. The chair. The phone."

"I checked for a pulse. Finding none, I called 911."

"You didn't touch or move anything else?"

"Correct. Oh wait. I pulled my gun in case the killer was still there *before* I checked for a pulse. After finding no pulse, I called 911 and my husband. Then I checked the lobby and breakroom for an intruder. As I was returning to the workroom, the lights went out, so I took a defensive position behind a workstation and waited for first responders."

Rodriquez's eyebrows raised. "I'm told you were in the salon lobby when the chief arrived."

"Yes. When I heard the elevator chime, I went to the lobby, put my weapon on the reception desk, and stood in plain sight with my arms up."

"Did you hear anything unusual while you were waiting for the first responders?"

Patricia tried to recall. "No. I don't think so. Natural sounds like the elevator, the windows against the wind. Nothing that seemed unusual."

"Were you and Mr. Li on good terms?"

Patricia bit her lip. She still couldn't accept Ken was gone. Her chin trembled. She turned away and stared unseeing into space, taking one deep breath after another. Once she regained her composure, she returned her gaze to Rodriquez. "Yes. He was a close friend for twenty years. I also know his wife very well and know most of his fourteen children."

"Did Mr. Li and his wife get along?"

"As far as I know, they were best friends. Ken always spoke highly of Cora, as did she of him."

"Did you ever see them argue?"

"Never."

"Do you know of anyone who might want to kill Mr. Li?"

She paused to make sure she didn't overlook anything. "Not a soul. Ken was kind to all and beloved by most."

Rodriquez switched off the recorder and stood. "Thank you, Patricia. You can leave now."

"I know you're exceptionally busy, Detective, especially with all the events surrounding Saint Patrick's Day. If I can be of any assistance what-so-ever on this case, don't hesitate to let me know."

"I appreciate that." He gave her a rare smile. "From experience, I know you're an excellent investigator. If I need the extra eyes, I might take you up on your offer."

Heaven had gained a magnificent new angel in Ken, but his precious wife and children had lost a devoted husband and father. Such a loss for them. Sadness swelled. "Who's going to tell Cora about her husband's death?"

"I am. I'm going over there now to notify her and take her initial statement."

Patricia took a deep breath. "Cora is a close friend. I'd like to go with you and be there when you tell her."

He nodded.

CHAPTER 2

"That's my car," Rodriquez said to Patricia.

They stepped out of the Hyatt Hotel lobby into the unseasonably warm evening air and waited for the valet to bring the Chevy Impala to a stop.

"I appreciate you letting me come with you to break the news to Cora," Patricia said. "She'll need all the support she can get tonight."

The valet popped out of the car and waited for Rodriquez. The doorman rushed to the passenger side and opened the door for Patricia.

She slid into the Impala. As the door closed and quiet settled over her, Patricia was suddenly aware of being thoroughly drained from the emotional turmoil of the past hour or so. Utterly depleted, she leaned her head back on the headrest.

Rodriquez got in, started the car, and pulled onto Bay Street. His head and shoulders were a black silhouette against the well-lit city street.

Patricia massaged her tense, tired shoulders, finding some relief. Knowing all too well the evening's emotional rollercoaster was far from over, she needed to take full advantage of whatever peace she could find. But first, she needed to let Trey know where she was.

She turned on her phone and noticed she'd missed a call. She checked call history and found Lily Li, Ken's receptionist, had called at five. There was no associated voicemail, so Patricia assumed it was probably just a confirmation of her appointment.

Patricia texted Trey to let him know she was done at the Hyatt, was on her way to Cora's, and might be late coming home. She returned her phone to her purse just as Rodriquez pulled the Impala into the parking lot behind the Li's Barnard Street building. "How are you doing?" she asked Rodriquez.

"Death notification is the hardest part of my job." Rodriquez turned down the radio music. A smooth jazz. Soft. Soothing. "I'm glad you're along."

"I just realized there was something unusual about the salon tonight," Patricia said. "The music wasn't on. Ken always had relaxing oriental music during my visits. And the aromatic candles weren't lit. No music. No candles. No ambience. Not like Ken. I'm sorry I forgot that detail."

"That's okay. It happens all the time. That's one of the main reasons we interview people multiple times." Rodriquez brushed hair from his eyes. "During our discussion at the hotel, you mentioned you hid because you were concerned the killer was still in the salon. Why was that?"

"Initially, I was just being cautious. When I settled down, I left my safety spot and did a sweep of the lobby and breakroom. On my way back to the workroom, the lights suddenly went out. Just the salon lights. I could see the hotel hallway lights were still on. Right or wrong, I concluded it was possible the killer had turned the lights off, so I sought cover immediately."

"But you'd just done a sweep?"

"Yes."

"Hmm. Does the salon have a coat or equipment closet?"

Patricia whipped her face to him. "Yes. Both. And I didn't think to check either."

"You did the right thing to hide."

She massaged her forehead.

"Are you alright?" he asked.

She shook her head. "I'm worn out. Aftershock, I guess."

He nodded toward the building. "What's coming next will be even tougher."

A chill went through her. "I know. But we'll manage. For Cora's sake, we have to."

"Are you ready?"

Dread stirred in the pit of Patricia's stomach. "As ready as I'll ever be."

He turned off the car. They got out and crossed the parking lot to the entrance. Patricia pushed the button marked *inquiries,* gave her and Rodriquez's names, and the door lock released with a loud click. Rodriquez pulled open the heavy steel door and stood aside.

Patricia stepped into the huge, dimly lit lower lobby of Ken and Cora's penthouse. Though she'd been there many times, the luxurious ambience of the oriental-themed room never ceased to impress her.

A massive golden Buddha sat in one corner, flanked by golden temple dog statues. The vaulted ceiling seemed to go on forever. Floor-to-ceiling murals with columns in the foreground and stark mountains in the distance covered both side walls. Cora once told Patricia the murals were intended to give the feeling of being inside a temple looking out at the countryside where the Li ancestors lived. A light aroma of incense added to the illusion.

Directly in front of Patricia and Rodriquez was a replica

antique elevator fashioned after one in the Hong Kong building Ken Li once worked in. The ornate brass outer cage featured lotus blossoms.

They got to the elevator just as the teak car arrived. Rodriquez opened the door of the brass cage, they went into the car, and Patricia punched the upper of two buttons. The car only serviced the fourth-floor penthouse. As the car slowly rose, Patricia glanced out the beveled-glass windows at the elaborately decorated elevator shaft-mythical animals from China's past cavorting in mountain valleys.

Cora Li, dressed in a knee-length mint silk dress, was waiting for them at the top. Her gray hair was arranged in a neat bun. She looked regal and ageless.

Though it wasn't the Chinese way, Patricia gave Cora a big hug which Cora returned in kind. Cora had graciously accepted most Western customs years ago.

"Sorry to disturb you," Patricia whispered, overcome with sadness knowing the tragic message they were about to deliver.

Cora stepped back and ushered them into her home.

Patricia and Rodriquez followed her into the penthouse foyer. An altar with cut flowers, fresh fruit and joss sticks stood in one corner. Several ancestral photos were hung on the wall over a shrine beside the altar. Cora had told Patricia who each person was some time ago. Most were Ken's deceased forebearers. Patricia was struck by a deep sense of sadness at the thought his picture would soon be on the wall of reverence.

"I thought Ken had an appointment with you tonight," Cora said.

Patricia's throat tightened. She took Cora's hand and stroked it. "I ... I'm afraid we have bad news."

Cora brought her other hand to her mouth.

Patricia took a deep breath, folded an arm around Cora, and looked at Rodriquez.

"Mrs. Li, your husband is"-he tensed-"is dead."

"No. That's impossible," Cora said angrily voice.

Patricia stroked Cora's back. "I'm sorry, Cora. It's true."

Cora's wail could have been heard in China. Patricia had expected as much, having been with Cora through the loss of her youngest son.

When Cora's knees started to buckle, Patricia steadied her and drew Cora tighter to her as her friend's anguish continued in convulsions, sobs, and moans.

After several painful minutes, Cora wiped her eyes. "Wha ... what happened?"

"Is there somewhere where we can sit?" Rodriquez asked.

"Of course." Cora led them down a hall to a study.

Rodriquez waited for Cora to sit on a heavily padded sofa that seemed to swallow her tiny frame. After Patricia settled next to her, Rodriquez sat in an upholstered chair across from them.

"So, what exactly happened, Detective?" Cora asked in a sad, quiet voice.

"I'm afraid, well, we believe he was killed," Rodriquez said. "At the salon. We're treating this as a murder."

"Killed? How?"

"He was stabbed, ma'am."

Cora's tear-streaked, flushed face morphed to tight lips and fiery eyes. Her brow furrowed. Rage personified. "Who would do such a thing? Why?"

"We don't know," Rodriquez said. "We are still investigating, but—"

"Where is my husband? I need to see him."

"His body is still at the salon."

"I need to see him."

"I'm afraid you can't yet. We'll have to take your

husband's body to the morgue," he said, his voice gentle. "You'll be able to see him there."

Cora seemed to understand.

"If you don't mind, I'd like to ask you a few questions," Rodriquez said. He removed a small notebook from his pocket, opened it to a blank page, and placed it on the coffee table in front of the couch.

Ah Tim, the Li's maid, appeared.

"Is there anything you'd like?" Cora asked. "A drink? Perhaps a snack?"

Patricia took Cora's hand. "No, thank you."

"That's very nice of you," Rodriquez said. "But I'm fine."

"That will be all," Cora said to Ah Tim.

Rodriquez took a recorder from his shirt pocket and placed it next to the notebook. "We need as much information as possible, as soon as possible, to try to track down who killed your husband. I know it's a difficult time, but the more we know the better. Do you feel up to that?"

Cora straightened. "I'm ready to do anything necessary to speed the apprehension of the person responsible for my husband's death."

"Okay." Rodriquez reached for the recorder and turned it on. "March 4th. Eight-thirty. Barnard Street Building. Penthouse. Interview with Mrs. Li. Please state your full name for the recording."

"Cora Li," she said in a clear but faint voice. Not her usual authoritative tone.

"Thank you." He pulled a pen from his pocket. "When did you last see your husband?"

Despite the simple first question, Patricia feared this would become a long and torturous interview for Cora. She stroked the top of Cora's hand.

"As was our custom, Ken and I had dinner in the restaurant downstairs at five. He left for the salon at five forty-five."

Rodriquez made a note. "Do you know how he traveled to the salon tonight?"

"Weather permitting, he normally would walk." She paused as if deep in thought or grief … or both. "But no, I don't know with certainty how he traveled to the salon tonight."

"Does the restaurant have security cameras that will show him departing?"

Cora nodded. "The entire building has a closed-circuit television security system that shows everything outside the building for up to one hundred feet."

"I'll need a copy of those videos," Rodriquez said.

Cora nodded ever so slightly, picked up a phone from the table next to her, and sent someone a message. Moments later, she glanced down at the screen. "My security chief will bring it as soon as possible."

"Thank you. What did you do after your husband left?"

"My son Luke owns the restaurant. He came to the table after Ken left and had tea with me. Oh my. How will I tell the children?" Cora's face crumpled, and she let out a series of quiet sobs, her head bowed.

Patricia rubbed her back until Cora could regain control again.

Finally, Cora dabbed her eyes and lifted her head. "I'm sorry."

"No need to apologize, Mrs. Li," Rodriquez said softly. "I know this is difficult, but when did you leave the restaurant?"

Cora stared into space. "Probably around six thirty."

"Where did you go after dinner?"

"Here."

"Was anyone here with you?"

"Just Ah Tim, my maid."

Rodriquez cleared his throat. "Did you remain home until we came to your door?"

"Yes. I was reading a novel by Natasha Boyd." Outwardly, Cora now appeared the picture of control. Only the tapping of her right foot gave any evidence of her inner turmoil.

"I realize this is quite a strain for you, Mrs. Li," Rodriquez said. "Do you mind if I go on?"

Though Cora's shoulders had slumped, and her language had slowed during Rodriquez's questioning, she straightened. "To tell you the truth, I'm drained. And I still need to call the children." Her chin wobbled. "But I want you to have everything you feel you need from me. And I want you to have it as soon as possible. So drained or not, let's move on."

Patricia admired the iron determination of her friend.

"Okay," Rodriquez said. "Do you know of anyone at all who might want to hurt or kill your husband?"

Cora inhaled deeply, then interlaced her hands. "No."

A very large Asian man appeared in the doorway.

"My security chief, Chen Ming," Cora explained. She beckoned to the man.

Chen crossed the room to Cora, said something in Chinese and handed her a thumb drive, then departed.

Cora offered the drive to Rodriquez. "Tonight's security videos."

"Mrs. Li's security chief, Chen Ming, has provided closed circuit footage on a thumb drive at," Rodriquez glanced at his wristwatch, "nine-oh-two." Rodriquez took the drive offered by Cora and slipped it into a small evidence envelope. "Thank you," he said as he pocketed the drive. "Do you know if anyone has threatened your husband?"

Cora's brow furrowed. "No. I don't know if he has been threatened."

"Does your husband have enemies?"

Cora took some time before she answered. "Not that I know of. As far as I know everyone loves-loved-Ken."

"I'm sorry, but I have to ask, did your husband have any problems?"

"Problems?"

"Yes, like vices. Drinking, drugs, gambling."

Cora sat back. "Heavens no."

"Again, I'm sorry, but how was your marriage?"

Patricia, sensing Cora's turmoil, swallowed, wondering if she should even be present for these invasive questions.

Cora shot a questioning look Patricia's way.

"Cora, why don't I wait in the other room while you answer these personal questions. I'll be here for you afterward."

"No. Please stay." Cora's eyes searched Patricia's. "It's just that it makes me uncomfortable to talk about my marriage. It's so … personal."

Patricia gave Cora's hand a gentle, reassuring squeeze, then turned to Rodriquez. "Maybe you could reserve that question for another day?"

Rodriquez nodded.

"Another day?" Cora asked, sharply. "No. Let's get this done tonight. About our marriage." She paused. "I can't think of anything that would be problematic. All marriages have their ups and downs, but we were okay."

"How did Mr. Li get along with your children?"

"He loved them with all his heart and soul."

"Who would benefit in any way from Mr. Li's death?" His words were spoken soft and slow.

"Our daughter Lily would inherit ownership of the hair salon. Our son Luke would become the family patriarch." Cora stared off into space. "And I suppose I would benefit from inheriting his wealth."

Rodriquez turned off the recorder, pocketed it, and stood.

"That will be it for tonight, Mrs. Li. Thank you for your cooperation."

Patricia walked with Cora and Rodriquez to the elevator.

At the elevator, Rodriquez said, "At some point, Mrs. Li, I'll have to speak with each of your children." He handed her a business card. "Please email me their contact information as soon as possible."

As Patricia reached for the elevator gate, Cora touched her shoulder. "Would you stay a bit longer?" Cora asked.

"Of course." Heartbroken for Cora, Patricia stepped back from the elevator.

Rodriquez said his goodbyes and left.

After they returned to the sitting room, Patricia asked, "Would you like me to contact your children?" She knew the children all lived in Savannah.

"Thank you, Patricia. It's best I call them. Would you mind staying until Luke comes? Being the eldest, he'll know what to do. This is all so … so sudden. So confusing."

"Yes. Of course."

Cora pulled her phone from the side table and made a sobbing call, entirely in Chinese. As she returned the phone, she looked at Patricia with bloodshot eyes. "Luke is … he is on his way up. He'll handle everything. He's such a strong, honorable man. Just like …" She to a moment to catch her breath. "His father." Cora's tone was firm. Her flushed face had morphed from grim to stoic. The matriarch. The dowager. An outward tower of strength. It was as if she'd set aside her anguish in preparation for that of her children.

"Ah Tim has tea brewing." Cora wiped her eyes with a tissue. "Would you care for some while we wait for Luke?"

"Yes. Please." Patricia knew it wasn't about the tea. It was about structure. Ceremony. Something familiar Cora could anchor on.

As if on cue, Ah Tim brought the tea service in, darting a concerned expression toward her employer before she left.

"I'll have to let the staff know too," Cora said, as the door closed behind her maid. "They will be devastated. They have been with us for so long they are like family."

Cora poured fragrant jasmine tea from a cast-iron pot into delicate, blue willow teacups. Patricia glanced around the room as Cora poured. In one corner, a fountain cascaded water into a basin. Orchids filled several tabletops. No surprise as Cora was the president of the Savannah Orchid Society. Two of Ken's miniature *penjing* trees sat atop an ornate teak chest. He called them 'tray scenery'.

Cora returned the pot to the tray, offered one cup to Patricia, then sat motionless, staring into space. A tear escaped and trickled like a dew drop down her pale, flower petal cheek. Despite her effort to keep up appearances, reality hung like a shroud.

Patricia fought back a lump in her throat. A great man had died. Husband. Father. Civic leader. Close friend. The evening's events weighed heavily on Patricia. Though there was a burning behind her eyes, out of respect for Cora, she held her feelings inside.

Cora draped an arm around Patricia's shoulder. "He loved you like one of his daughters."

Luke, dressed in black slacks and a short-sleeved white shirt, strode into the room.

Cora and Patricia stood.

Luke took his mother in his arms and gave her a long hug. They spoke briefly in Chinese, then Cora began to sob.

"I should be going," Patricia said.

Luke looked at Patricia and nodded. "Thank you, Mrs. Falcon, for staying with my mother. Your kindness means so much to us."

Cora, her checks streaked with tear trails, stepped back

from Luke, moved to Patricia, and gave her a hug. "Thank you," Cora said, her voice barely a whisper. "Call me tomorrow. Please. I have something important to discuss with you."

"Certainly."

Cora walked Patricia to the elevator, where they said their goodbyes.

As the elevator descended, Patricia pondered Cora's strange parting words, and something uneasy settled on top of the grief of the evening.

CHAPTER 3

*P*atricia's taxi pulled to the front of the Hyatt Regency. She paid the driver and left the cab. The cool night air had an instantaneous cleansing effect on Patricia's troubled mind as the soft breeze seemed to momentarily sweep her grief away.

Then it all came back. Her mind teemed with a tsunami of emotions. Grief. Sorrow. Isolation. Loss. Emptiness. And the surreal images of Ken sitting in the chair and Cora wailing were stuck in her mind, like the image of her mother's funeral. Patricia's throat tightened.

She walked over to the valet desk and handed the attendant her ticket. Moments later, he was back with her Navigator. It only took ten minutes to drive home. She stepped out of her SUV, left the detached garage, and headed down the path to the house, where she unlatched the back door. A low hum reminded her the security system had detected her entrance.

As she walked into the kitchen, she felt anticipation to be in Trey's arms. He was the healing light at the end of her current grief tunnel. She so wanted to snuggle into and linger in the warmth and safety of his embrace. And, after that, to sit quietly in the same room with him. A familiar, peaceful place with no threats.

"I'm home," she shouted from the kitchen, noticing and appreciating the beautiful bouquet on the table.

Trey met her in the hallway and took her in his arms. "I'm so sorry you're going through this, Patsy." He rubbed her back.

Connectedness filled her. It was exactly what she needed. Safety. Security. She inhaled his familiar pine scent and nestled deeply into him, lingering in the tranquility, immobilized by her need, totally absorbed in the moment.

Then reality hit. This very experience, that meant so much to her, was something Cora would no longer have with Ken. And with that thought, Patricia's tranquility was shattered. When she stepped back from Trey, she could already see the questions in his eyes.

She let out a sob. "I can't stop thinking about Cora. And I can't imagine losing you."

"Do you want to talk about what happened?"

"Can we not talk about it tonight? I'm just too raw. I don't want to relive it right now."

"Of course," he said as he led her down the hall to the reading room where they spent most of their evenings.

She knew Trey could get all the case facts from his friend Chief Patrick, if he hadn't already done so. And she knew the police investigative team certainly knew far more than she. So she didn't feel bad about keeping Trey in the dark because she wasn't really doing that. She was just protecting herself, and she knew he understood.

He paused as they entered the reading room. "If you'd like, I'll draw you a warm bath. Or if you're not ready for that, I'll get you a drink."

"Thank you. But I'm going to pass on the bath and alcohol."

"Would you like something to eat? A snack? Pimento cheese? A tomato sandwich? Leopold's ice cream?"

"Oh, Trey, you're so thoughtful. But no, thank you."

"Herbal tea?"

She gave a nod. "Now that sounds great."

"Any particular tea?"

"Peppermint would be perfect."

"Coming up," he said, then headed for the kitchen.

She slowly walked to her chair and sat. She drew a long breath, closed her eyes, and leaned her head back, seeking without finding the calm she'd enjoyed moments before in Trey's arms. Though gone, the elusive tranquility still cast its shadow, and her need was great.

Patricia kicked off her shoes. She'd sit for a while and drink tea, then suggest they go to bed, where she'd cuddle close to Trey. Hopefully, the tranquility would return there to settle her need. Her troubled mind took solace in that.

She opened her eyes at the sound of Trey returning from the kitchen. He handed her a steaming mug.

"What time do you want to head upstairs?" he asked as he sat, mug in hand.

"After I finish this tea. Maybe fifteen or twenty minutes."

He nodded.

A HALF HOUR LATER, PATRICIA STEPPED INTO THE SHOWER AND sighed with relief as the warm water pelted her tense body. She didn't normally take a shower before bed, but she figured the diversion might help her shake off the evening's tragic experience. She set the shower heads on 'pulse' and let the water massage her tight shoulders. Then she soaped up and washed off the grime of the evening. If only she could wash off the images of Ken sitting in that chair and of Cora wailing.

She spent a good fifteen minutes in the luxurious indulgence of the shower and got out feeling much less tense and decidedly refreshed. She slipped into clean pajamas and went into the bedroom.

Trey looked up from his phone. "Do you feel better?"

She dipped her chin in a nod. "Definitely."

He scooted to the center of the bed and lifted the covers on her side, inviting her in. She turned off the bed light, slipped into bed, and cuddled close to him. Everything converged. Him. Her. Peace. Security. His strength. Her need.

Trey's breathing slowed as he drifted off to sleep. Sleep was always easy for him. Not because he was chronically tired, but rather because he was a master of relaxation. She hoped one day some of that would rub off on her. So far, so good. She kept her mind focused on Trey, savoring every nuance of their closeness. The slow rise and fall of his chest. The solidness of his curves. The warmth of his skin. His pine scent.

Serenity.

Patricia woke with a start well past her normal waking time the following morning. She was still tucked in beside Trey. It wasn't the weekend. Why was he still in bed?

She tapped his shoulder. "Trey. It's eight o'clock."

He turned on his back and blinked his eyes. "Okay."

"You overslept."

"No, I'm taking the day off." He sat up on the side of the bed.

She rolled on her back. Images of last night washed through her, making her cringe. The overhead fan washed cool air over her face. After a night of cuddling against him,

Patricia suddenly felt different. The warmth was gone, as well as the peace that came from the warmth. "Why'd you take the day off?"

He turned to face her with a delightful smile. "I didn't want you to wake up alone."

"That's so sweet of you. Thank you."

"My pleasure." He gave her a kiss. "Would you like to go out for breakfast?"

"I'd love to." This thoughtful man had already made the morning as perfect as she could have wished.

The new day brought with it new purpose and fresh opportunities. Chief among them was to get back to Cora on the matter she had mentioned, though that could wait until after breakfast, when she was fed and could give Cora her full attention. Equally important, Patricia wanted to check on Cora's well-being.

Trey shuffled to the bathroom and turned on the shower. Patricia followed.

Once they had completed their morning tasks and dressed, they went downstairs. She fed the two feral cats who had made the Falcon patio their home, then they headed for the garage.

"Thank you for being so understanding last night," she said as Trey backed the Bentley from the garage.

"You're welcome."

"I know I have to talk about last night, because the more we talk, the more I'll recall and maybe come up with something important to help solve the crime."

"Now?"

"Not quite yet, but soon."

"Sure." He guided the Bentley into traffic. "Where would you like to go for breakfast?"

"I don't know," she said. "Where would you like to go?"

"It's your day, Patsy. What do you feel like having? Something familiar? Chicken and waffles? Biscuits and gravy? Ham and grits?"

"No, I'd like to do something new. Different."

"Didn't you tell me Meredith recently found a French creperie."

Patricia paused in thought. "Yes. A place called *Le Café Gourmet*. Helen is the owner. Meredith said the food was great."

"Sounds perfect," he said. "Let's give it a try."

Patricia googled the restaurant, found the directions tab, and hit *start*. Five minutes later, Trey deftly pulled the Bentley into a parking space. They got out and headed down the block to *Le Café Gourmet*.

The small restaurant was busy, and there was a bit of a wait. Something you'd expect of a well-regarded facility. Before too long, they were shown to a nice, tile-topped table at one of the front windows. A waitress brought water and menus. A few minutes later, the woman returned. "Do you have any questions about the menu?" she asked, her English carrying a pleasant French accent. Meredith had said the female owner often served guests.

"Are you Helen?" Patricia asked.

"Yes, *Madame*."

"We're heard marvelous things about your food."

Helen smiled. "Is this your first visit?"

"Yes. It was recommended to me by my friend Meredith."

"Wonderful. Let me point out that we make everything from scratch and use the best available ingredients. We import the flour for our crepes from France." Helen removed an order pad and pen from her spotless apron. "How might I serve you?"

Patricia ordered the Gourmet White crepe and a latte. Trey ordered a ham and brie crepe and a French press coffee.

After Helen left, Patricia said, "What a charming place, and I can't wait to try their food."

"Hungry?"

"Very."

"Me too."

Their coffees came right away. Patricia sipped her rich, delicious latte and, from a distance, watched Helen pour batter on the round griddle at the counter. Five minutes later, their crepes arrived. True to Meredith's review, they were awesome.

Once they finished eating, they ordered more coffee and talked for a while about the various Saint Patrick's Day parties they'd been invited to attend. There were more than they could possibly fit in so, as always, they narrowed their choices to two galas and a couple of house parties. Patricia found the conversation comforting, much as she had found the breakfast.

After breakfast, they walked hand-in-hand to City Market.

Along the way, Trey squeezed her hand. "I'd give anything for you to not have witnessed what you did last night. But I'm so grateful you arrived when you did and not earlier. Murderers don't leave witnesses."

A chill went through her. "Well, I'm not sure the murderer wasn't still there."

"What?"

"It was weird. The lights went out. I thought I had looked everywhere before they went out, but I was nervous and just looking for clues. I think there was a supply closet I didn't check."

"The lights went out after you arrived?"

"Yes. But shortly after they went out, the police arrived. They made a thorough search and didn't find anyone still around."

"Yeah, that does sound weird," Trey said. "How about Cora? Were her kids with her?"

"No. I waited with her until Luke, her eldest, arrived. Then she said the oddest thing. She said she needed to speak with me today, and I have a feeling it was something she didn't want to say in front of Detective Rodriquez."

"Patsy, be careful."

"I know, Trey. I will."

Patricia glanced at her phone. Ten thirty. Cora hadn't specified when she'd like to talk, but Patricia sensed it should be soon. "I should check on Cora in any event. See how she's doing." Patricia took a steadying breath, squeezing her husband's hand. "I can't imagine what waking up was like for her this morning."

They completed a full circuit of City Market and then headed back to the Bentley. Once they settled into the car, Trey asked Patricia, "Is there anything else you'd like to do before we head back to home?"

"I'm ready to go home," she softly said. "Thank you so much for making this morning perfect."

"You're welcome." Trey stared the Bentley and pulled into traffic.

"When we get home, I'm going to call Cora. I'd like to visit and give her some additional one-on-one support, which I'm sure she needs."

"That's thoughtful of you." His voice was deep and calm.

"I'm just hoping to repay a portion of what the Li family has given to me over the years." Cautious by nature, an uneasy feeling descended on Patricia. She hoped that was all attending to Cora would entail.

CHAPTER 4

As soon as they got home from breakfast, she called Cora.

"Good morning, Cora. It's Patricia."

"Oh. Hello, Patricia," Cora said in a flat voice that was so unlike her. "I was expecting a call from the funeral home. If I don't keep busy, I'll ... Well, I don't want to think about that."

Patricia gritted her teeth imagining how Cora must have felt waking up. "I'm so sorry, Cora. Is the anything I can do to help with arrangements?"

"The kids are helping. Thank goodness we have each other."

"And how are they all doing?"

"As well as can be expected. Luke has taken charge for which I'm so grateful. I was wondering though if you had a moment to pop over?"

"That's actually the reason I'm calling. You mentioned last night needing to talk with me."

"Do you know when you might come over?"

"How about now?"

"I'd *love* that," Cora said. "We can talk about the matter I mentioned last night."

"About that—"

"It'd be better done in person," Cora said in a hushed voice.

"I understand. I'll be right over." Patricia's mind raced to think of some dish she could take with her. There was nothing suitable in the refrigerator, and since she was leaving right away, it was too late to cook up something.

"When you come over, don't come in through the first-floor lobby. Go to the Ellis Square Garage. Go down to level three. Find parking space Z949. It's a reserved space. Park there. My security chief will meet you and bring you in."

"Why all the—"

"I'll explain when you get here. Trust me. It's for your protection."

A chill swept through Patricia. She swallowed back the emotion as she completed the call, made a note of the parking space number, and headed to the great room to let Trey know she was off to Cora's.

The doorbell rang.

Wondering who it could be, she scurried down the hall, unlocked the deadbolts, and opened the door to see her florist, Sheila Ainsworth. Sheila's yellow shirt dress was covered with a spotless white apron, and her smile was as bright as her dress.

Patricia's morning had been so busy, she'd forgotten it was the day Sheila delivered her weekly display for the foyer. "Good morning, Sheila."

"Morning, Patricia. I came by earlier, but you weren't here." Sheila stepped into the foyer and removed the spent arrangement from the table.

"I'm sorry. I forgot about the delivery. Trey and I went out for breakfast."

"Sounds like fun."

"It was."

Sheila took the old flowers to her van and returned with a dazzling display of yellow Fuji mums and bright green ferns.

"They look lovely," Patricia said as Sheila placed the huge bouquet on the foyer table.

"I was looking for something bright and cheerful to celebrate the arrival of warmer weather." Sheila puttered with the flowers. "Oh, by the way, an Asian man stopped by my shop an hour ago and seemed quite interested in you."

Patricia blinked. "Did he give you a name?"

"No." Sheila removed a damaged fern and put it in a pocket of her apron. "He asked about what kind of flowers you enjoyed and how long you've lived in the neighborhood. That kind of stuff."

Patricia wondered if the man's interested in her had something to do with Ken Li's murder. "Was he a detective or maybe a reporter?"

Sheila shook her head. "I honestly don't know. He didn't offer any identification."

Rattled that someone was checking up on her, Patricia took a calming breath. "What did you tell him?"

"Since he was a stranger, I didn't tell him anything."

"That's it?"

Sheila nodded. "Oh. He did ask if you have children."

Patricia shuddered. "Did you mention Hayley?"

"No."

An uncomfortable silence hung while Patricia contemplated next steps. "Do you have video security at your shop?"

"Sure do. Just got a new system."

"Would you mind making a copy of his visit for me?"

"No problem."

Patricia looked at her phone. "I have a meeting I have to

go to, Sheila. Thanks for letting me know about your inquisitive visitor. If he shows up again, try to get a name."

"Will do."

Once Sheila left, Patricia closed the front door, told Trey she was on the way to Cora's and headed out.

As Patricia drove to Ellis Square, she tried to figure out what was so important that Cora needed to speak to her and exactly why Patricia had to visit in such an unorthodox way. Cora had said it was for Patricia's protection. Did Cora know or have suspicions of who might have killed Ken? If so, why not tell the police? Nothing made sense, but somehow all this was connected, and she couldn't wait to find out how.

Patricia took a parking ticket at the Ellis Square garage entrance and drove down to the third floor. It took a while, but she finally found the Z949 parking space, and sure enough, Cora's burly security chief, Chen Ming, was waiting for her. She wondered if Cora always had this level of protection or if was it new after Ken's murder?

She parked the Navigator and followed Chen to a steel double-door in the concrete block wall. After surveying the dim parking lot behind them, he punched in numbers on a security panel, opened the door to a brightly lit concrete block hall, and gestured Patricia to enter. The door clunked closed once both had stepped inside.

The air in the long, wide tunnel was cool. The walls were painted yellow. Florescent lights covered the ceiling punctuated with closed-circuit television cameras. One way in. One way out. Nowhere for danger to hide.

Patricia's shoes clicked on the concrete floor. At the end of the hall, Chen Ming punched in a code and pulled open a second steel door to reveal a storage room. From the looks of things, it was where Luke Li stored dry goods for the restaurant. They walked through the storage room and down a narrow hall to a sprawling kitchen.

As they entered the chaotic space, busy cooks parted to allow Patricia and her escort to move through. She smiled at each and nodded as she passed them. The kitchen smelled heavenly, rich with Asian spices. Chinese versions of American country music blared from overhead speakers. At one side of the kitchen was a freight elevator that Patricia assumed would give them access to Cora's home.

Chen Ming pushed the call button and soon they were on the way up. On the second floor, apparently another dry goods warehouse of some sort, they transferred to a second, fancier elevator of teak, brass, and beveled glass, similar to the one Patricia normally used to visit Cora. The elevator took them to the fourth floor, where Cora, dressed in a black cheongsam, stood. Her eyes were red. Her shoulders slumped. She looked sad and fragile.

As soon as Patricia stepped from the elevator car, she gave her friend a warm hug.

The massive security man disappeared wordlessly into the quarters.

"I'm so pleased you came," Cora said as she led Patricia through the corridors into the household. "We have so much to discuss."

At the end of a long hall, Cora opened a carved mahogany door and gestured Patricia into a small sitting room with a sofa and two large stuffed chairs. Heavy drapes were pulled aside, bathing the ornate room in sunshine.

When Cora indicated the sofa, Patricia took a seat at one end and Cora sat on the sofa as well.

Ah Tim appeared in the doorway.

"Is tea okay?" Cora asked Patricia.

"Yes. Please."

The maid left.

Cora, her back ramrod straight, turned to Patricia. "In all the shock of last night, I didn't ask how you were doing. It must have been an awful thing to experience." Cora shuddered, her eyes pressing closed against whatever imaging had surfaced.

Patricia squeezed her friend's hand. "It was. Awful. I'm okay though. More worried about you."

"I'm not doing well. Though the children have been excellent at taking care of everything and making sure I'm never alone. They're good kids. Their father raised them well. I see so much of him in them. Not just physically, but also their words and behaviors." A solitary tear glistened on her porcelain cheek. "Like you, they are a blessing."

"How are they handling Ken's death?" Patricia stroked the top of Cora's hand.

"Like me. Not well. But we're relying on each other for strength." Cora pulled her hand back, brushed the tear from her cheek, then let out a sigh. "We will get through this."

"Cora, I have to ask, why all the secrecy about me coming over? You said protection. Protection from who?"

"You came here on the night of Ken's death with a detective," Cora said with warmth in her voice. "The killer could have followed the detective and noticed you. It wouldn't take the killer much effort to determine you're an excellent amateur sleuth. You found the body. You came here with the detective assigned to the case. I would image the killer could view you as a threat. Hence, I asked you to come over surreptitiously."

"I appreciate your concern. Do any of your children have any idea who might have killed their father?"

"They speculate. But what do they know? That's why I wanted to speak with you. I want you to investigate Ken's death. I need someone I can trust."

Patricia understood the invitation but questioned how effective she could be. "The police—"

"We don't trust the police," Cora said firmly.

"Why?"

"We're immigrants. Outsiders. We're not part of the local power elite."

"The police work for all of us, regardless of our heritage or social standing."

"With all due respect, Patricia, I don't believe that and neither does my family. We've repeatedly experienced prejudice firsthand, and we know we'll never be insiders like you and Trey."

Patricia sat in silence, understanding all too well what Cora was saying. "I don't know. The police are on this. They have the expertise and the tools."

"They also have half a million tourists to police during the Saint Patrick's Day festivities. Don't you think that's going to stretch their resources?"

"Of course but, talking about resources, what do I know about investigating a murder?"

"You solved your mother's murder."

Tangled memories surfaced. "I didn't solve it. I was lucky."

"You survived your mistakes and got ahead of them."

Patricia nodded.

"I hate to burden you, Patricia, but I *need* you to do this. You're our only hope. Please. If not for me, do it for Ken."

The pull of Cora's pleading was more than Patricia could resist. "Okay. I'll look into Ken's death. And I'll help you with the police."

Cora leaned over and gave Patricia a hug. "Thank you. Ken was always a worrier after we left China. We have resources. If you needed anything, just ask."

"Do you understand that I'll need to take a close look at

your family and staff in order to do a thorough investigation?"

Cora's thin eyebrows elevated. "I can assure you that *no one* in my family or staff had anything to do with my husband's death."

"I'm not saying that they do," Patricia said, surprised by Cora's defensiveness. "But they might have knowledge of some fact or event that could lead to who the murderer is. So I'll need to know everything, Cora."

Cora shook her head. "Why can't you leave us out of this?"

"I don't want to be difficult, but it doesn't work that way. I must be thorough. I need to know the good, the bad, and the ugly."

"Cora sighed. "Maybe this wasn't a good idea."

"If you, your family, and your staff won't be candid with me, it's definitely not a good idea."

Cora buried her head in her hands. "This is all so difficult."

Patricia rubbed Cora's back. "I'm in this with you, Cora. We'll figure it out."

Cora dropped her hands and looked up. "Okay. Let's do it. No limits."

"Good decision."

Cora nodded.

"So. What is it that you didn't want to tell me?"

Cora let out a long breath. "Ken gambled. Big stakes. Often."

CHAPTER 5

"Is there anything else you want to share with me, Cora?"

Cora, who sat with her slim hands folded in her lap, shook her head. "The children don't know about Ken's gambling. And I don't think they should. I don't want to damage his legacy in their eyes."

"I understand," Patricia said softly. "But I will have to tell Detective Rodriquez."

"Oh, I wish you wouldn't."

"I really want to help find out what happened to Ken. The detective may come across a puzzle piece, and I may come across another, but without us sharing our information, we may never get to the answer. If Rodriquez is going to trust me with case information, we'll have to trust him too."

"The information will get out and be a great embarrassment to the family."

"Ken's gambling might never get out unless it's eventually relevant at trial. And I *really* need Rodriquez on my side."

"Okay. I suppose if you have to, you have to."

"Thank you, Cora. I'm grateful for that." Patricia took a

slow breath. "What form did Ken's gambling take?"

"Ken started when we lived in Hong Kong. From time to time, he and a few friends would take the boat to Macau and spend the day gambling, mostly Fan Tan and some baccarat. When we moved to Savannah and money was tight, Ken stopped gambling. However, once he prospered, he returned to gambling with friends in Macau, halfway around the world."

"Oh yes. I know how it is when Trey goes on one of his guys' weekends. They go hunting or fishing. It's important for them to have those long-standing friendships."

"Indeed. And while I always wished they didn't bond over gambling, it was lovely that Ken kept up with his longtime friends and they continued to spend time together."

Patricia took comfort that Cora appeared to be open with her and that the conversation was flowing freely. At least with regard to Ken's gambling. "You said Ken's gambling was big stakes. How big?"

Cora's cheeks blushed. "I think it was hundreds of thousands. I know it's a lot of money, but Ken often said there was no point in small stakes gambling."

"So, and this is important, did Ken have any sizable gambling debts?"

Cora paused as if scouring her memory. "Not that I know of. But to be perfectly honest, I don't know for sure. He didn't discuss finances with me. What I *can* tell you is that everything we've done here in Savannah has been self-financed." Cora took a breath. "That is, after Ken paid back a Hong Kong investor who helped finance Ken's first business here, a machine shop. Ken never really liked that business and sold it for a nice profit once he paid off the loan."

"I do want to talk about how Ken got his start in Savannah, but let's get back to Ken's gambling first."

"Two or three years ago, Ken started taking more trips to

Macau and began staying longer."

"How long?"

"A week or ten days, where before it was just a long weekend."

"Why do you suppose he increased the frequency and duration?"

"I think he enjoyed his trips. Well, not the actual air travel, just the gambling time with his friends in Macau."

"Did anything happen in your marriage around that time?"

Cora frowned. "Heavens no. Our marriage was solid."

"Was he gambling all the time he was in Macau?"

"That's what he told me. He said he was staying longer so he could attend the Tuesday horse races on Taipa Island." Cora took a sip of tea.

"Did he ever gamble by himself?"

"No. Always with the same set of friends from his early days in Hong Kong."

"Tell me about these guys."

"They've known each other for decades." Cora rubbed her chin. "I think some of them went to college with Ken. One invested in Ken's first business here in Savannah."

"Have you ever met them?"

"No."

"Do you have their names?"

Cora nodded.

"If you don't mind, please email me their contact information." Patricia made an entry in her notebook.

"Okay."

Ah Tim appeared at the doorway.

"Yes?" Cora said.

"Would you care for more tea, madame?"

Cora nodded and Ah Tim left.

"Do you know if Ken ever received any threats?" Patricia

asked.

"Not that I'm aware of. And I believe he would have told me if something like that happened."

"Did he have a bodyguard?"

"No. He didn't carry much money. He felt safe on the streets here."

"I know you said he didn't discuss money with you, but might Ken have had any other financial difficulties not related to gambling?"

"He always promised me that if there was something to worry about, he would let me know, but that we were well off. It's a pride thing, and maybe a cultural tradition, but many Chinese families of our standing operate the same way. We wives put faith and trust in the honorable men we married."

"I've done lots of investigations, and while I'm not dismissing the big picture, Ken's murder could be something very simple," Patricia said. "Often family is involved. If you don't mind me asking, did Ken have a will?"

"We both do."

"How is Ken's estate to be distributed?"

"I get half. The other half is split equally between our children. Plus, Ah Tim, Wu, and Chen Ming each get one million."

Patricia knew her friends had done well, but still she tried not to show surprise at the obvious size of the estate. People had killed for much less, as well she knew. "I'm sorry, but I have to ask. Do the children or staff know about their inheritance?"

Cora shook her head. "We never discussed it with them."

For a few moments, the two just sat there, looking into space. Then Patricia recalled learning last year that the Barnard Street building was protected with military grade perimeter security when the building's state-of-the-art system zapped one of Patricia's high-tech drones during a massive Ponzi scheme investigation. Why would Ken Li need that kind of security, particularly when he was willing to walk the streets of downtown Savannah alone at night? What was in his building that demanded so much security, and could it have anything to do with his mysterious trips to China and murder? The thought that she was on the trail of something significant was almost palpable.

"Cora, it's pretty clear Ken felt personally safe here in Savannah. Yet the family has a security chief, and this residence has a secure secret entrance. What's in this building that requires so much protection?"

"Gold," Cora said. "A fortune in gold."

Totally surprised, Patricia took a moment to absorb the revelation. "Who knows about the gold?"

"Just Chen, our head of security, and I."

"How much gold is there?"

"More than one hundred million."

Patricia's jaw dropped as she considered the enormity of what Cora had just revealed. No wonder the building had such elaborate security. "I think the less I know about the gold, the better."

"I agree," Cora said. "And I certainly hope you don't plan to mention it to Detective Rodriquez."

"I appreciate the need for secrecy. I'll only mention it to Rodriquez if it becomes germane to the investigation. And I'll tell you before I do."

"Thank you, Patricia."

"Tell me about your staff. Of course, I know of Ah Tim and Chen Ming. I assume there are others."

"We have a butler, Wu, who runs the household. And we have a housekeeper, Jenny. We've had a cook and a driver in the past, but we found we didn't have enough work for them."

"Who attended to your husband's needs?"

"Wu."

"If you don't mind, I'd like to talk with Wu before I leave."

Cora dipped her chin slightly. "Of course. If you have no further questions for me, I can summon him right now."

"Please."

Cora picked up her phone and sent a text message.

Moments later, Wu, a tall, slender Asian with gray hair, appeared in the doorway. "Yes, ma'am."

"Come in," Cora said. "This is Mrs. Falcon. She's an investigator looking into Mr. Li's murder. She'd like to ask you some questions."

"Please be seated," Patricia said.

Wu sat ramrod straight in a stuffed chair across from the two women.

"How long have you worked for the Li family?" Patricia asked.

"More than thirty years," Wu said stiffly.

"When did you last see Mr. Li?"

"I assisted him when he dressed for dinner with Mrs. Li last night."

"What was his temperament at that time?"

"Serious. Perhaps preoccupied."

"Was that normal?"

"No, ma'am. Mr. Li was generally a happy, cheerful man."

"Do you know what he was preoccupied with?"

"No, ma'am."

"Were you and Mr. Li close?"

Wu nodded. "I believe so. After thirty years, one gets to know another quite well. We have shared some confidences."

"Did Mr. Li ever speak ill of anyone?" Patricia asked, fully aware she was pushing Wu's boundaries but hoping he would answer.

Wu looked at Cora.

"It's okay, Wu," Cora said. "Please tell Mrs. Falcon whatever you know."

Wu took a breath and let it out slowly. "Mr. Li didn't like the police. He didn't like bankers. And he had a strong distain for politicians."

"Anyone in particular?"

Wu shook his head. "He never once mentioned a name to me."

Patricia looked back and forth from Wu to Cora. "Do either of you know if Mr. Li expressed his distain publicly?"

Wu looked to Cora.

"Ken was quite open about his views," Cora said. "He expressed them politely when appropriate. Lately, he's been critical of the strong-arm tactics of the Chinese Communist Party."

"Was there an inciting incident for his criticism?"

"His anger ratcheted up significantly after the arrest of one of his friends in Hong Kong."

"Well, that's understandable," Patricia said. "Did anyone take offense at his political views?"

"Not that I know of," Cora said.

"Okay. Wu, do you know of anyone who would want to harm Mr. Li?"

"No, ma'am."

"Thank you, Wu. You've been very helpful. If you think of anything else I should know, please contact me." Patricia handed Wu her card.

Wu looked at Cora.

"That will be all," she said.

Wu stood and left.

After he was out of the room, Patricia said, "Wu said Ken was preoccupied when he was getting ready for dinner last night. Did you see any of that preoccupation at dinner?"

Cora bit her lip.

CHAPTER 6

*A*h Tim brought a fresh pot and clean cups into the lavishly appointed sitting room. Patricia checked her phone while Ah Tim exchanged the tea services. It was well past noon. Cora seemed to be handling the questioning well, and a meaningful suspect list was coming together nicely.

Once Ah Tim left, Cora offered tea, which Patricia graciously accepted. The ladies took time to sip tea, then Cora resumed the conversation.

"You were asking about Ken's temperament at dinner last night. Usually, our dinner conversation is Ken discussing one of the kids. He was always so proud of their accomplishments. He loved to tell me about something he'd discovered about one of them," she said with a soft and wistful laugh, "thinking I didn't know." Then her face turned sad. "But last night, Patricia, he was distraught."

Patricia leaned forward.

"Ken had learned that afternoon that one of his closest friends, a freedom fighter, had just been arrested by the Hong Kong police for insurrection. Ken feared for the man's life and felt powerless to save his friend from certain death." Cora's gaze sharpened. "Patricia, I have *never* seen Ken so distraught. Well maybe when I lost my child, but not since."

Patricia took Cora's hand and stroked it. "I'm so sorry."

"Thank you." Cora straightened. "Of course, since the Chinese Communist Party takeover of Hong Kong this kind of arrest has occurred frequently, but the arrests have never involved one of Ken's friends."

"That's terrible. Did Ken have any way to help him?"

Cora thought for a moment. "No. And it was the lack of a clear way forward that most troubled him. He was, more than anything, a problem solver. A man of action. And when his friend most needed help, he was powerless. It tore him up."

"So he left for the hair salon in that state of mind?"

"Not really, though I'm sure he carried his frustration with him. Toward the end of our meal, he received a text message that seemed to further upset him."

Patricia lifted an eyebrow. "In what way?"

"I think anger, but I'm not sure."

"It's good to know about that message," Patricia said, making a starred entry in her notebook. She had a strong feeling this could be the clue that cracked open the case. "The police have Ken's phone. They'll probably ask you if you know the password and, if not, they'll ask the carrier to let them in. Did Ken tell you anything about the content or sender?"

"Not a word." Cora grimaced. "But the message clearly bothered him."

"Did you see if he sent a response to the message?"

"He didn't when he was with me. If he did after, I wouldn't know. He just sat there, cheeks aflame and eyes on fire."

Not knowing how long Cora would tolerate questions,

Patricia felt the pressure of time and the need to focus. Still Cora seemed open to the questions and seemed to be handling her emotions well. "Do you mind a few more questions?"

"No. Not at all."

"What was Ken's position in Savannah's Chinese community?"

"Over the years, Ken sponsored many of the Chinese immigrants now living in Savannah. He gave them their first jobs in Savannah and helped them start their own businesses. And many have prospered and raised large families who have aligned themselves with Ken."

"So he's the leader of the community?"

Cora nodded. "Unofficially."

"Are there others who would like to lead the community?"

Cora looked at Patricia with understanding. "Yes."

"Were they a problem for Ken?"

"Ken seemed to have a gift for keeping the community unified. If there was conflict, it was dealt with. Are you thinking someone in our group might have wanted him dead?"

Patricia waved her hand dismissively. "I'm just exploring possibilities. You said there were people who wanted to lead the Chinese community. Does any particular name stand out?"

She shook her head. "You know, Patricia, Ken abhorred discord and felt it was a wholly ineffective way to bring about meaningful progress. So he confronted discord whenever it emerged in our community. And he had many allies joining him in taking that kind of positive, healing action."

"How did he put down discord?"

"Diplomatically," Cora said. "Once he became aware of unrest, he promptly sought out and addressed what gave rise to the unrest. Then he lobbied his peers to make changes across the community that would undermine the very basis for the discord. Because he had the support of so many, he was very successful in those undertakings."

"But he had rivals."

"Yes."

"Any enemies?"

"Not that I'm aware of," Cora said.

"Did he have any close advisors? People he relied on for advice?"

"He consulted with Luke a lot. It was his way of grooming our eldest son to take over the family business."

"Did Luke's favored status create any friction with your other children?"

Cora nodded. "Yes, but Ken smoothed it out. He was good at appeasement."

"What about non-family advisors?"

Cora thought for a moment. "As a matter of fact, he did. A woman, Felicia Chow, and Paul Ng. Ken valued their opinions greatly. But I must tell you, most of Ken's important decisions were entirely his own. He was very knowledgeable and extraordinarily wise."

Patricia added the names to her meeting notes. "What did those two advise Ken on?"

"The way he told it, he'd be faced with a decision and come up with a few options of what to do. If one option didn't jump out at him as best, he'd call in his advisors one by one and hear their advice. Then he'd make the decision."

"Did he meet with them often?"

"Ken and Paul had coffee weekly. I think it was more social than business for them. As for Felicia, I doubt Ken met with her as much as once a month. Their meetings were always on an as-needed basis."

"How long had Ken known them?"

"I'm pretty sure he knew of Paul back in Hong Kong. Paul was a young, hotshot Economics professor at Ken's university. Paul is at least ten years older than Ken and was one of the first immigrants Ken sponsored to come to Savannah. Ken met Felicia sometime in the last ten years and was very impressed with her advertising savvy."

"Would it be safe to say these two had insight into what was going on in Ken's business life?"

"As much as any," Cora said. "With the exception of Ken's accountant. Ken didn't do anything important without discussing it with his accountant."

"Who would that be?"

"Tom Lo."

Patricia added the name to the growing list of people to follow up with. "Is Tom based in Savannah?"

Cora nodded.

"How far back did Ken and Tom go?"

"From day one in Savannah." Cora paused. "I think Tom was the person who guided Ken toward some of his early commercial successes here. And I know over the ensuing years Tom helped Ken avoid some serious financial disasters. Well, apart from that Maynard Jackson scheme that everyone got caught up in." Cora shook her head. "That was one of the few times Ken invested in something other than a business, and he took his loss as a lesson to stick with what he knew."

"It was a harsh but important lesson for all of us." Patricia nodded, clearly remembering the case that had almost gotten her killed.

"I hope our conversation is giving you some leads."

Patricia turned the page in her notebook and nodded. "Yes indeed. And I'll follow up on them once I receive the contact information from you."

"I realize you'll be sharing much of what we discussed

this morning with Detective Rodriquez, but I want to again request you avoid any mention of the gold stored here."

"Speaking of which," Patricia said, dodging the issue. She'd already gone over her intentions regarding the gold. Patricia held up her notebook. "Why didn't you give Detective Rodriquez this information?"

Cora shrugged. "I don't know. Maybe he didn't ask the right questions."

"Well, I'm glad this worked out as well as it did."

CHAPTER 7

etective Rodriquez strode into the lobby of the police station and headed toward Patricia. He wore a blue, short-sleeved shirt and khakis. Typical dress for March in Savannah. His biceps and forearms were muscled. His dark eyes were intense.

Patricia stood. Was he annoyed she had dropped by? If so, he wouldn't stay annoyed for long when he heard what she was about to share with him.

"Nice to see you again, Mrs. Falcon."

She gave him a smile. "Thank you. You as well."

He escorted her back to a simple conference room. They sat at the scuffed table in worn chairs.

"How can I help you today?"

"Actually, I think I can help you."

He straightened in his chair and tilted his head.

"Apparently, Mrs. Li doesn't trust the police, so she asked me to investigate her husband's murder."

He frowned. "That's, uh, unfortunate. Her right, of course. It was obvious she had some issues, but she seemed forthcoming to me."

"Well, she opened up even further to me. Though she wasn't sure if any of it was necessarily relevant, but I did tell her whatever she shared with me, I would share with you in case it was relevant. And she agreed."

He nodded, shoulders relaxing somewhat. "I appreciate that."

"For one thing, Mrs. Li didn't tell you about her husband's state of mind before he left for the salon."

Rodriquez stroked his dark stubbled chin. "Okay."

"He received a text message just before he left that appeared to have upset him."

"Does she happen to know who it was from?"

"No."

"We'll check it out." Rodriquez jotted a note. "Alright. Anything else?"

"Yes. And this is where she's not sure it's relevant. A close friend of Ken Li's was recently arrested in Hong Kong for sedition. Ken felt the arrest meant certain death for his friend. He also believed the Chinese government would investigate his friend's acquaintances for collusion. What if Ken was involved? Would the Chinese government send someone to kill him?"

Rodriquez's eyebrows rose, and he drummed his fingers on the table. His nails appeared manicured. "That's news to me. I'll have to look into it."

Patricia noticed he didn't write that down in his notebook. It did sound farfetched and irrelevant. She changed the subject. "Have you made any progress?"

Rodriquez grimaced. "With the Saint Patrick's Day parade just a couple of weeks away, it's been kind of chaotic around here. As usual, a wide spectrum of criminals are converging on our city for a shot at our half million visitors. You know?"

Patricia nodded. "There are always bad apples in crowds

that size. So you're bogged down?"

"Afraid so. To be honest, what you told me about Mrs. Li not trusting the police wasn't surprising. In my experience, those who don't trust cops have something to hide. Do you think that's the case here?"

"Ken and Cora? Never." Patricia shook her head emphatically. "I know they're a very private family, but I don't believe they're hiding anything."

Rodriquez nodded. "That's good to know."

"Have you talked with the kids?"

"Most of them." His face remained unreadable, giving no clue as to whether the interviews had been useful to him.

"Any leads?"

"One," Rodriquez replied nonchalantly. "A Mr. Feng. Turns out Mr. Li had a serious rival in the Chinese community."

"So, there was bad blood between them?" Patricia asked.

"Yeah. Really bad. Apparently, Feng blames Ken Li for all his business failures."

Patricia chewed her lower lip. "Enough to murder for?"

"That's what we aim to find out." Rodriquez looked at his watch, a military-style chronograph, and stood. "Let me know if you come across anything else that could be useful."

"You too. Oh, actually just a brief request. Could I have copies of your crime scene photos?"

"Sure." Rodriquez sent a text message. "It will take a few minutes to print them out. Anything else?"

"Nothing else." Patricia stood.

"You can wait here for the photos."

She returned to her seat.

Rodriquez took the notebook he hadn't written her hair-brained theory in and left. Again, she felt a bit foolish for bringing it up. She needed to find out more about Feng. That was a good lead.

Ten minutes later, Rodriquez returned. "The copies you requested," he said as he handed a folder to Patricia.

She opened the folder and paged through the assortment. When she paused on an 8 by 11 photo of the murder weapon, sadness flooded her anew. The resolution was surprisingly sharp, causing her to grimace at the thought of Ken Li being stabbed with it. She pulled the photo from the folder and showed it to Rodriquez. "Have you done any follow-up on the murder weapon?" she asked.

"We sent the knife to the Georgia Bureau of Investigation for analysis. If we're lucky, we could get some finger or palm prints. Maybe even some DNA."

"Good," she said. "It's so ornate. Makes you wonder if it's something other than a design. Have you determined its origin?"

He ushered them toward the door. "Not yet."

"Do you mind if I take a crack at it?"

He gave a smile. "Knock yourself out."

She tucked the photo back in the folder.

He walked her back to the lobby. "Thank you for sharing your information, Mrs. Falcon."

"Anytime," she said on her way out.

As she headed for her car, she thought about going back and telling Rodriquez about the Asian man who had contacted Sheila. However, she decided she'd let Rodriquez know the next time they talked.

Once back in her car, Patricia sat in thought before pulling into traffic. Cora was right. The cops were too busy. If she left this investigation up to them, this case would most likely slide into the cold case files. A primal drive blossomed and swelled within her. It was up to her to find Ken's killer.

· · ·

As luck would have it, Patricia found a parking spot just in front of Cathay Antiques. She turned off her Navigator, grabbed the page-sized enlargement of the handle of the murder weapon, folded back the part with the police case number stamped on it, and headed toward the shop. Birdsong from the square across the street filled the spring air.

It never ceased to amaze Patricia how so many antique shops thrived in Savannah. It probably had something to do with the hundreds of restored historic homes in Savannah's ubiquitous urban Historic District, the largest in the United States.

The shop door was locked, but she had an appointment. She used the call box.

A woman answered.

When Patricia gave her name, a buzz sounded, and the lock released with a click. She opened the heavy door and stepped into the dimly lit, musty interior. Traces of incense and furniture polish tainted the air. A petit, middle-aged woman stood just inside. Patricia assumed she was Mrs. Zao, whom she had spoken to earlier. The shopkeeper looked on the high side of middle age. Her platinum hair was done in a tight bun. Small gold hoops hung from her ears. She wore a simple black cotton mandarin pants suit and black flats.

"Welcome to our little shop, Mrs. Falcon. I'm Mrs. Zao. Feel free to look around. If you have any questions, I'll be at my desk in the back."

Patricia gave the woman a smile. "Actually, Mrs. Zao, I'm not here to shop. I have a question about an object I recently ran across I hoped your expertise could help me with."

"Do you have it with you?"

"I brought a photo."

Zao gestured to the back of the shop. "The light is better at my desk."

Patricia followed the woman through a maze of oriental

furniture to a large teak desk carved with strange animals. From the looks of the papers strewn on the top of the desk, Patricia assumed it was the woman's work desk. It was well lit.

"That's such a unique desk," Patricia said.

"British Colonial. Pre-war. The provenance lists some British taipans, the last of whom sold it just before the Chinese takeover of Hong Kong."

"That's quite a history."

"That's why we're here. The story behind the antique is as important as the antique itself."

Patricia nodded.

In unison with the cathedral down the street, a clock inside the shop chimed noon. Zao gestured to a carved teak chair with red silk cushions.

Patricia sat.

Zao took a seat in a matching chair next to Patricia and lifted her eyes. "You have the photo?"

Patricia removed the copy from her purse and handed it to Zao. She saw the woman's small body tense. "Is something wrong?"

"Where was this photo taken?" The woman's voice was tight.

"Here. In Savannah. A couple of days ago."

"Do you have this knife in your possession?"

"No."

"Good." She shoved the photo back to Patricia like she couldn't wait to get rid of it. "I urge you to avoid having anything to do with this knife or anyone associated with it." Zao's voice was so tight the warning sent a chill through Patricia.

Patricia took a moment to regain her composure. "Why?"

Zao held a hand up in a pause gesture. "You don't want to know. Just distance yourself from it."

"I must know," she gently pressed.

Zao shook her head with a sharp snap. "Not from me."

Patricia shrugged. "If not you, who?"

"I wouldn't know." Zao stood.

Nothing like a summary dismissal. Patricia stood and followed the shopkeeper to the front door. Where Zao opened the door.

As Patricia stepped out, Zao said, "Be careful, Mrs. Falcon. Be very careful." Then she closed the door in Patricia's face.

This time the chill darn near froze Patricia on the spot.

PATRICIA'S MIND WHIRLED WITH UNSETTLING QUESTIONS about the mysterious weapon as she headed to the Ellis Street garage and the Lis' Barnard Street building. She debated calling Rodriquez, but ultimately called Cora and asked if she could swing by. Cora was free, so Patricia headed over.

Chen Ming met Patricia at the access tunnel door and escorted her to Cora's penthouse.

Cora, dressed in black, greeted Patricia with a warm but somber hug as she got off the elevator and guided her to the sitting room. Ah Tim brought tea as soon as they were seated.

Patricia assumed any discussion of the murder weapon would distress Cora, but Mrs. Zao's dire warning demanded answers. Cora was Patricia's best bet for advice on who in the Chinese community to turn to for those answers.

"Cora. I need to talk to you about the weapon involved in your Ken's death."

Cora's porcelain face pinched. "The knife?"

Patricia nodded. "Have you seen it?"

Cora crossed her hands in her lap and shook her head.

"It's an extremely distinctive knife and may lead us to Ken's killer. I visited an antique shop earlier today and was told, no *warned*, to dissociate myself from the knife and anyone associated with it."

Cora's eyebrows lifted.

"Exactly. The shop owner, Mrs. Zao, wouldn't give me any additional information. I was hoping you might be able to direct me to someone in your community who might be more open with me."

"Can you describe the knife?"

"Better, I have a photo." Patricia removed the enlargement from her purse and handed it to Cora.

Cora looked over the photo then, with shaking hands as if the photo was venomous, carefully placed it face down on the mahogany end table next to her. "Triad," she whispered.

Patricia arched her eyebrows, hoping Cora would continue to explain what a triad was.

Cora paused, her eyes moist, then withdrew a tissue from her sleeve and dabbed her eyes. She dropped the tissue on the end table and slowly shook her head, her brows knitted in confusion. "This is impossible. Ken would *never* involve us with a triad."

"What is a triad?" Patricia asked, her heart aching for her friend.

Cora let out a long breath. "Well, since you're actively investigating Ken's death, for your protection we need to get you up to speed on them."

"Okay."

"Triads date back almost four hundred years. They were the unofficial power brokers for various Chinese dynasties. They wielded vast power, capable of overthrowing or resisting rulers. Patriotic resistance fighters."

"That doesn't sound bad."

"That came later. When the communists took power in

1949, they cracked down on the triads and many fled beyond China's borders. Once settled elsewhere, they gained territory, engaged in criminal activity and used violence to expand. They remained splintered into separate groups until the communist government realized they could use them and invited them back home to China. Now, I'm afraid they're inextricably linked to the government."

This was getting more discomforting by the second. Patricia thought back to what she'd told Rodriquez. It was now very clear that Ken's dissident friend could be a clue in Ken's murder. "You're saying that based on this knife a triad is here in Savannah? What are they doing here?"

Cora shook her head. "No idea." She studied the photograph again and brought it closer to inspect the design.

"What are you looking for?"

"There are unique designs among the triads, but I am not trained to tell which triad this might be from."

Patricia leaned forward. "Who can we ask about it? I've already struck out with Mrs. Zao."

Cora sat back in thought. "I have a friend in Hong Kong who might know. If you let me copy your photo, I'll have Chen email it to my friend right now."

"This is a police photo. I don't feel comfortable having it circulating."

"Okay," Cora said. "Maybe Chen might know which triad."

Cora texted Chen, who instantly appeared in the doorway. She spoke to him in Chinese and handed him the photo.

Chen stiffened as he stared at the photo. "This knife was used to kill Master Li?" his voice was filled with alarm.

"Yes. Do you know which triad it came from?"

He dipped his chin. "Maybe, madame. And it is a dragon master's knife."

"Why would they send a dragon master to kill my husband?" Cora asked.

"I will ask some questions," he said somberly.

"Do so. And report back to me as soon as you have something substantial. And, Chen, do not share this information until we know what is happening. We must not panic anyone."

"Of course." Chen left.

"As you heard," Cora said. "Chen believes the knife in the photo is in the style of those used by dragon masters. A dragon master is the head of a triad. When his knife is used in a crime, it is like a calling card, meant to instill fear. To retaliate against a triad is understood to be certain death. Ken died at the hand of a triad associate, or at least someone who wants us to think so." Cora shivered. "This is so much larger than I thought."

Silence lingered for a moment.

"I'll let you know what Chen comes up with. In the interim you must be very careful, Patricia. This community talks. The wrong people may already know you're asking questions about this triad knife. Go straight home and lock your doors. Please."

For the second time that afternoon, Patricia felt a chill sweep over her.

CHAPTER 8

It was already late afternoon when Patricia left
Cora's. The exact origin of the knife was still
sketchy, but they'd made some progress.

The air was warm, a typical March day in Savannah, but
the chill of Cora's parting warning still clung. The sun was
low behind the office buildings, casting long shadows over
the streets.

Patricia guided her Navigator down Jones Street, finding
calm in the familiar vibration of tires on the old cobblestone
roadway. Awareness had long ago become a way of life for
her. Her father had made sure of that. She noticed things
most others missed. Closed storefronts that were normally
open. Changes in traffic light cycles. Even headlight design.

The use of LED-embedded lights to distinguish the front
end of cars fascinated Patricia and fed her attention to detail.
Because each manufacturer tried to make their light displays
unique, she'd learned to identify most common vehicle
models by their light patterns. Borne of hypervigilance and
necessity, it was a useful skill.

Which was why she noticed the late model Escalade

behind her had made every turn she had taken since leaving Cora's and now trailed two cars behind. There had been-Patricia counted-four turns.

She glanced at her purse on the seat beside her, thankful she had her gun inside. Patricia looked in her side mirror, and then flicked on her blinker. The Escalade behind her did the same thing.

Oh my gosh. Could Ken Li's killer be watching anyone visiting Cora? Or have they been following me since I left Ken's salon last night?

The dreaded yet familiar tingle raced up her spine. She called Simon, her part-time bodyguard. He lived close by.

"I'm working on Ken Li's murder, and now I'm being followed," she explained. "Are you available for an apprehension in front of your condo?"

"Sure," he said. "What am I looking for?"

"I'm being followed by a black Escalade. I want to ID the driver. I'll jam the car up in the traffic in front of your condo. I just need you on the sidewalk as backup. I'll do the talking."

"I'll be right down. A minute. No more. That work?"

"Perfect."

Patricia drove the Navigator to Simon's always heavily congested street.

Simon, dressed in a black hoodie, black tee-shirt, and distressed jeans, was already in front of his building. The hoodie, no doubt, concealed his pistol and armor.

After taking her gun from her purse and clipping the holster on her belt, she slowed in the heavy traffic, then jammed the brakes on. Tires squealed. Hers and those behind her. Horns blared.

She flung her door open and checked to make sure Simon was in place on the sidewalk next to the Escalade, which was pinched in traffic with no way to escape. Then, with adrenalin coursing through her, she confidently strode back to the suspicious vehicle.

As she approached, she saw the shocked driver, an Asian man, and his petite Asian female passenger staring out the windshield at her. Pulse racing, hand resting on her gun, he walked to the back of the car and took a photo of the license plate. She returned to the driver's door, stopping short of it in case the driver decided to swing it open.

Her shoulder muscles bunched as she unsnapped the flap securing her seven-round 45 automatic in its holster and gripped the butt.

When she tapped on the dark-tinted side window, the glass descended. As the window came down, she quickly scanned everything she could see in the dark interior-the occupants, a woman and a man, and the area under their control. No immediate threats. The tension in her torso loosened incrementally.

Both of the driver's hands rested on the steering wheel. The passenger's hands were equally visible. Two half-empty Sentient Bean coffee cups sat in the console cup holders. An open Byrd Cookie Company bag was also on the console. A six pack of Red Bull lay on the backseat.

"Why'd you do that?" said the round-faced driver with a drawl.

"You were following me," she said with all the authority she could muster. Then, keeping an eye on the driver's hands, snapped a photo of him. "I don't like stalkers." She sent the photos to her secure cloud storage.

The passenger, her face too shadowed for a decent photo, stared into the distance.

"It's a public road," the driver said.

"Stalking is still stalking. I'll be making a police report of this incident. The second time you follow me—"

As soon as the driver's right hand left the steering wheel,

she had her gun in his face.

His passenger snorted, her mouth clearly suppressing a laugh.

"Cut it out," the driver said with authority, but without any apparent impact on the passenger.

"You're so screwed," the passenger said and let loose the laugh she'd been struggling to hold.

"Keep your hands in sight," Patricia demanded.

"You have a permit for that?" the driver asked.

"Sure do."

"Look, lady. This is official business."

"What kind of official?"

"FBI."

Patricia raised her eyebrows. "Why are you following me?"

The driver frowned. "Like I said, official business."

"You have ID?" Patricia asked.

"That's what I was going to show you before you went crazy on me."

"Open your coat with your right hand."

He rolled his eyes, then pulled his lapel to the side, revealing his shoulder holster.

"Take your ID out with your left hand."

The driver slowly removed an ID case from his inside jacket pocket and flipped it open to reveal an official-looking badge and a photo ID. The name was Franklin Chow.

"Hey. I know your boss. I'm surprised he didn't tell me he had someone following me."

The driver's face remained blank. "We just set it up."

"Yeah. Right."

She holstered her gun and took a picture of Franklin's ID.

"Oh no, lady. You shouldn't do that," he said with a growl.

"Why not?" Patricia said. "You're stalking me and claiming to be FBI. You produce a hunk of metal that says

FBI and an ID card you probably bought off the internet. And you're armed. Now let me reiterate how this is going down—"

"Franklin, you're so screwed," the passenger said. "When the boss gets wind of this, you're gonna end up freezing your butt off in Anchorage."

Patricia glared at the passenger. "I was talking to Franklin. Understand?"

"Sorry," the passenger said, then pressed her lips together.

"Here's how it's going down, Franklin," Patricia said. "I'm making a police report tonight, and I'm sending a formal complaint to your boss. If you or anyone else from the *FBI* follows me again, I'll sue you civilly for stalking, harassment, and intimidation. And don't try any of that 'official business' stuff on me. If you want to know where I'm going, just ask."

"So, where are you going?"

"Am I under arrest?"

"No."

"Then where I'm going is none of your business."

He glared. "You're refusing to talk with me?"

"That's right. I'm not talking to you without a lawyer present. And knowing my lawyer, she'd advise me to remain silent. Now, I suggest you guys get back to the office and start working on your explanation for getting your cover blown."

"Anything else?" the driver said, a grudging respect lacing his tone.

"I hope the rest of your evening goes better than this."

"Me too," he said grimly. The window went up.

She gave Simon a smile and an okay sign.

He went back inside.

When Patricia returned to her car, a policeman was directing traffic around her car.

"Everything okay, Mrs. Falcon? Have you broken down?

Can I call for some assistance?"

"Sorry for blocking traffic, Charlie. Just dealing with a stalker."

"Pictures?"

"Sure 'nuff."

Charlie gave a huge belly laugh.

Patricia climbed into the car, put her gun back in her purse, and started the engine. Charlie stopped the traffic, then waved her into the interval.

Once moving, Patricia called Simon, debriefed him, and thanked him for the backup. She'd just finished with Simon when Sheila called.

"I have the thumb drive for you with the security footage of that inquisitive visitor who was asking about you."

"Any more visitors?"

"No."

"Thanks, Sheila. I'll be right over."

There were plenty of cars on the streets. Tourists were already arriving for the Saint Patrick's Day festivities, though the half million crush wouldn't peak until ten days or so. The stop and go traffic allowed her mind to wander.

She thought of Ken's brutal murder and hoped she would quickly bring his killer to justice. She thought of Cora and prayed God would cloak her in calm during her emotional storm. As concrete as these thoughts were, something else niggled. The 'why' of Ken's murder, and equally important, the 'why' of the FBI following her. If it had even been the FBI.

Patricia had confidence she would eventually get to the reason for Ken's murder, as well as the FBI following her. She'd known Algenon Melfive, the resident agent in charge, for a long time. He'd become a good friend and a person she could trust. He'd be open with her. She'd call him first thing in the morning.

Patricia stopped by Sheila's shop and picked up the thumb drive with the security video of the man who inquired about her that morning. She'd sent the file to her friend, Timnit Araya, a recently retired special ops veteran. She'd ask Timnit to run the man's face through the special facial recognition programs she had access to.

Patricia was eager to get home to Trey, so she left Sheila's as quickly as decorum allowed. Sheila, herself busy with preparations for the next day's deliveries, seemed to understand.

As soon as Patricia walked into her home, Trey took her in his arms. "Simon called me. Are you okay?"

She looked up into his imploring eyes, knowing how sincere his question was. "It's been a long, long day." She gave him a smile. "First thing this morning, Sheila told me someone stopped by her shop, asking about me."

Trey's brows elevated. "Not good."

She held up the thumb drive. "I just picked up a copy of Sheila's security tape of the visit. Then I got crime scene photos from Detective Rodriquez. He's not making much progress on the investigation, so I offered to look into the origin of the murder weapon. I was told by an antique dealer to avoid anything to do with the knife, so I dropped in on Cora. She said the knife appeared to be the type used by Chinese triad leaders."

"Really!"

"And if that wasn't enough, on my way home from Cora's, two FBI agents followed me. It's all left me with more unanswered questions."

He kissed her on the forehead and stepped back, his six and a half feet towering over her. "That *is* a long and strange day. Actually, an upsetting set of circumstances. What exactly did Cora say about the knife?"

It was so Trey to pick up on the one thing she'd held back

in her summary. She took his hand. "Are there any Chinese gangs operating in Savannah?"

He took a moment, clearly in thought. "Not that I'm aware of. But that doesn't mean there aren't."

Patricia knew his organization, the Cotton Coalition, kept close tabs on organized criminal activity in Savannah and moved quickly to nip it in the bud. "The knife used in Ken's murder has been identified as typical to those carried by leaders of triads."

"So either a triad assassin is here in Savannah, or someone wants us to think one is here." Trey's brow furrowed. "Do you know which triad?"

"Cora's security chief is checking and will get back to me."

"You shouldn't do this investigation by yourself. It's too dangerous. I have a massive deposition pending that will take at least a week. Can you delay for that long?"

"No, but I think I can safely get enough information to assess how dangerous it is."

"Okay, do that," he said, rubbing his chin.

She nodded, knowing she'd see little of him during that time. Normally, Trey was good about avoiding spending evenings and weekends at work. So, she knew the depositions had to be terribly important.

"Tell me more about the situation with Sheila," Trey said.

"Like I was saying, someone showed up at Sheila's this morning asking questions about me. I just picked up a thumb drive with her video surveillance. And I have a clear picture of one of the two following me this afternoon. I need to see if we can get facial recognition on any of them."

Trey frowned and remained silent for a moment. Then he pulled her tight. "I don't like this, Patricia. I'm going to ask Simon to be by your side until this is over. Let's debrief every day, and I'll be here to help more actively in a week."

"Okay. I must admit, I'm also concerned."

CHAPTER 9

With the demands of Trey's pressing deposition schedule, this would be Patricia's last full evening with him for at least a week. Once Trey was off a call to Simon, she patted the sofa cushion to her right where she was sitting. "Come sit with me."

As Trey settled on the sofa, Patricia leaned into his body, resting her head on his chest, and looked up. "I'm going to miss you."

He gave her a hug. "It's just a week. And we'll still be next to each other every night."

"A long, long week. It's strange how easy it is to take our time together for granted. Then when something like your or my work takes one of us away, the together time becomes so precious."

He stroked her back. "I was thinking the same thing. Together time is indeed precious."

When he kissed on her forehead, she gave him a tight hug and released a thoroughly contented sigh. They sat in silence and bliss for what seemed to be an eternity. She awoke in his arms, disoriented. "Have I been asleep for long?"

"Just a few minutes."

"I'm sorry, Trey. But your arms are just so comfortable."

"I enjoy our closeness too, Patsy."

She straightened. "What did you work out with Simon?"

"He'll be over tomorrow morning at ten to recheck our home security."

"I have a meeting with Luke Li at Sentient Bean at nine."

"I don't think that's a good idea. Too dangerous."

"You've never known me to sit by when threatened and cowering isn't going to happen now. Besides, this is only a *potential* threat."

He raised his eyebrows. "If you must go, I'd feel better if Simon went with you." Trey pulled out his phone and punched in some numbers. After discussing the subject with Simon, Trey put away his phone. "Simon will come over at eight thirty and go with you."

Patricia nodded. She knew it was necessary and had long accepted that heightened security was a way of life for them. And Simon was the best security anyone could have.

Simon poked his head around the kitchen door as Patricia cleaned up the mugs and plates from her early morning breakfast with Trey. "Are you ready to go meet Luke?"

Patricia closed the dishwasher. "Sure am."

They made their way out to the Navigator. "How's Trey doing? I haven't seen him for a few weeks." Simon opened the passenger door. "I'll drive today."

"He's busy," Patricia said as she climbed up into the vehicle and then waited for Simon to jog around. "This morning we had a hasty coffee before the sun came up. He can't talk about the case."

Simon backed out and merged into traffic, then he

glanced in the blind spots and checked the review mirror for tails. "It's the one where he's defending his longtime friend Beau Simpson, isn't it?" he asked.

"That's the one. He said it should be straightforward, so hopefully he'll be back to normal hours soon."

A couple of minutes later, Simon pulled into a parking space across from the Sentient Bean. "Right on time."

PATRICIA DIDN'T KNOW LUKE WELL, BUT SHE KNEW KEN HAD immense confidence in his eldest son and had been grooming Luke for years. She hoped Ken had confided in his son information she could use in her investigation. If she could get Luke to open up, he might be a gold mine of inside information about Ken and his possible enemies.

Luke, a tall, trim version of his father, stood as Patricia and Simon approached his table. He wore white linen slacks and a pale-blue golf shirt. He took her extended hand.

"I'm so sorry for your loss," she said, still holding his hand. "Your father was a wonderful man, and a dear friend. If there is anything Trey or I can do to help, don't hesitate to ask."

He pushed thick glasses up his nose, looked down and dipped his chin ever so slightly. "Thank you, Mrs. Falcon, for the comfort you've provided to my mother."

"Luke, this is Simon." Patricia gestured toward Simon. "He's helping me with my investigation. Simon, this is Luke."

The two men shook hands.

When Patricia turned toward the sales counter, Luke touched her forearm. "Please. Sit. Let me get it. What do you prefer?"

"Thank you. I'll take a dark roast. Black. No sugar or milk."

He gave an acknowledging nod.

"Same," Simon said.

As soon as Luke left for the counter, she and Simon sat. Moments later, Luke was back with three mugs and a carafe of coffee. He sat and poured, a touching echo of Cora pouring tea. Propriety coupled with humbleness. He slid a mug across the table to her. Patricia, remembering the Chinese manner the Li family had taught her, tapped two fingers on the table to show appreciation.

Luke smiled, the first since her arrival. "You know our ways well," he said.

"Thank you."

After pouring coffee for Simon and himself, Luke said, "You can speak freely here."

Patricia looked around. Three stout Chinese men sat at tables close to them. She nodded toward the men. "Yours?"

"Yes. In view of recent events, one cannot be too careful." Luke sat up straight. "Mother said you are investigating Father's death. How might I assist?"

It was reassuring to hear his offer. "Who do you think took your father's life?"

"The Forty-four Brothers triad," Luke said without hesitation.

"Are you sure?"

"One hundred percent." Luke calmly took a sip of coffee.

"How can you be so sure?"

Luke tipped his head. "The knife."

"If the Forty-four Brothers triad were in Savannah, I think the authorities would know about it."

Luke leaned forward. "Trust me. The triad is here."

"Who's running it?"

He shook his head. "Don't know."

"How many people?"

"Don't know."

Patricia opened the photo app on her phone and scrolled

to the pictures she took the day after the killing, stopping at the photo of the driver. She held up the phone for Luke to see the screen. "Do you recognize this man?"

Luke studied the photo. "No. Why?"

"He could be the person who killed your father. But I'm not certain. Let's say he's a person of interest. Great interest."

"Where did you get this photo?"

"I took it."

"Why do you think he could be the killer?"

"He followed me after I met with your mother the day following the murder."

Luke studied the screen. "Please send me a copy."

"Sure. By the way, have you been looking for your father's assassin?"

Luke gave a wry smile. "A unit of the family security team has."

"Is this a new security team or one your family has had?"

"To maintain independence from the Chinese Communist Party, we've always had extensive security. With my father's death, we tasked a couple of our finest to find the assassin."

"And?"

"So far, they've found nothing. But they didn't have your photo."

"Do you think the assassin could still be here?"

"We have to assume the people behind this have a bigger plan. Perhaps more killings."

An icy chill went down Patricia's spine. "Who else would be a target? You?"

"Anyone who gets in the way of their plan, whatever that is."

Anyone would include Patricia and her team. Trey and the Coalition. Chief Patrick. Anyone who was protecting the status quo in Savannah. Even her FBI friends. Everyone. "What's their endgame?"

"Don't know yet."

Out of the corner of her eye, Patricia caught movement toward their table. Her skin pebbled, and she instinctively dropped her hand onto her gun-carrying purse as she turned her head, only to see a woman's back rapidly heading toward the door. Patricia scanned the petite profile trying to see if the retreating female looked familiar. She considered following her out, but felt it was too risky to attempt without consulting Simon. Feeling vulnerable, she turned to Simon. "Did you see her?"

Simon locked eyes on Patricia. "Who?"

"The woman who approached our table."

Luke's brow furrowed.

"No," Simon said.

"A woman with waist length black hair approached our table. When I turned to get a better look, she spun on her heel and abruptly left."

"Did you get a look at her face?" Luke asked.

"No. Just her back."

Luke stood. "I'll check with my security team. They may have noticed something."

"What was she wearing?" Simon asked.

"Black. All black. Tapered pants. Long-sleeved shirt." Patricia stared off into space. "Black boots, I think."

"Purse?"

"Don't think so."

"Okay. We'll check the store's security video if they even have one and give us permission. With any luck, they'll cooperate, and we might get a decent facial."

After a few moments, Luke returned. "Sorry. They didn't see anyone approach our table."

"Why would someone approach us, then rush away?" Patricia wondered out loud.

"It may be nothing," Simon said. "But considering the current situation, we have to treat *everything* as significant."

"I agree," Luke said.

"The tactic you observed," Simon said, "is a classic move adversaries use to test security. And we failed."

"She didn't get too close," Patricia said.

"Good thing, but I had a bad angle and didn't notice the approach. If you hadn't, who knows what might have happened?" Simon paused. "I'm sorry. Terribly sorry," he said in a voice more gravelly than normal. "I shouldn't sit with you in the future. I should sit separately. Close enough to protect you, but far enough to identify and intercept adversaries. And I need to be much more aware."

"We don't know I was the target."

Simon shook his head. "You might have been. That's all that matters. And I didn't handle it properly."

Patricia put her hand up, palm toward Simon. "That's okay. We can't be right all the—"

"It was a rookie mistake."

"Then let's learn from it and move forward. No shame in that." She paused. "Besides, it could be nothing."

That evening, Patricia and Trey had a late dinner of crawfish etouffee carryout from Huey's. Afterward, Patricia called her friend and former special ops operative, Timnit, to set up a breakfast meeting with her at Goose Feathers for the following morning.

"Make sure you bring your gun," Patricia said.

"Why?"

"I'm being followed, and I think the follower could be Ken Li's killer."

"Are you sure Goose Feathers is the best place to meet?" Timnit asked.

"Goose Feathers is fine. It's public and will be crowded with the breakfast crowd. Plus, I'm going to ask Simon to shadow us. We three against one or two of them sounds doable. And, if they show their hand, it could help us identify who they are."

CHAPTER 10

The following morning, the doorbell chimed at eight thirty.

Patricia checked the front porch camera and saw Simon. She released the deadbolts and opened the door to him. He was dressed in SWAT black and carried two large duffle bags.

"Good morning. I understand we have a nine o'clock meeting. I'll just drop my gear in the guest room and be right back."

Moments later, Simon was back with a scanner of some sort.

Patricia grabbed her purse from the kitchen counter.

He pointed at her bag. "Gun?"

"Always."

They headed through the kitchen to the garage.

Simon moved around her Navigator, crouching every few feet as he ran a scanner back and forth and under. At the back passenger side wheel well, Patricia saw his shoulders stiffen, and his arm reach into the darkness.

"What is it?" she asked.

Simon brought his arm back out and stared at a tiny metal circle in his palm. "A tracking device. New. Not one of ours."

"Shoot," Patricia said, nerves jangling. "I wonder how long it's been there."

"No telling." Simon put the device on the work bench. "I'll check the source once we get back. It could give us a clue on who's following you." He ran the scanner over her and her purse, finding nothing unusual, then put the scanner on the work bench. "Do you want me to drive today?" he asked.

"I'd prefer to." She went around to the driver's door as Simon climbed into the passenger seat.

As she waited for the garage door to go up, Simon said, "If you notice anyone following you, mention it. I'll keep a lookout as well."

Patricia nodded, fired up the SUV and drove them the five minutes to the Whitaker Street garage.

"As far as I can tell, no one followed us into the garage," Simon said. "I think it's strange they would follow you one day, then not follow you the next." He punched the elevator call button. "How did you arrange your meeting with Timnit?"

"Phone. My cell."

He glanced at the phone she held out. "We'll check your phone and home to see if there's any indication of a wireless phone tap. Meanwhile, let's assume you're still being followed. I'm glad Trey called me in on this."

"Me too," Patricia said and meant it with every fiber of her being.

The elevator arrived. Simon stepped in, then motioned Patricia in. At ground level, he was the first out. Before they left the parking garage, Simon reviewed protocol with Patricia.

As per protocol, they walked to Goose Feathers well apart from each other, and Patricia went in first.

Simon waited outside. Patricia ordered a latte, then took a table at the back of the restaurant that gave her a good view of the entrance and waited for Simon and Timnit to arrive. Simon came in and sat to the right of the entrance.

A waiter had just delivered Patricia's latte when Timnit walked in. Patricia stood and Timnit crossed the room to the table. They embraced. "It's so good to see you, Timnit," Patricia said. "It's been a while. What's been keeping you so busy?"

"Nothing much," Timnit said. "My husband has been doing a lot of contract work."

"Interesting."

"Dangerous too." Timnit pointed to the counter. "I'm going to go order."

"Are you eating?"

Timnit nodded.

"I'll hold our table." Patricia handed Timnit a ten. "Would you mind ordering me an egg croissant?"

Moments later, Timnit returned with a streaming mug of coffee and sat. "So, you're working a new case?"

Patricia nodded. "Ken Li's murder."

"When I saw that on the news, I thought you might pick it up. You found the body, right?"

Sadness surged. "Yeah. That was quite a shock."

"I bet. We dealt with plenty of death during my military career, and I *never* got used to it. Mr. Li was a good friend, wasn't he?"

"Very good and too young to die. Quite a tragedy for all of us, particularly his family."

Their breakfast arrived.

"Any suspects?" Timnit asked between bites.

"Plenty."

Timnit's brow furrowed. "Really? How can I help?"

"I know you have your hands full right now with your husband's comings and goings, so I'll just limit my requests to—"

Timnit held up her hand in a 'pause' gesture. "That's not necessary, Patricia. I'm fully available to help you. To be honest, I'd welcome any opportunity to work on something other than sitting at home waiting for him to return from another overseas assignment."

Patricia tilted her head in understanding and appreciation.

Timnit laughed. "When I was just at the counter ordering, I actually considered ordering an ice cream sundae rather than the French toast. Ice cream for breakfast. Can you imagine?"

"Yeah."

Timnit leaned forward. "What do you have for me?"

Patricia pulled the photographs of the so-called FBI agents from her purse and pushed them across the table to Timnit. "These two claimed to be FBI agents. The male had FBI identification that said his name was Franklin Chow. No name for the other. They were following me yesterday. And just before coming here Simon found a tracking device on my SUV. I'd like you to run facial recognition."

"So, you don't think they're FBI?"

"I'm skeptical. I've known the resident agent in charge for years. Surely, he would have called me if he wanted something. But I'd rather know for sure they aren't his people before I talk to him."

Timnit put the photo in her purse. "Timing for results?"

"Yesterday."

Timnit smiled. "How about by five this afternoon?"

"That works." Patricia pulled Sheila's thumb drive from her purse and handed it to Timnit. "This is security footage of someone asking about me at Sheila's flower shop. I'd like facial recognition on that person too."

Timnit dropped the thumb drive in her purse.

A waiter came by and refreshed their coffee.

"You could have emailed all this to me." Timnit forked the last bite of French toast.

"What fun would that have been?" Patricia moved her empty plate to the side.

"Exactly," Timnit said. "I'm so glad we see eye to eye on that. Don't let anyone think they can intimidate you, or the next thing you know they'll own you. By the way, I noticed Simon sitting by the door."

"Like I told you, we're uncomfortable with these people following me."

Timnit nodded knowingly, then finished off her coffee. "Well, I better get going." She patted her purse. "I have some work to do." She stood, as did Patricia. "Be safe and call me if you need anything else. I'm here for you." They hugged and Timnit departed.

Patricia remained at the table and watched to see if anyone followed Timnit out. Satisfied Timnit wasn't being tailed, Patricia finished her coffee and headed out, checking all the new customers. Once outside, she checked both sides of the street and, with Simon, headed toward the parking garage.

Considering the potential danger involved in her morning meeting with Timnit, Patricia felt relief when she pulled the Navigator into her garage.

Simon turned to her as she turned off the SUV. "Let's keep conversation to a minimum inside the house until I finish searching for bugs one more time. We do it weekly for all the Cotton Coalition directors, but I want to be certain. No point in tipping off the bad guys that we're onto them."

Patricia nodded her understanding.

As Simon got out, he went to the work bench, grabbed the tracking device he'd removed from her car earlier, and removed the battery. "Time for some quick research on this device and how available it is to the general public." Simon examined the tracker. "Concox. Hmm. That name's familiar, but I can't place it."

On the way from the garage, Simon left the walkway and went to the back patio, where he dropped a small green cylinder next to the house. Dense, white smoke spilled from the container and quickly filled the air behind the house, obscuring the bank of back windows.

"What's going on?" she asked in complete surprise, stepping back and fanning the smoke from her face.

He scanned the cloud that was beginning to dissipate. "Checking for lasers. Smoke makes them visible. Good news is that I don't see any."

"Why lasers?"

"They're a well-established and virtually undetectable way to listen to conversations inside a house. The laser, located outside your home, is focused on a window and detects vibrations in the glass caused by conversation. Software at the laser source translates the vibrations back into conversation."

"And the smoke tells you there are no lasers here?"

"Not really. They could be motion activated, making them even harder to detect. Once we get inside, I'll install laser surveillance countermeasures on each of your back windows. They generate white noise that will render the lasers useless."

Simon opened the back door, and they stepped into the kitchen. "I'll get the countermeasures." He returned a few minutes later and started placing the thumb sized devices on the windows.

"Do you want some coffee?"

"That'd be nice."

Patricia shoveled ground coffee into the coffee maker, filled the well with water, and turned the device on. "If there's any way I can help, let me know."

"You could check out this company on the internet." He pointed at the Concox logo on the tracking device.

"Will do." She eyed the coffee maker. "I'll bring you a cup when it's done." Patricia sat at the kitchen table and opened the lid of her laptop.

Simon held his hand up. "Hold on."

She froze. They'd been through this before. Every electronic device in the home that connected to the internet could be intercepted, including her laptop.

Simon left, then returned with a small black duffle, from which he removed a slim laptop.

She smiled as she took the computer. "The last time we did this, the secure laptop was much bulkier."

He nodded. "You've got to love technology." He wrote down a password to open the laptop, then handed her a sleek cell phone and a smartwatch. "Same password for each." He placed her laptop into the duffle. "I need your phone and watch."

She removed her smartwatch and gladly handed it over. She had no desire to have her activities monitored by bad guys. Parting with her cell phone was more problematic, only because it contained all her contacts. "My contacts?" she asked as she handed the phone to Simon.

"They're in the cloud. They'll transfer to your new phone seamlessly." Simon removed a black box from the duffle, plugged the cord into a wall socket and placed the device out of the way on the kitchen counter.

"What's that for?" she asked.

"It transmits data that will mislead anyone monitoring your internet activity."

She loved that.

"Do you have any Alexa or Siri devices?"

"Yes."

"Turn all of them off and pull the plug on every one of them."

She did as he asked. "Done," she said as she returned to the kitchen.

"I'll secure your home security system."

She frowned. "I thought it was already secure."

"It was when we put it in, but security technology evolves rapidly. We can lock all the doors, physically and electronically, but a determined adversary will find a way to get in. Capabilities are constantly changing. There's never a moment we can relax. So be careful."

He left.

As soon as Simon disappeared into the rest of the house, she sat at the kitchen table and opened the new laptop. She quickly learned that Concox Information and Technology was established in Shenzhen, Guangdong, China, in 2003 as a manufacturer of fleet tracking systems. Over time, they expanded and acquired several smaller companies. Concox's website claimed they were now the top GPS tracking company in China. In late 2020, they merged with Jimi IoT. Jimi was founded in 1999 as a small telephone producer and grew to become a key player in China's wireless telecommunications sector and electronic vehicle parts. There were long lists of products produced by the company, but she found no financial nor structural information.

Once she'd finished her research, Patricia got up from the table, poured two mugs of coffee and took one into the dining room, where Simon sat at the table with three laptops. A couple of long guns were stacked in a corner and an armored vest hung on a chair back. She handed him a mug.

"How are you coming on the tracker?"

"Chinese military issue. Not available to the public. According to Cyber Command, it's the latest technology. What did you find on the manufacturer?"

Patricia shared what she'd learned about Concox. "I apologize I didn't find more."

"That's okay. Chinese companies tend to be very private about company details." Simon stood and grabbed a wand from the table. "Let's see if the bad guys have placed any transmitting devices *inside* the house since our last scan. It's old technology, but sometimes it's the old technology that works best. Particularly if we don't look for it."

She followed him into the library. "You're good at this."

Simon finished his scan of the fireplace and moved to the bank of windows overlooking the patio. "This kind of work comes naturally to me." The wand chirped each time it passed over one of the laser surveillance countermeasures he'd placed.

"Scanning?"

"Counterintelligence." Simon stepped out to the patio, pick up the expended green cylinder and scanned the outside of the patio window set. "I put myself into the mind of my adversary. I ask myself, where would I put bugs that would be effective but hard for me to detect."

"You give your adversary a lot of respect."

Nodding, he came back in and scanned the kitchen. The wand screech when it passed over the black box scrambler he'd placed on the counter. "If I don't respect my enemy, I'll probably miss something. And in this business, that could be fatal."

"Like those self-contained listening devices Judy put on

our window a couple of years ago," she said, referring to her first serious investigation.

He nodded. "That was embarrassing. I try to do my best, but my best isn't always good enough."

"So when you're done scanning, there could still be active bugs?"

"I'm afraid so." He let out a frustrated breath. "We never know for sure that a place is bug free."

"How does that happen?"

He rolled his eyes. "Sometimes, human error. Sometimes, brilliant adversaries. But usually, if it happens, the other guys simply have superior technology." Simon headed upstairs. She followed. "Did you do counterintelligence in the service?"

He shook his head. "Rangers. Special Ops."

"Why'd you get into this technology?"

His body stiffened. "I lost a best friend," he said in a flat voice. "He died in my arms. Everything I'd ever trained for, worked for, wasn't enough to prevent his death. I don't want to lose another." Simon cleared his throat. "That's when I realized I had to change my focus."

"I'm sorry for your loss."

He went into the master bedroom and continued scanning.

She stood at the door out of his way.

He looked up. "Why do you sleuth?"

She hadn't expected the question, and it took her back. She rolled some answers around before settling on one. "Justice. If each of us don't combat evil with everything we have, it could take over our lives, our community. And I don't want that. I'm blessed with resources, time, and a deductive mind. I suppose sleuthing is the best use for those resources."

He smiled. "You're definitely good at it."

She returned his smile. "Coming from you, I'm flattered."

Simon looked around. "Well, we're finished up here and downstairs."

Patricia looked at her new smartwatch as she went down the stairs with him. It was already eleven thirty. "Do you feel like lunch?"

"I got filled up at Goose Feathers. I think I'll pass."

"More coffee?"

He smiled. "Always." He grabbed his cup from the dining room table and walked to the kitchen with her. "What do you have planned for this afternoon?"

"I want to bring my case file up to date and talk to Cora about a Mr. Feng."

"Who's that?"

She frowned. "A not-so-nice rival of Ken's."

Patricia worked on her case file for the next hour or so. She knew it was important to go over and over her information, but nothing jumped out at her. Patricia clenched her teeth. She'd been through her notes three times. Her suspect list was huge, and so far, she'd been unable to narrow it down. Every conversation seemed to yield more suspects. An involuntary sigh escaped her. Though her file was growing in thickness, she had nothing solid.

Annoyed at her lack of progress, she closed the laptop, pushed back the chair, and jaw twisting, paced the kitchen to clear her mind. She reached the back door, turned, and paced back to the entrance to the library. She had a slew of suspects. But what if Ken Li's murderer wasn't on her list? That would certainly explain her failure to lock down on one or two highly promising suspects. Darn. She'd been thorough. Who had she overlooked?

She went into the dining room to get an update from Simon. Perhaps he'd stumbled on something.

Simon sat at one end of the table, well away from his open laptops, wearing magnifying glasses and holding a miniature soldering iron in his hand. The room had a faint acrid smell. In front of him lay the open case of the Comcox vehicle tracker. Pieces of the interior electronics lay next to the case.

She cleared her throat so as to not startle him.

He looked up and put the soldering iron down on an asbestos pad.

She gestured to the disassembled electronics. "What's going on?"

"Something about this tracking device bothers me. It's battery operated, which means it's temporary. I suspect whoever planted this device just wanted to determine your address. If they wanted to track your comings and goings for the next week or two, they would have hard-wired a tracker to your car and run it off your car battery."

She nodded her understanding and sat.

"A big problem for temporary trackers is they not only have a short life, but they're also relatively easy to detect. Therefore, once they've served their purpose, it's best for the bad guys to remove it from your car and save it for their next tracking situation. Which is what all this"-he gestured to the electronics-"is all about. I'm wiring a sub-miniature tracker inside the Comcox tracker. When the bad guy retrieves his tracker, we'll be able to track him."

"Sweet," she said with enthusiasm. "That's a brilliant idea."

He nodded and gave her a rare smile. "Once I'm done with the rewiring, I'll return the Comcox tracker to your car. The next move will be up to them, possibly tonight, while your car is in the garage." Simon took a sip of what was almost certainly cold coffee.

"Do you want more coffee?"

"I can get it."

She stood and held her hand out to his mug. "I can get it while you finish off your electronic trap."

He smiled. "You don't mind?"

"Not at all."

He handed her the mug.

She took off to the kitchen, poured fresh coffee and returned, placing the steaming mug in front of him.

"Thank you," he said. "I've been wondering about where you might have picked up this tracker. Please tell me again everywhere you and your Navigator have been since Mr. Li's murder. And don't skip anything, however minor."

She thought for a moment. "My SUV was in valet parking at the hotel the night of Ken's death. After discovering the body and giving my statement, I rode to Cora's in Detective Rodriquez's car. Then I took a cab back to the Hyatt to pick up my car after consoling Cora. I went straight from the hotel to here. The following morning, Trey and I went for breakfast. Trey drove his Bentley. The Navigator remained here in the garage. After we returned from breakfast, Sheila dropped off our weekly flowers and told me about someone asking about me. Then I drove to Cora's in my car."

"Hold it," Simon said. "At that point, they already knew who you are and where you live. Otherwise, they wouldn't have been able to ask your florist about you. They had to have put that tracker on your car at the Hyatt. Possibly while you were waiting for the police to take your statement or while you and Detective Rodriquez were visiting Cora."

"How would they know which car? I had my valet ticket in my purse all the time."

"Did you ever put your purse down?"

She tried to recall. "I had my purse with me all the time I was waiting for the police to take my statement." Then it hit her. In the distress of finding Ken dead in the salon chair, she'd pulled her gun and abandoned her purse. "I lost track of my purse when I found Ken dead. I recall having to search for it before the cops came. If the killer had been in the salon with me, he could have had time to search my purse and find the valet ticket. I'd just tossed it into my purse, so it would have been in plain sight."

It was pretty clear the killer had identified her pretty early. Perhaps, as Simon had suggested, at the scene. So why would the killer put a tracker on her SUV? That was really the crux of the matter.

Patricia had learned that in-depth discussion of case facts and possibilities with an expert was a good way to move a case forward. And no one was better at brainstorming a case with her than Simon. He always seemed to be able to help her see more clearly. "I think we may have gone down a rabbit hole in our thinking about the tracker," she said.

His brow furrowed. "Really? Why?"

"First, whoever placed the tracker had to identify which vehicle was mine. Once he knew that, it would be simple to find my address. But I didn't return to my car until after visiting Cora. Second, a guy showed up at Sheila's shop the day after the murder. Let's assume the killer figured out who I was and where I lived as early as the night of the killing. Then why put a tracker on my SUV?"

"If not to get your address, then you were being tracked to see where you went, and more importantly, *who* you interacted with immediately following the murder."

"I didn't go anywhere with the Navigator."

"Precisely." He smiled. "That probably pleased the killer. Your behavior subsequent to the murder posed no threat to him."

"Do you think he followed me and Detective Rodriquez to Cora's that night?"

"Probably, but Rodriquez going to the widow's home the night of the killing would be completely expected."

"Wouldn't the killer wonder why Rodriquez took me with him?"

"Probably. Which would explain why the killer continued to follow you."

"And all I did after picking up my car was go home. Then out to breakfast the following morning with my husband."

"Perfectly normal behavior."

"But then I went to see Cora again. This time in my SUV, which probably had the tracker on it by then."

"Yeah," he said. "That trip could have concerned the killer."

"But not enough to take any direct action against me other than follow me from Cora's."

"That's an important point, Patricia. The tracker was doing its job."

CORA CALLED EARLY IN THE AFTERNOON. "CHEN MING HAS finished up investigating the dragon master's knife. Unfortunately, he was unable to tie it to a particular gang."

The antique dealer seemed to have recognized the knife. Why not Chen Ming? Was Cora's security man withholding information from them? And Luke said the knife came from the Forty-four Brothers triad. How did he know that and not Chen Ming? She'd try elsewhere. "Cora, have you heard of a man known as Feng?"

Cora's gasp was audible. "Yes," she said in a weak voice. "Why do you ask?"

"The police have identified him as a person of interest in their investigation. What can you tell me about him?"

"Master Feng is the Savannah patriarch of the Feng clan. His clan is as large as our extended family and has been in Savannah almost as long as us. However, they haven't been anywhere as successful, and some of their children have repeatedly engaged in serious crimes. Ken was a staunch law-and-order advocate and did everything he could to weed out the criminals in our community. I know he and Master Feng didn't see eye to eye on many matters affecting our population."

"Would Mr. Feng be capable of murder?"

"I don't think so, but I have no doubt one or more of the Feng children could be. And would be, if directed by their father, who always blamed Ken for the Feng family's inability to prosper."

"I'll need names." Patricia jotted a note. Her task list had already morphed into two pages, which was good, but would take a lot of time to follow up on. And time eroded data and gave the killer opportunities to escape or maybe kill again. She'd have to prioritize the tasks and bring in some helpers-the girls she'd worked with previously-provided they were available.

And there was always Rodriquez. She'd continue to coordinate with him as much as possible, which could allow her to cross off some of the tasks on her list. But realistically, he was stretched thin too. Some stuff wasn't going to get done. At least not anytime soon. She just hoped she would prioritize the right tasks to solve the case.

"I'll text the Feng family names to you as soon as I get off this call. I'm sorry. I don't know why I didn't think to mention the family when you first asked. I know some of them, but I'll have to look up the rest."

Patricia's spirits rose. Finally, she'd have some suspects with motive and means. Proof would follow. Of that she was certain.

CHAPTER 11

It didn't take Cora long to email Patricia the thirty or so names of the extended Feng family in Savannah which Patricia promptly transferred to her case file suspect list. As she gazed at the long list, a sigh escaped. Too many.

In all probability, the best piece of evidence Patricia had was the so-called dragon master's knife.

It troubled her that the killer had clearly left the knife as a triad calling card yet, if she were to believe the feedback, no one knew specifically who to associate with the knife. What kind of 'calling card' was that?

Perhaps it was meant to communicate to a very small audience. An audience the killer knew would be terrified on seeing the triad knife and would be completely unwilling to cooperate with the police. The antique dealer seemed to get some sort of a fearful message from seeing the knife, as did Cora and Chen Ming. And none were cooperating. Except, perhaps Cora. But even then, Cora had held back, initially 'forgetting' to mention the Feng family. So clearly the knife was recognizable.

Patricia opened the secure laptop and searched on the topic of Chinese criminal gangs. The FBI's Violent Gang Task Force and the national Gang Intelligence Center topped the search results. Next came the Georgia Bureau of Investigation's Gang Task Force and the Georgia Gang Database. When she probed deeper, she found the databases listed gang members and identifying attributes of particular gangs, but not the Forty-four Brothers triad. Also, there was no mention of dragon masters, nor their unique knives. She decided to discuss the FBI gang data with her friend Algenon at the Savannah FBI office tomorrow. Perhaps there were other gang databases that he knew of. She read further in the search results, hoping for a breakthrough.

Buried on the third page of the results was a reference to Doctor Bai Yi, a professor in the East Asian Studies program at Emerald University in Atlanta. Patricia clicked on the citation and read, with delight, that he had authored a recent paper on modern Chinese criminal organizations. More in-depth research revealed Doctor Yi was a well-regarded academic on the subject.

Patricia called Doctor Yi's office at Emerald University and made an appointment to see him in person the following day during his afternoon office hours. Then she called Trey's secretary to make sure his jet would be available for the round trip to Atlanta. Once all was set up, she made a lunch date with their daughter, who attended Emerald University, then made a late afternoon appointment to meet with Algenon at the FBI office in Savannah. It was an extremely tight schedule, but workable if there were no complications.

Timnit called while Patricia was scrolling through the last of the search results. "Are you available to meet?"

"Is it something we can discuss now?"

"I don't want to talk over the phone, but we really need to talk."

"Sure. My place or yours?"

"You have better coffee than me. How about your place?"

"Okay. I don't have anything else on my calendar this afternoon, so come on over whenever."

"I'll be right over."

"Simon's here."

"With everything going on, I thought he might be."

"See you soon." Patricia disconnected the call.

About the time the fresh coffee had brewed, the doorbell chimed. "I'll get it," Patricia shouted to Simon as she headed toward the front door. "It's Timnit."

"Yeah. I can see her on the security camera."

Patricia released the deadbolts and opened heavy door.

Timnit, dressed in black pants and tee-shirt stood in the doorway, laptop in hand. Her eyes were bloodshot, and her face looked haggard. Not at all usual for Timnit, who normally projected excellent mental and physical fitness.

"Are you okay?" Patricia asked, concern in her voice.

"Didn't get much sleep last night, and a long day at the computer," Timnit replied as they headed back to the kitchen. Timnit placed her laptop on the kitchen table and made a beeline to the coffee maker. "Do you mind?" she asked, gesturing to the full pot.

"Not at all."

"Can I pour you one?"

Patricia nodded.

Coffee mugs in hand, they moved to the table and sat.

"How'd your research go?" Patricia asked.

"I've exhausted all my facial recognition resources." She shook her head. "No hits."

Patricia's stomach sank as she shared Timnit's obvious disappointment. "Well, you should have called me with the bad news and caught on some sleep. Coffee is the last thing you need."

"No, you see, it doesn't make sense. If they are permanent residents here or visa holders in any way, there'd be facial recognition in at least the TSA database. For there to be nothing is actually rather alarming."

"Maybe there was a problem with my images." Patricia had counted on the government's ubiquitous, highly classified facial recognition resources to make an identification of the man and woman who'd followed her, and the man who'd interrogated Sheila about Patricia and her family. It wasn't a matter of competence. Patricia knew Timnit was fully competent to exploit all the facial databases.

"No," Timnit replied. "Your image of the driver was splendid, and the image of the female passenger was more than adequate. Plus, I was able to pull a fine image of Sheila's visitor from the security video. Safe to say the authorities don't have a reference photo of either individual."

"There were three people."

Timnit again shook her head. "The man who visited Sheila was the man who drove the car that followed you."

Patricia gasped. "Really? I guess I should have looked at the security video before I gave the drive to you. Well, that makes one less person to worry about."

"He made a big mistake visiting Sheila. Her new security system got excellent images of him from all angles. Plus, the system recorded his entire conversation with Sheila. I ran the conversation through voice recognition. The system couldn't identify him as a particular person, but Predictive Attribute Analysis identified his voice patterns to Savannah, China." Timnit paused for a moment. Her gaze fixed on Patricia's face.

Patricia stopped her coffee midway to her mouth. "Wait. Did you say Savannah, *China*?"

"It's a spy school where they train agents for duty in Savannah, Georgia," Timnit said.

Patricia had a sense of foreboding. "A trained spy. And no photos in any government database?"

"Happens all the time," Timnit hastily added with a reassuring smile. "They just sneak in across the Canadian border."

"Why's there a Chinese spy school modeled after Savannah, Georgia?"

"To prep spies for missions in Savannah."

"What on earth for?"

Timnit shrugged. "No one I contacted seems to know. But it can't be good."

"If the driver is from a known spy school, wouldn't our counterintelligence people have photos of *everyone* coming and going from that place?"

"I checked. Turns out the compound is so special they have built a wide perimeter of secure, uninhabited territory around the school. Actually, the school is a village designed after part of Savannah. Trainees live there for years. We have no record of comings and goings."

"Satellite observation?"

Timnit nodded. "They're useless for facial observation unless the subject angles their face up at the right moment, but we have a good idea of how many people are there."

"Surely they need food, clothing, and energy. How do they get supplies?"

"Same undetected way the trainees come and go."

"Tunnels?"

"Probably."

Patricia was relieved for that explanation, but still disappointed by the lack of names for the two. "Thank you, Timnit. Excellent work."

Timnit smiled. "Glad to be of some help. How is your part of the investigation going? Any luck with the knife or who might have killed Ken?"

"The knife is attributed to a particular triad, but I have no additional information about the triad. I did find out from Cora there's a rival family business to the Lis' and got a list of names of the local members of that family. I could really use your help if you've reached the end of your own search. But only after you get a good night's sleep."

"No bother at all. I love sleuthing with you."

"I'll email you the names." Patricia picked up her phone and forwarded Cora's email to Timnit. "You take the first half. I'll do the rest."

"What are we looking for?"

"Criminal past," Patricia said. "Even better if they were involved in violent crime. Possible gang involvement. And, of course, no alibi for the night Ken was murdered."

"That will involve interrogation."

"Just of the violent ones."

Timnit wrinkled her brow. "Why would they cooperate?"

"It's all in how you put it to them. You get them talking freely, perhaps over a beer, then encourage boasting. Before you know it, the information you're after pours out of them."

"It's that easy?"

Patricia shrugged. "I wouldn't say it's easy, but it's often doable and certainly worth the try."

After Timnit left, Patricia reviewed the crime records of those Feng family members she was assigned, shocked to find how violent three of the Feng cousins had been, but were back on the streets. The remaining Feng suspects seemed to be remarkably ordinary. Almost too ordinary. And it occurred to Patricia that some of those ordinary profiles she'd found could possibly be fabricated to cover up an assassin.

Patricia and Simon had takeout pizza for dinner, then she worked on further profiling the three Feng cousins she would be chatting up. At nine, she called it a day and got ready for bed. It was odd crawling into bed without Trey beside her. He'd said his depositions could go as late as eleven. Sleep evaded her. She couldn't stop mulling the case through her mind. And Trey's absence didn't help.

Patricia rolled over, picked up her phone from the nightstand and messaged Trey.

PF: Turning in. Please wake me when you get home. I love you.

TF: Will do. Will be here at least two more hours. Love you, too.

Just reading his text settled her somewhat but not completely. She lay in the dark and quiet wondering if someone was in her garage to retrieve the transmitter.

Though Simon was downstairs, she got up, retrieved her Kimber, and put it under her pillow.

The shrill sound of Patricia's five-thirty alarm jolted her awake. Still groggy, she rolled to her back. The shower rumbled in the distance. She blinked and rubbed her tired eyes, wondering why Trey hadn't woken her when he got home.

All night, her sleep-robbing mind kept going back to Ken's body. The blood. The knife. His slack face. And the anguish of telling Cora the terrible news. Dear Cora. Patricia yearned to roll over and try to snooze, but just as she closed her eyes, she thought of Cora waking up this morning without Ken, and Patricia's chest clenched. Poor Cora.

Patricia was no stranger to death. Her mother and father had died. Trey's parents had both passed. Some of her friends had died. But Ken's death was different. Like her mother, Ken had been murdered. He had been healthy and in the prime of life. Her eyes welled. She brushed a tear from her cheek.

She knew Ken as a simple, kind man. Devoted to his family. Always supportive of his friends. He never seemed like the type to be harsh, regardless of circumstances. Sure, he'd had a tough life, what little he shared with her in over twenty years in his styling chair, but he retained a gentle soul through and through. Yet for some unfathomable reason, he had been murdered. Bitterness surged at the utter unreasonableness of his demise. There was something, perhaps a lot of somethings, she didn't understand about Ken and the world he lived in, but she was determined to find out.

She sat up and hung her legs over the side of the bed. Awakening. Focusing. Redirecting her thoughts. Her body ached from fatigue. If there ever was a morning she needed to sleep in, this was it. But with the trip to and from Atlanta on her schedule, she had a full day ahead. Even with the convenience of Trey's jet.

The shower went off. Light spilled from the bathroom. Her turn.

Trey wrapped in a white terry bathrobe came into the bedroom. Water dripped off the cowlick he disliked so much onto his forehead. She smiled at his handsome, tired face. He was just the distraction her mind needed.

She stood, wrapped her arms around Trey and gave him a kiss, then eased back. "Good morning, sweetheart."

"And good morning to you, beautiful. You're up early. I'm glad I got to see you." There was so much warmth and affection in his voice.

"I'm catching the jet to Atlanta today, remember?"

"Oh yes. Who are you seeing?"

"Doctor Yi at Emerald University."

"I know Doctor Yi," Trey said. "Tell him hello for me."

"Will do. What kind of guy is he?"

"Easy going, but he's definitely an academic. If you get him going on Asian affairs, you'll likely get a lecture. Are you seeing Hayley?"

Patricia nodded.

"Give her a hug for me."

Though she wanted to linger with him, she reluctantly headed into the bathroom.

AFTER GETTING READY FOR THE DAY, PATRICIA WENT downstairs, fed the cats, and doled out a few scratches behind their ears. She started the coffee maker, turned the oven on rapid preheat and removed some biscuits from the freezer.

Trey came into the kitchen dressed for work and gave her a quick kiss. "What time are you and Simon leaving for Atlanta?"

"Ten, but Simon isn't going."

"I think that's a mistake."

"I can take care of myself."

"Text me when you land so I know you got there safely."

She nodded.

The oven chimed the end of its preheat cycle. Patricia put the frozen buttermilk biscuits in the induction oven and set the timer. Trey went to the counter and poured two cups of coffee, as well as one in his travel mug. "What time are you seeing Algenon?" He handed the second cup to Patricia.

"I'm seeing him at four. What's on your schedule today?"

"More depositions and Saint Patrick's Day parade details."

"Problems?" Patricia sat her coffee on the counter, removed the biscuits from the oven, and put four of them on the table. Then she made a plate of two for Simon.

Trey shook his head. "There are always problems. Pimps, prostitutes, and pickpockets pour into town for the event. But as long as it's not organized crime, it's nothing we can't handle." Trey wrapped a biscuit in a paper napkin, grabbed the steaming travel mug of coffee, and headed out. "Patsy," he yelled from the mudroom. "Did you go out and get the paper this morning?"

"No. Why?"

Trey returned with a questioning look. "The back door is unlocked."

A shiver ran though Patricia.

"Maybe Simon went out." She went into the dining room and handed Simon the plate with the biscuits. "Did you use the backdoor this morning?"

"Yes. Checked to see if the tracker was missing from your SUV."

"And?"

"Still there."

"Did you lock the door when you came back in?"

"Probably."

"Sure?"

"Not sure." He took a bite of biscuit. "Why?"

"Trey just found it unlocked."

"Oh." Simon keyed one of his laptops. "I'll check the security log. Here it is. The back door was locked all night until I went out. When I came back in, I forgot to lock it."

Patricia's shoulders relaxed. "Thank you, Simon."

"Since you're going to Atlanta today, do you mind if I borrow your Navigator? I want to take it out in public for a while so the bad guys will have a chance to retrieve the tracker."

RAYLEE PENG FINISHED THE LAST *TAI CHI* POSTURE IN HER regular series. With her body cleansed and her life force elevated, she thanked her instructor. Then she picked up her backpack from the park bench and made her way past the glorious, pink azalea bushes in full bloom toward the Sentient Bean coffee shop. A familiar route. One she'd taken nearly every morning since joining the class six months ago. On the way, she paused to once again admire the Candler

Oak, Savannah's largest oak and at 300 years old one of the oldest living landmarks in the city.

She loved being able to attend private school in Savannah. Her freshman classes in fashion design were beyond exceptional, but what really brought her pleasure was how thoroughly Savannah revered its history. Her gaze roamed the broad canopy of the Candler Oak. Raylee let out a whistle in admiration. This magnificent oak was growing in this spot before Savannah was settled in 1733 and had been lovingly cared for ever since. Joy filled her heart at the thought.

Savannah, China, the training city she grew up in, didn't have the Candler Oak, but they had done a very good job of duplicating the homes, businesses, and parks of a large section of the historic district of Savannah. Everyone spoke English with a drawl, routinely ate shrimp and grits, and attended Savannah Bananas baseball games. There as here, Forsyth Park was her favorite place, and March, with all the azaleas in bloom, was her favorite month.

Rumor back home was that there were quite a few similar Americanized training villages in China, each fashioned after a targeted American city. She wasn't sure what they were targeted for. Nor was she aware of what her role was beyond attending fashion school at the Savannah Design Academy, an assignment she'd only known about since last summer.

So here she was in a place that felt like home, attending college, and checking the dead drop at the Sentient Bean each morning.

Raylee walked into the coffee shop and saw with relief the table she was supposed to visit each morning was empty. She went to the counter and ordered chai and a barbeque tofu taco. After receiving her food, she crossed to the table, put her food down and sat. While taking her drink with her right hand, she casually reached up under the tabletop with her left. Her heart sped on finding something there, a very rare occurrence. She palmed the message and brought her hand up to the tabletop. After sipping her chai for a few more moments, she sat her chai drink down and picked up the message.

She'd always thought it strange in this modern electronic era that her control officer used handwritten messages. She'd been told such messages were much more secure than any other communications, particularly when written in the obscure Chinese dialect she'd been schooled in since she first started reading back home. She unfolded the message.

Go to 1020 Abercorn at 6:30 a.m. on the morning of the Savannah Saint Patrick's Day parade. Check in with the receptionist. Code word: Dragon.

A LIMO MET PATRICIA AT THE GENERAL AVIATION TERMINAL AT Atlanta's DeKalb-Peachtree Airport and dropped her at Hayley's dormitory at Emerald University.

Patricia texted Hayley to let her know she had arrived. "I'll wait for you in the lobby."

A few minutes later, Hayley walked into the lobby with a big smile and outstretched arms. "Mom!"

After a warm embrace, Patricia stepped back to admire her daughter, who was dressed in a green Emerald University hoodie and distressed jeans. "It's so good to see you."

Hayley gave an even broader smile that accentuated her dimples and scrunched her brown eyes. You couldn't fake happiness like that. "I thought you might like eating at the food court. You know, a taste of college life. My life."

"Of course."

They walked to the food court, and both ordered salads.

"How's school going?" Patricia asked.

"Wonderful," Hayley replied in a bright tone that warmed Patricia's heart.

They talked about courses and sororities and college life. All seemed to be going smoothly. Patricia knew Hayley had been seeing a classmate named Shawn but, knowing how fluid college life could be, avoided asking about him. And Hayley didn't bring the subject up. After a half hour, Patricia looked at her watch. "What time's your next class?"

"I'm done for the day." Hayley began to gather up her dishes. "How about you? What time is your appointment?"

"Fifteen minutes. Do you want to walk with me to the Asian Studies Department?"

"Sure. I looked up this professor and know exactly where his office is. If we leave now, we should be able to get there in plenty of time." Hayley stood and gathered her tray. "Why are you meeting with him. And don't tell me it's a case you're working on like you did on the phone. Why him and for what?"

Patricia gathered her tray as well, and they headed to the discard station. "We might have a Chinese gang forming in Savannah, and he's an Asian gang expert," Patricia said.

"Why are you interested in gangs?"

She held the door for her daughter as they headed outside. "One of their members might have killed a friend of mine."

"Someone I know?"

"No."

After a pleasant walk across the campus, they parted with a long hug outside the building where Doctor Yi's office was located. It was, as always, too short of a visit with Hayley, but it was time well-spent that once again reassured Patricia that her daughter had acclimated to college well.

Patricia had no problem finding Doctor Yi's well-marked office on the first floor of the building. The door was ajar.

When she rapped on the doorjamb, a male voice with a Southern drawl beckoned her in.

As she entered, his dark eyes took on a feral alertness. What about her had provoked that look? Or did he level it on everyone? She took a moment to study him, then her focus shifted to her surroundings. A steel desk was straight ahead, a window overlooking the quad behind it. A conference table was on the left. Bookcases filled the walls. The office felt cozy.

Smiling broadly, Doctor Yi came around the desk with his hand extended. Taller than she had expected, he had a full head of gray, conservatively cut hair and wore a short-sleeved light blue shirt and khakis. His size clashed with his broad shoulders and thick, hairless arms.

"You must be Mrs. Falcon."

She took his hand. His grip was firm. "Please, call me Patricia."

He nodded his understanding. "My pleasure." He gestured to the small, round table in the corner.

She took one of the chairs.

He settled into the other. "Are you related to Trey Falcon?"

"He's my husband. And he sends you greetings."

"We've occasionally worked together. He's a very nice man. So, what can I do for you, Mrs., Patricia?" he asked.

Patricia removed one of the eight by ten knife photos from her purse and handed it to Doctor Yi.

His forehead creased as he examined the image closely. "There appears to be blood on the knife." In contrast to the antique dealer, Yi's voice was confident. No fear there.

"Yes."

He gestured to the photo. "What is your relationship to this knife?"

"It's evidence in a case I'm investigating."

His bushy eyebrows raised. "Are you police?"

"No. Private investigator working with the Savannah Police."

He looked down and his lips pursed for a moment, as if contemplating whether to cooperate of not. Then he looked up. "Okay. How can I help?"

"Do you know anything about this kind of knife?"

"This appears to be a dragon master's knife."

"Does the specific design mean anything to you?"

"Maybe." He stood, went to his desk, found a magnifying glass in a drawer, and returned. He examined the photo under magnification. He looked up to Patricia. "It would be better if I could examine the actual knife. The resolution of this photo isn't the best. However, based on what I can see in the photo, I'd say this knife is from the Forty-four Brothers triad. It's an elite paramilitary organization that supports certain international activities of the Chinese Communist Party. And if it is from the Forty-four Brothers, I would say that as a layman you're playing way out of your league."

"What sort of activities?"

"Everything from intimidation to assassination. What Chinese diplomats fail to accomplish is turned over to the Forty-four Brothers."

"Why do they use such a distinctive weapon?"

"To send a message to the local Chinese community that people will continue to die until whatever is requested is achieved."

Patricia recalled the antique dealer's reaction. "Intimidation."

"Where did you say you're from again?" he asked.

"Savannah."

Yi rubbed a finger over his eyebrow. "A small, easy to control city," he said absently.

There was something welcoming about Yi's manner. She

couldn't quite put her finger on it, but it encouraged dialogue, so she pressed on. "How would Savannah stop the triad?"

He folded his hands on the table. "Many have tried. All have failed."

She didn't bother to hide her frustration. She wanted a plan to cope with the triad. "What did they do wrong?"

"They probably didn't realize how important successful missions are for the triad. They absolutely must succeed and will simply pour more resources into the mission to achieve success. Remember, this is a Chinese organization. The triad has an unlimited supply of assassins and will take all the time they need for success. They definitely take the long view."

She shook her head in despair. "Given your knowledge, how would you recommend trying to stop them?"

"You have to stop them from within," Doctor Yi said. "The same way the FBI brought down the Italian mobs. Infiltrate. Map the organization. When you're certain you know all the leaders, take them out all at once."

"Short of that?"

"I'm afraid they'll run your city."

A shiver went through Patricia. Thank God Savannah had the Cotton Coalition. But would the Coalition be strong enough for this particular threat? And Trey could become a target. Her heart pounded. She took in a deep breath, trying to get her system calmed.

She returned the photo to her purse. "You say run the city, and you mentioned control? What exactly do you mean by that?"

Silence hung for a moment. Was he trying to decide how much to share? She was, after all, a stranger. "Based on their camps in China, we know they've been training operatives for work in Savannah. Several years ago, they built a rather large village resembling a portion of Savannah's historic district and populated it with at least a couple hundred people. In some instances, complete families. That village replaced a much smaller one built thirty years ago in the wake of the Tiananmen Square massacre."

"What are they training for?"

"We don't know."

"We?"

"A government agency that keeps track of such things. I consult with them frequently."

With the triad now present in Savannah, she had no doubt the Cotton Coalition could find out whatever the secret government agency knew. "How long has the Forty-four Brothers triad been in Savannah?"

"That knife is the first evidence I've seen that they've finally arrived. And as I mentioned before, once they arrive, they'll be there forever."

She resisted the temptation to tell him about the Cotton Coalition. "Not what I wanted to hear."

"I know. But it's the unfortunate reality."

"Is there any way to identify members? Like tattoos? Distinctive clothing? Hand signs?"

"Tattoos of the Mandarin characters for forty-four on their lower back." He drew the two symbols on a blank piece of paper and handed it to her. "Plus, we're told the dragon master usually wears a distinctive dragon ring."

"Is there a list of known or suspected members of the triad?"

"No. Not a single name."

"So there would be no organization chart?"

"Correct."

"How do you know they actually exist?"

"To some extent, the Forty-four Brothers are active in most large Chinatowns in America and have been, in one form or the other, since the nineties. We've seen duplicates of your knife at some crimes in those communities and have numerous anecdotal accounts of the triad's existence and practices. Though, I have to say, getting people to speak of them is extremely difficult."

"So I've learned."

He gave her a smile.

"This government agency you spoke of, have they infiltrated the triad?"

"It's not for me to say. I hope you understand."

"One more question?"

"Go ahead."

"The day following the assassination, I was followed, and a tracker was placed on my vehicle. I confronted the stalkers, and they identified themselves as FBI, but they might have been triad. If they were triad, why wouldn't they just kill me at the scene?"

"Did you witness the murder?" he asked, obviously shocked.

"No. But I was the first on the scene. I called 911."

"That's why you're alive. You can't actually identify the killer."

"Then why follow me?"

Yi paused for a moment, probably considering his words. "As you say, the people following you could be FBI. But if they were triad, they might have just been being thorough. The triad has maintained secrecy for decades by meticulously tying up loose ends. As long as you stay out of their hair, you're okay. But as soon as you get too close to them, you'll become a liability, and they won't hesitate to kill you."

"I'm investigating the assassination. Why not kill me now?"

"Every one of their assassinations have been investigated. That's no problem for them. Preemptively killing investigators would simply attract more attention, and they don't want that. But don't get me wrong-get too close to them, and you'll become a target."

"I understand."

"Be circumspect in the rest of your investigation," he said gravely. "Like coming here. Were you followed? Was your car tracked to the university? For your own safety, you must always endeavor to mislead the triad."

"I came by private jet."

"Your phone," he said. "It's easily tracked."

"It's secure."

Yi cocked his head and looked at her appraisingly. "Are you sure?"

CHAPTER 13

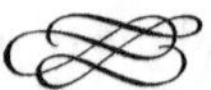

The Savannah FBI field office was in a suburban area outside of Savannah. The limo with Patricia and Timnit was on the onramp to I16 when Patricia's phone rang. The display read Willie Maye, a reporter for the *Savannah Post* she'd communicated with for years. She'd known Willie long enough to know he didn't make social calls at three forty-five in the afternoon.

"Hello, Willie. What can I do for you?"

"Can you talk?"

"For a moment," she said. "I have a meeting at four." She glanced out the window of the limo and got her bearings. Still at least ten minutes to the FBI building.

"Do you want me to call back later?"

"Is your business going to take some time?" she asked.

"Probably. If you cooperate," he said with an expectant lilt to his voice.

She chuckled. "I generally cooperate with you, Willie. What's this about?"

"Ken Li's murder. I heard you found the body. Can you fill me in?"

"Yeah. Off the record." She wasn't surprised Willie was following up the case, he was an investigative reporter after all, and there were no suspects. Besides, Willie, who had the most amazing contacts, might have some additional insight into how the city's murder investigation was going and might even have some theories she'd not considered on why Ken had been killed. "I'll call you after my meeting."

"An hour or two?"

"Probably less. Goodbye, Willie. Stay out of trouble." She ended the call.

A few minutes later, the limo pulled into a parking spot in front of the FBI office.

"This shouldn't take much time," she told Timnit.

"I'm sure the FBI office is secure. I'll wait here and keep an eye out for any unexpected visitors."

Patricia climbed from the limo. Pink azaleas were in full bloom and the hardwood trees were beginning to leaf out. March in Savannah was so heavenly.

She stepped into the FBI lobby, surrendered her gun to security, and was escorted to Algenon's office.

Algenon, the consummate gentleman, stood at the sight of her and came around the desk. He wore, as always, a black suit, white shirt and, today, a blue tie. "Good afternoon, Patricia."

"Algenon."

They embraced briefly, then he gestured to a chair at the front of his desk.

"Coffee?" he asked.

She nodded.

He stepped to the office door. "Rita. Would you please bring us two coffees?" He went to his desk and sat. "How are things with you today?"

"A lot going on."

He chuckled. "Patricia, you're always looking into something. Especially when you visit me. So what's it today?"

She pulled the stalker photos from her purse and handed the picture of the driver to Algenon. "Let me tell you a story. The afternoon after I stumbled on Ken Li's murder, my car was followed by two people in an Escalade. When I stopped and confronted them, they said they were FBI agents."

Algenon's white eyebrows shot to his hairline.

"Are your people following me?" Patricia pressed.

"No." He took a closer look at the picture, then grimaced as he placed the photo on his desk. "This guy doesn't work for me."

"He had an FBI ID." She handed him the photo of the man's FBI ID.

Algenon examined it closely. "The ID looks authentic, but, like I said, this man doesn't work for me. Perhaps he's part of a special unit." He keyed his computer. After a moment, his face soured. "Nope. Not FBI. It's a serious offense to impersonate an FBI agent. Given the circumstances, this man could be Ken Li's murderer or someone working with the murderer. I suggest you be careful." His voice ended on a firm tone. "And I need to take a report from you and make a copy of those photos." Coming from him, it was an important warning. He never exaggerated.

"I am careful and will continue to be. I have a strong husband who has trained me to deal with fear, as well as aggressors." She patted her purse. "I always carry my Kimber and know how to use it. And if cornered, I *will* use it. And I have an associate with me, a former special ops person. Well trained. Together we are awesome."

"Live with your pistol. Even sleep with it. Vary your traffic routes. And vary your vehicles, if possible."

Which was why she used a limo to visit him. No way was she going to use the Navigator and tip off the triad she was talking to the FBI. Patricia offered him the photo of the stalker vehicle license plate. "The guy was driving this car."

"I'm reluctantly impressed you had your wits about you so much, after witnessing a murder scene no less, to get all this information and confront your follower. But it was extremely dangerous. Please be more careful from now on. Let me get a trace on this plate." He keyed it into his computer. "It'll take a moment."

Rita came in with the coffee and put the tray on the conference table wordlessly. Rita had worked for Algenon for as long as Patricia had known the man.

"How's your husband doing?" Patricia asked her.

"He just got out of the hospital. Thank you for asking. How's Trey?"

"Busy as usual."

"Enjoy your coffee," Rita said as she turned to leave.

"We have a match," Algenon said. "The plate is registered to a local rental agency. Not much help there. Let's see what the rental agency has." Algenon pursed his lips. "The car was rented by an Emma Zhang. They're emailing me a copy of her driver's license and credit card. Was there a woman in the car also?"

"Yes. But the picture of her is low quality."

"I'll have one of our guys check her out and let you know what they come up with." Algenon's laptop signaled a notification. He worked his keyboard. "I just forwarded the rental documentation to you."

"Thank you."

"And I'll submit this photo of the driver and Emma Zhang's driver's license photo to facial recognition. That should help narrow this down."

There was a sense of external calm brought on by his full cooperation, but internally Patricia was still unsettled. She picked up the coffee, blew over the top to cool it a bit, and took a sip. Algenon always had the best coffee.

The triad connection to Ken's death troubled Patricia, particularly now since Algenon had confirmed the stalkers didn't work for him. Had she stumbled into an international plot or a triad mission of some sort? Had she captured photos of two photo-shy triad members? She took a deep breath and let it out slowly. Doctor Yi had said he was unaware of *any* photos of members of the Forty-four Brothers triad. No wonder they were tracking her. How far would they go to get those photos back?

She sensed the photos would become important pieces of evidence. But presently it was one step at a time. She leaned forward a bit. "Are there any Chinese gangs active in Savannah?"

His lips curled downward as he thought. "There's certainly crime within the Chinese community. Ordinary stuff, like in any community. But nothing I'd say was gang related."

She sat back, took a photo of the dragon master's knife from her purse, and handed the glossy to Algenon. "This is the weapon used to kill Ken Li. As you can see, it's quite distinctive. I'm told by a Chinese gang expert that it's a weapon used exclusively by the Forty-four Brothers triad. Have you heard of them?"

His face pulled into a frown as he examined the photo closely. "No. I haven't. Can I make a copy of this too? I want to forward it to our Violent Crimes Task Force in Atlanta. They'll run the knife though our weapons database."

She nodded.

He summoned Rita and asked her to make a couple of copies.

"What agency keeps track of foreign spies operating in the United States?" she asked.

Algenon looked at her thoughtfully, as if he sensed there was more to the question. "The Counterintelligence Division of the FBI's National Security Branch is tasked with protecting the United States from foreign intelligence and espionage."

"What about the CIA?"

"They operate exclusively overseas."

"And the National Security Agency?"

"They monitor international communications. Why?"

"I'm just trying to get straight who is responsible for getting control of this triad. Based on what you just told me, the FBI would keep track of the Forty-four Brothers triad when they operate in the United States."

"Correct." He jotted a note she couldn't read.

"Does the FBI maintain a gang database?"

His dark eyes focused on her like a laser. "Yes."

"Is the Forty-four Bothers triad listed?"

"Is there a reason you think they would be?"

"I'm told they are active in most of the large Chinatowns in the United States."

His brow furrowed. "Who have you been talking to?"

"Doctor Bai Yi. He's a professor at Emerald University and is known as an expert on Chinese gangs."

He didn't reply straightaway, apparently considering all she'd just shared. "Okay." Algenon's eyes fixed on the screen as he keyed his computer. He squinted to read whatever came up and clicked on his mouse. Eventually, he looked up. "The Forty-four Brothers triad is in our database."

"So if the triad is in Savannah, y'all would track their activities, figure out what they were up to, and take action to counter their mission?"

He gave a skeptical look. "Yes and no. We might try to confirm they were here and perhaps even investigate them a bit. But the reality is we're chronically short of manpower.

So we can only track the biggest threats. It's always been that way. If our initial assessment of the triad concludes they don't pose much of a threat to Savannah, we probably won't do anything about them being here."

Unwilling to give up, she pointed to the knife photo. "They murdered Ken Li. The knife. It's not something they carry at Walmart."

"The knife itself isn't really evidence that a member of the triad stuck that particular knife into Ken Li. I know you know that. Sure the knife is a lead. Possibly a good lead. But before we could take any action, we'd need much more evidence."

He was right, of course. The FBI would be powerless to apprehend the stalker without rock-solid evidence he committed a crime. "Okay. Now this next part is going to sound farfetched, but I've corroborated it. And honestly, with the lead on the knife, it's starting to seem more plausible. Are you aware there's a spy school in China training spies for missions in Savannah?"

He drew a sharp breath. "No."

"If there was such a school, would that increase your sense of urgency to investigate the killing of Ken Li with this knife and the people following me?"

He looked at her for a long moment, then made a note that she could see was the name of the triad. "I can't promise anything. And this is … a lot. But I trust you not to come to me with frivolous claims. Thank you for bringing this to my attention."

Her persistence had paid off. "Thank you, Algenon." She grabbed her purse and stood up.

He walked her to the lobby and bid her goodbye.

She retrieved her pistol from security and stepped outside. The sunny day was bright and dazzling. She blinked while her eyes adjusted.

She settled into the backseat of the limo with Timnit. She wasn't wild about getting tangled up with the triad, but with the FBI and police focused on keeping an eye on the half a million visitors who were flooding Savannah for the Saint Patrick's Day festivities, she knew it was likely up to her, and her alone, to come up with solid evidence on the killer. She'd find a way to neutralize the inevitable fallout.

CHAPTER 14

Returning Willie's calls could be as dangerous as playing golf on Skidaway Island with predators lurking in the undergrowth and lagoons. Big hungry alligators. And venomous snakes. Willie was a good contact and, after decades of covering the news, knew more about the dark side of Savannah than most. He'd given Patricia a hand on some of her tougher cases, and she'd helped him out when she could. But every now and then he violated her trust, like when he wrote a disparaging article about her mother. Patricia asked the driver to raise the privacy screen.

Willie picked up on the second ring.

"Good afternoon, Willie. Patricia Falcon, I'm returning your call."

"I heard you found Ken Li's body." Willie always cut to the chase. Expediency was his bonus maker. "Does that mean you were one of his clients?"

The mention of Ken's body brought the whole murder scene to life. Her longtime friend sitting lifeless in a salon chair. She took a deep breath in the hope it would calm her, but it didn't. "He did my hair for twenty years. Ken was an exceptional hairdresser, a good friend, and an extraordinarily kind man. Such a sad thing to happen."

"Any idea who would want to kill him?"

It was the same painful, frustrating question the police had repeatedly asked at the scene. She'd grown to hate it. "Nothing yet. Do any of your sources know anything?"

"The police say they're stumped. Apparently, he was a model citizen with no known enemies. Did you know his family?"

"Yes."

"I was hoping he or they might have said something to you that might be useful."

"I'll tell you the same thing I told the police. Ken Li was indeed a model citizen. He was honest, ethical, and extremely generous."

"He was also immensely successful, Patricia. Surely he stepped on some toes on his way to Savannah's economic summit."

She shifted uncomfortably. "As far as I know, all my friends had nothing but respect for Ken. You know, he didn't inherit his money. He and Cora immigrated to the US with five children and the clothes on their backs. He worked hard. He educated his children and instilled a strong work ethic in each. You can't fault him for that."

"I heard that he started with a small machine shop."

She sorted through her memory and came up blank. "I've heard that."

"According to state records, after he arrived, he incorporated the machine shop business and then he brought in immigrants from Hong Kong to operate it. It made money right from the start." Willie didn't wait for Patricia to respond. "My problem is I can't figure out how a dirt-poor immigrant could afford the overhead, like the lease, machinery, and the rest of the investment to get started. There are no records of secured loans to his company. Not a dime. The German equipment maker was paid in full by the Savannah Mercantile Bank a year after delivery. I'm having trouble getting information from the bank. They don't like dealing with me since that story I wrote about their mob connections."

For a second, she lost her focus. She blew out a held breath. "So how can I help you, Willie?"

"Could you check around and see if you can find out who bankrolled Mr. Li when he arrived?"

"Trey and I will be socializing some this week and next. Saint Patrick's festivities, you know. I'll ask around. Do you think his mystery backer might have something to do with his death?"

"Too early to tell, but I'm betting that Mr. Li, like many successful people, has some unflattering secrets. Prominent people don't get murdered randomly. There's usually a reason. That's the story I'm after, and I'd guess the story lies very close to someone's money."

Patricia bristled at Willie's harsh assessment. That was exactly how he'd handled her mother's death. What did he have against rich people anyway? On the other hand, in this instance he could prove to be useful to her own investigation.

She thought briefly of telling Willie about the triad link, but worried he'd mishandle the information. It could upset her investigation, not to mention needlessly damage Ken's reputation. But if Willie came across some information that could help her, like the machine shop history, she'd need to keep lines of communication open.

"You still there, Patricia?"

"Yes, sorry, just navigating traffic." He didn't need to know she wasn't driving.

"Did you know Ken Li owned a building on Barnard Street?" he asked.

"As a matter of fact, I do. The family lives on the top floor. One of his sons operates a Chinese restaurant on street level."

"There are two other floors in that building," he said. "Do you have any idea what they're used for?"

"No." The limo pulled up in front of her house. A while back, she'd learned there was an extraordinary amount of advanced electronic security on the perimeter of Ken's building. Far more advanced than was normal for commercial establishments in Savannah. And, of course, there was the gold Cora had mentioned. There was no way she was going to tell Willie about that.

"Just because someone owns two extra floors in a building doesn't make them suspicious, Willie. They have a huge family."

"No one's perfect. There's so much bad in the best of us, and so much good in the worst of us that it's often hard to tell the difference."

"For now, Willie, you need to report it as a burglary gone wrong," she said. "At least until the funeral. Any speculation about a link to a criminal element is going to make Ken look bad, and right now, he's just a victim. His family is grieving his loss, and they deal with enough prejudice, despite their financial success. I agree we need to find the truth of what happened, but let's be very, very sure before we ruin the man's legacy."

She heard Willie exhale. "If we want to find his killer, someone is going to have to locate the mud and plow through it."

"The police can do that. There's no reason to pillory a good man in the press."

"The police told me they don't have a clue. And with the

Saint Patrick's crowds building, they won't have much time to properly delve into his murder until after the tourists leave town. That's two weeks away, and I have a job to do."

Patricia sighed.

"Look, Patricia. If he was your friend like you say, then I know darn well you're looking into his death too. Don't pretend otherwise. So you help me with anything you find, and I'll keep you informed of what I come up with in my investigation, good or bad."

"No muckraking though," she warned, neither confirming nor denying.

"Agreed. I've learned the hard way that tearing down good people is short-sighted for an investigative reporter."

Patricia flexed her jaw. "All right. I'll ask around."

Once she completed her call with Willie, she got Meredith Stanwick, her best friend and a banker, on the line. "I need a favor," she stated after their usual pleasantries. "Unless you're too busy today."

"Sure. What do you need?"

"I want a financial profile on someone. I'm texting you the name right now."

"Like a Dun & Bradstreet report?"

Patricia moved the phone to her other ear. "Yes. But a historical perspective as well."

"No problem. Is there anything in particular you're looking for?"

"This person started a machine shop when he first immigrated here. It would be good to know who backed him."

Patricia heard clicking. "Okay. When do you need this?"

"Today. If that's at all possible."

"That shouldn't be a problem. I'll see what I can come up with quickly. Since he is a business owner." Meredith paused. "*Was* a business owner, there should be a fair amount of reliable financial information on him. Give me an hour. Okay?"

"That's great. Thank you, Meredith." Patricia looked at her watch. Two o'clock. "Are you free for dinner?"

"Yes. Is Trey out of town?"

"No. He's just working late. I'll meet you at 17Hundred90 at six."

Once the call was over, Patricia asked the limo driver to take Timnit home, said her goodbyes, and headed up the walk to her home. Once settled inside, Patricia contacted Isabel to thank her for the use of the limo and to set up a midmorning meeting the following day at Huey's. Then she called Summer to arrange getting together at Summer's home after the Isabel meeting. And finally, she scheduled a midafternoon meeting with Lily Li. It would be a busy day, but each meeting was critical to advancing Patricia's case.

Next, she spoke with Simon about transportation. "I need to get back to driving my own car."

"I'd rather you not do that. It's too dangerous."

"Come on. If Ken's murderers wanted me dead, I'd be long gone by now. They have no reason to believe I'm onto them. From their point of view, I'm no threat. They have bigger fish to fry. The more normally I operate, the more they'll lose interest in me. I'm using the Navigator tomorrow."

"What about the tracker?"

"I'm having coffee with my lawyer in the morning and meeting a good friend afterward. There's nothing suspicious about that."

"We have Isabel's limo for the rest of the day."

"Okay," Patricia relented. She knew Simon was just doing his job of keeping her safe. "I'll use the limo for my dinner with Meredith."

. . .

THE LIMO PULLED UP AT 17Hundred90 JUST AS A NEARBY cathedral chimed six. Patricia headed into the restaurant.

"One for dinner?" the maître d' asked.

Patricia searched the dining room for Meredith. "No. I'm dining with a friend, but she doesn't seem to have arrived."

"Miss Stanwick?"

"Yes."

"She asked to be seated privately. Please follow me."

The maître d' led her down a hallway toward the rear, then opened a well-disguised door to a small, tastefully decorated room the size of a small bedroom and stepped aside. One table with two chairs was placed by the window. A crystal chandelier illuminated the mahogany-paneled space. Twilight poured through the lace curtain to illuminate the table and its occupant. Meredith, her smile genuine though slightly uneasy, stood on seeing them. She wore a black suit, and her dark hair was twisted up into an elegant chignon.

Patricia had known Meredith for twenty years, first meeting the banker to discuss investing some trust fund money she'd come into from her father.

They embraced momentarily, then Patricia went around to her side of the table. "Any luck getting a financial profile on Ken Li?" Patricia asked once the waiter had departed.

"Plenty of information, right back to his start in Savannah." Meredith passed a file folder to Patricia. "There was a big transfer of funds to him shortly after he arrived in Savannah and then smaller, but still sizable, amounts quarterly afterward for three years. All done according to international banking standards and our laws."

"Legitimate?"

"Appears so. But …" Meredith shrugged.

"Dirty money?" Patricia bit her lip.

"I don't think so. According to my Hong Kong contact,

the money was transferred from a Chinese government account with a nine-figure balance."

Patricia's mouth dropped again, her mind reeling. "A government investment? Or a loan?"

"Possibly a loan," Meredith said. "My source reports that similar transfers are routinely made to other Chinese individuals in the US."

"Business people?"

"Apparently."

"Did Ken make any payments back to the bank?" Patricia asked.

"There's no record of that."

"So what now?" Patricia asked, eyebrows raised.

Meredith shook her head. "Making more inquiries could alert the Chinese authorities and be traced back to me. And until I know it's above board or sanctioned, my gut tells me not to poke my head up too high. Or get the bank into trouble."

"I understand." Patricia nodded. "I don't want to put you in an awkward position."

Meredith flicked her black hair off her face, exposing the scar on her forehead from where she had been shot. Every time Patricia saw the remnants of the attempted murder of her best friend, a slug of guilt dumped into her stomach. Meredith had been shot and nearly killed because Patricia involved her in the investigation of Patricia's mother's death.

"As much as I'd like to help you, Patricia, I'm a banker, and I can't afford to get crosswise with big money Chinese."

She certainly understood Meredith's reluctance. "Alright, I'll look into the Chinese government connection myself, but can you help me get information on some old transactions involving Ken at the Savannah Mercantile Bank?"

Meredith's dark eyes widened. "I didn't see those in his profile. If Ken did business with them, that's dirty money for sure. They have a long history of money laundering. I doubt that I can get information on those transactions. They were probably off book."

"I'm told Ken did business with them twenty years ago. Possibly a sizable business loan for some German machinery he imported to set up a machine shop."

Meredith shook her head. "That doesn't make sense. Why would he do business with Savannah Mercantile when he had Chinese government backing?"

"Hopefully, that's what you and I are going to find out. Are you in?"

Meredith smiled. "I'll help as much as I can as long as it doesn't involve direct contact with Chinese banks."

Though Raylee Peng had been schooled from birth to keep her emotions in check, she couldn't suppress her elation each time she received a letter from home. Her hands quivered as she opened the envelope and unfolded the two sheets of family stationary covered with the obscure Chinese dialect that kept their messages private. Warmth radiated through her body as she recognized her father's characteristic writing.

Dearest Ying. He never used her Western name. *We are moving to Savannah—*

Her heart drumming in her ears, Raylee dropped the letter to her desktop, brought her hands to her face and sobbed tears of utter joy. Her family was coming to Savannah. They would be reunited. When? Why? With shaking hands, she picked up the first sheet and read again.

Dearest Ying,

We are moving to Savannah. I am opening a branch office of the Hong Kong and Macau Bank there. We believe it is essential to your education that you continue to live at school but are grateful for the opportunity to be closer to our beloved daughter. Details of the move are uncertain. We will contact you on arrival.

The lack of a specific time disappointed Raylee. She picked up the second page, a letter from her mother.

My precious daughter,

My prayers to be reunited with you have been answered. While we will miss our friends here, it is minor to the joy of having our family together again. I realize your studies are most important and will take priority. But we can now spend holidays and special occasions together once again. Your father is excited about his new opportunity. Your brother is not happy to be leaving his friends but understands his duty. The Songs and Wangs are also moving to Savannah.

Raylee's thoughts raced as she folded the letters and returned them to the envelope, noting the Atlanta postmark and US postage stamp. More security she supposed.

She knew the Songs and Wangs from home. Their daughters had not only been in training with her in China, but were now also in the same school with her in Savannah.

CHAPTER 15

Trey had already left for work when Patricia awoke the following morning. Though disappointed to have missed him, she knew he still had a busy week or two of depositions. At least they'd have some time together at the evening's gala. Though they both tended to treat galas as networking events, she hoped they'd get a chance to catch up with each other. There was so much she was trying to get her head around.

She did a light treadmill workout, showered, and dressed for the day. Once downstairs, she greeted Simon, fed the cats, and caught up on her text and email messages. At nine thirty, she left for River Street, where she found a parking space in a lot just down the road from Huey's, thankful to be driving her own car again, even above Simon's protestations.

The cool, dark interior of Huey's bar provided respite from the bright sunshine. It took a moment for Patricia's eyes to adjust.

Isabel, her close friend and lawyer, was seated in the shadows at the far end of the bar well away from the front of the house. It was the bacchanalian week before Saint

Patrick's Day, so Patricia wasn't surprised the front of the bar was crowded, but the stools Isabel had secured looked relatively isolated. Patricia saw no signs of Isabel's security detail, which was as it should be.

Once they greeted each other, they ordered chicory coffee and beignets, skipping Huey's signature pecan caramel syrup. Isabel's gray hair was pulled up into her trademark bun. Her nails were black, as always.

The bartender poured coffee for them, then returned to the customers packed into the front of the bar. Patricia glanced around the room as the Cajun vibe sharpened.

"Our own slice of New Orleans," Isabel said as the bartender placed the basket of warm beignets between them. They each lifted a powdered sugar-coated pillow of goodness from the basket.

Patricia took a bite, savoring the sweetness, then wiped the excess powdered sugar from her mouth and fingers with her napkin. A swallow of rich black coffee cleared her palate. "How's your father doing?" Patricia asked.

Isabel's attentive face became somber as it always did when discussing her father's long battle with cancer. "His cancer is growing again, so his oncologist is switching his medications." Her voice caught on an emotional wave. "Apparently, the cancer adjusts to treatments, so it was anticipated that sooner or later he'd have to switch to a new drug routine. But it's disappointing, nonetheless. There are only so many drugs that work on his form of cancer. After that, all that are left are some experimental drugs."

Patricia took Isabel's cold hand. "Every extra day you get with your father is a blessing," she said, missing her deceased mother fiercely.

Though Isabel's hazel eyes were moist, she managed a faint smile. "I know, Patricia. We're so blessed to have these medications, and Father seemed to tolerate the first one well." She wiped her eyelids with her fingertips. "I hate to see him so incapacitated, and I know he hates it more than I. Oh, Patricia, we're such a sorry bunch."

Patricia gently squeezed Isabel's hand. "You give him a reason to go on."

"I suppose." She sounded uncertain.

Patricia gave another squeeze. "You *are* his rock."

Isabel nodded. "Enough of me." She pulled her hand from Patricia's. "How are you?"

"I'm fine."

"And to what do I owe this meeting?" Isabel's face filled with anticipation.

Patricia knew Isabel was exceptionally well-informed about Savannah dynamics, particularly since she was the head of the Cotton Coalition. And that meant Isabel might have information that could help her investigation. Patricia pitched her voice low. "I think a Chinese triad might be behind Ken Li's murder."

Isabel's hazel eyes narrowed slightly. "Why do you say that?"

"The murder weapon is a triad calling card, so to speak."

"Okay." Isabel's gaze was focused. "What are we talking about?"

"A knife, a dagger really, known to be used by triad assassins. What do you know about Chinese gangs in Savannah?" Patricia asked in a whisper.

Isabel shook her head. "There aren't any that I know of."

"Have you heard of a city in China training spies for missions specifically in Savannah?"

Isabel stiffened, then immediately relaxed. "That's outrageous."

"Maybe," Patricia said, fully aware her question had struck a nerve. "But it's fact."

Isabel frowned. "According to who?"

"Timnit. The camp is one of many in China. Each fashioned after a major US city."

"Patricia, listen to me." Her voice was quiet, but forceful. "If these camps exist, and I'm not saying they do, it's something you don't want to stick your nose into."

Patricia paused to absorb Isabel's message and the warning therein. "If they're implicated in Ken's murder, I have to."

Isabel leaned forward and gripped Patricia hand. Hard. To anyone watching, it would be seen as comforting. "Listen to yourself. You're talking spies. Chinese spies. There are entire branches of our government who deal with these matters. For good reason. As your friend and attorney, I'm telling you-no, I'm imploring you-drop it."

Patricia had never seen Isabel so adamant.

Isabel, normally a paragon of patience, let out a long breath and released Patricia's hand. "You're investigating this possibility, and you came here alone? Based on my knowledge of US triads, you should have a SEAL team with you and still be worried." Isabel slowly scanned the crowd. "You know, dear friend, if you're right, you've put me at risk as well."

Patricia surreptitiously flexed her fingers beneath the bar top, absolutely rattled. But rather than being warned off, she was suddenly very sure she was on the right track. The question was how did she move forward and who could she trust to help her?

LATER THAT MORNING, SHORTLY BEFORE NOON, PATRICIA drove to Summer's home on Jones Street. She hadn't seen Summer for a while so, after some small talk, she brought Summer up to date on the possible triad presence in

Savannah and what she was doing on the Ken Li murder case.

"My biggest problem is getting the Li family to open up with me," Patricia said as she concluded her update. "I have the feeling they know more than they're sharing. As my friendly neighborhood psychologist, do you have any suggestions?"

"You have to get each of them to trust you," Summer said. "Even though you know them, you'll have to build that trust through increased familiarity. One on one. It will take time. Possibly a lot of time."

"I don't have time. Ken's killer is out there, and I need to track him down before he kills again."

Summer shook her head. "You can't rush building trust. I'm sure you have a measure of trust with Cora and possibly with her daughter Lily. Recruit them and ask them to speak to others on your behalf."

"Summer, I'm at my wits' end. I thought we'd throw some ideas around and see if we can come up with some new ideas. Do you have any thoughts on how I can find the guy who was stalking me? The one who posed as FBI?"

"He could have left town as soon as his mission was complete. That assumes his mission was to kill Ken, which I rather doubt. If his mission was something else and Ken's murder was just one unfortunate step toward his mission goal, then I'd guess your stalker is still here."

"Let's assume he's still here," Patricia said. "Psychologically, how do I find him?"

"Well, he's already displayed an interest in you by following you and by putting a tracker on your car. By the way, brilliant idea to put a tracker in his tracker. I hope it works. But getting back to your question, it's possible he's going to continue tracking you. But if he has an unfinished mission, he'll probably prioritize that. He can't be in two places at once. And if you want to go totally deep, you could begin to scout the places your stalker is likely to frequent in his downtime. But as a white woman, that would be practically impossible. You'd be more successful with a local Chinese scouting for you."

 Tea Room for her meeting with Lily Li. Sunlight poured through the stained-glass windows into the dining room. Overhead, Tiffany lamps cast more direct light on each table.

Lily, who was seated at a table close to the door, stood when she saw Patricia.

"Lily," Patricia greeted, and they embraced. As Lily stepped back, Patricia noticed how tired and strained her normally vibrant eyes were. "Thank you for agreeing to meet me."

"Of course," Lily said weakly.

Compassion consumed Patricia. "Are you okay?"

Lily shook her head. "I can't believe my father is gone. We worked side by side in the salon all these years. It's not the same without him. It's lonely. He is-was-my foundation. He taught me to be strong. But I'm not strong enough for this."

"I'm sorry, Lily. He was an extraordinary man," Patricia comforted, feeling powerless to help her.

"You need to find his killer," Lily begged.

"That's the plan," Patricia said softly. "And I need your help. Perhaps you could tell me about the people your father recently saw at the salon."

She pressed her lips together for a moment. "Which people?" "Anyone who visited your father who wasn't a client."

She stroked the tablecloth with her thumb. "There are a few, but not many. More visitors recently."

"Who?"

"I don't know all their names. It was so unlike Father. He wouldn't tell me anything about a few of the visitors. It was so disconcerting."

"Local?"

"I don't think so."

"Men or women?"

"All men."

"Chinese?"

Lily nodded.

Patricia searched her mind for more identifying questions that could help her understand who these visitors were. "Could you guess what age?" Patricia wondered if they were young agent recruits or more experience officials.

"Older," Lily answered. "Like closer to sixty than forty. Some had facial lines and graying hair. You know?"

Patricia pulled the photo of her stalker from her purse and showed it to Lily. "Is this one of the men who visited your father?"

Lily's back straightened. "Yes. He visited my father three times in the weeks before Father's death. I think his first name is Franklin. Father was upset that I had heard his first name. I don't recall his last name." Lily fixed her bloodshot eyes on Patricia's. "Do you think he may have been the killer?"

Patricia kept her expression neutral. "I don't know. But I'm not ruling anyone out yet."

The waiter came. They ordered tea.

After the waiter left, Patricia continued, "You said three times. Did each time seem normal? Did he come unannounced or have an appointment? How did your father act when Franklin showed up? Had you seen him before the recent meetings?"

"There was nothing normal about the visits or Franklin,"

Lily said. "I felt my father was surprised and upset each time he showed up. And, no, I had never seen him before."

Patricia jotted down Lily's answers. "On a different line of thought, what can you tell me about where out-of-town Chinese visitors might go in Savannah in their spare time?"

As Lily rattled off a short list of restaurants and bars, Patricia jotted the names down. "Where would they be able to buy a Chinese newspaper in Savannah?"

"Only two places," Lily said.

Patricia recorded those locations as well. "You've been very helpful, Lily. Would you be willing to help me track down some leads? I think people might be more willing to talk to you than me, particularly if they know you. You'd have to be careful though."

"I'd be happy to help in any way I can."

Patricia gave Franklin's picture to Lily. "Show this picture around to people you trust and see if anyone recognizes him. If anyone does, get details. Then let me know."

Lily nodded her understanding.

They chatted for a while over the rest of the delicious tea and then left the Gryphon.

As Patricia pulled her Navigator into the driveway and the garage door rose, she was surprised to see Trey's Bentley parked inside. She knew he was going to come home early for the gala, but not so early. Eager to see him, she parked and hurried inside.

Trey was seated in the family room and stood on seeing her.

She crossed the room and gave him a kiss, then a big hug. "What an unexpected pleasure."

He returned the hug and stepped back. "We need to talk."

Her heart skipped a beat. "Are you okay?"

"I'm fine." He took her hand and stepped closer. "Isabel told me you asked her about a Chinese spy school this morning. Where did you get the idea there was a school in China training spies for missions in Savannah?"

She hesitated. She wanted to protect Timnit, but she couldn't lie to Trey. Not even a lie of omission. Transparency was an integral part of their relationship. "Timnit told me. She got a voice sample, and it matched to a database she got access to about a Chinese spy school. Look, Trey, there can't be any repercussions to Timnit for being an excellent investigator. It's all on me. Not her."

He nodded. "Thank you for your candor. Timnit is good at what she does. That's why we suggested her to you. Nothing bad will happen to her. Regarding the school, I want you to forget you ever heard about it."

"But I think the Chinese government could be behind Ken Li's murder."

"Do you have any evidence Chinese spies are involved in Ken's death?" Trey asked.

"I just learned my stalker saw Ken three times before his murder. And he was the match in Timnit's voice analysis. It establishes he likely learned English at the Chinese spy school. I think that's pretty good evidence."

Trey gave a frustrated sigh.

"What can you tell me about the Chinese spy school?"

"Nothing right now, but I'll talk with Isabel."

"At least tell me what's going on, Trey."

"I can't, Patsy. I'm sorry. And more than that, I don't want to. I think the more you know, the more dangerous it could be for you." He reached out and took her shoulders, squeezing gently. "I think you need to carefully back out of this investigation."

"What? No!"

"Patsy—"

"Please, Trey. What can you tell me? You know you can trust me."

"Isabel told me you met her this morning without Simon. Is that true?"

"Yes, but—"

Trey swore and dragged a hand through his hair. "This is dangerous."

Eyes fixed on Trey's, Patricia brought her fist to her mouth, then dropped her hand. "I *have* to get to the bottom of Ken's murder. I have to talk to people unfettered. I have to operate spontaneously when necessary. Waiting for Simon's background checks slows everything to a crawl. I don't have time for that. I have to solve this puzzle."

"This isn't a puzzle, Patsy. It's your life, and it's too dangerous for you to relax your security. Tell me you'll give this up."

She shook her head. "I need time to figure out what I'm going to do. Surely you can give me that."

"It's not safe for you to be out alone. Can't you see that your life is in danger?"

"The day I married you, my life went into danger. There hasn't been a day since then that it's been otherwise."

"You haven't been a witness to a murder before. You haven't been followed by a trained assassin before. And you haven't had a murderer put a tracker on your car before. This is different, Patsy. Vastly different and much more serious than ever before."

She looked him squarely in the eye. "Ken needs justice. Please don't make me let down Cora and the Li family when I've promised."

"Please don't let *me* down, Patsy. I love you. I need you. I can't lose you." Trey stared at her, his eyes stark.

"Oh, Trey." She stepped toward him, and he folded his arms around her.

"Let the authorities find his killer," he begged.

"But they're not." She pulled back to look at him. "No one is doing anything. They're too busy with the parade."

"They will. When they have the resources, they will."

"By the time the authorities get to work after the parade, the killer could be completely off their radar. I'm the only one currently committed to this investigation. And I'm making progress. If I back off now, it's likely the killer will go free. Maybe even kill again."

"I can't force you to stop, Patsy, but I'm begging you. Something is off about this. And the thought of you out there on your own, I feel ill just thinking about it."

"I'll take Simon or Timnit from now on."

"I think you should interview people here."

"It's clear to me that people are holding back," she said. "I need people to relax and talk freely. They're more likely to cooperate with me in their homes, or at least in a neutral setting."

Trey shook his head. "Why are you so insistent on taking this kind of risk?"

"It's what I do. It's my truth. And while I appreciate your concern, I need *your* support. The sooner I solve this case, the sooner our lives can get back to normal. I can't do this alone. Please help me."

"That was a terrible thing for me to say." Trey buried his face in his hands for a moment, then looked up. "Of course, I'll support you. One hundred percent. But please limit your risks and keep Simon close."

She pulled him into a hug. "Thank you, Trey. I'll be careful, and I'll keep Simon with me."

CHAPTER 16

Shortly after 6:00 p.m. on March 12th, Simon pulled Trey's Bentley up to valet parking at Savannah Station, a renovated turn-of-the-century stable in downtown Savannah.

A uniformed greeter opened Patricia's door. Patricia hiked up her long, Kelly-green gown, stepped out with the help of the greeter, and waited for Trey to come around the car. Trey, dressed in one of his dinner jackets, also wore a bowtie to match Patricia's dress. She smiled, straightened his tie, and took his arm.

With Simon following at a distance, they made their way into Savannah Station to mingle with the sellout crowd at the annual Saint Patrick's Day Fire Ball, one of the many charity events they attended every year.

After checking in, they bid on some of the silent auction items, then found their table and greeted the two couples, the Hempfields and the Potters, already seated there. Hempfield and Potter served on the board of directors of the Cotton Coalition with Trey. An eight-piece band played "Georgia

On My Mind". Patricia sat and scanned the crowd, recognizing several couples.

"Would you like something to drink?" Trey asked.

"No thank you, honey. I'll stick with water for the time being."

"Have you read any good books lately?" Anna May Potter asked. Anna May, a retired forensic pathologist, was the current president of the Jones Street Book Club.

"The last book I read was *Indigo Girl*," Patricia said. "It was excellent. Such great attention to historical detail."

"I was so impressed by that book." Clarise Hempfield, a former actress, placed her hand over her chest for additional drama.

Anna May ran her fingers over the edge of the table. "What do y'all make of Ken Li's murder?"

Shocked that the subject came up, Patricia froze, hoping someone would fill the void.

"Shocking," replied Clarise, glancing around before continuing. "Benton says the Cotton Coalition is looking into it."

Anna May nodded. "Augustus told me it looked like some sort of ritualistic assassination."

"Oh my." Clarise's hand returned to her chest.

A fourth couple, who wasn't affiliated with the Cotton Coalition, arrived at the table and was introduced by Senator Hempfield as their new neighbors, Eloise and Lester Crandal. Lester was a recently retired general who last worked at the Pentagon. With the arrival of the Crandals, conversation switched from Cotton Coalition business and on to Lester's assessment of various military hot spots.

Patricia spotted Meredith chatting with an older woman in the corner of the ballroom. Patricia leaned toward Trey. "Meredith is right over there. I'm going to talk with her. Care to join me?"

"Tell her hello for me, but I'm going to get a drink while there's a lull at the bar." He stood and gestured toward one of the bars.

When he took off, she headed to Meredith, who looked up and smiled as soon as she saw Patricia. "Patricia, darling, you remember Nancy Demeci. She and her husband own the Savannah Mercantile Bank."

Nancy extended her hand.

Patricia took the older woman's frail hand. "How lovely to see you again. I didn't know you'd be here."

"Well, this old body will only come out for a few of these dos. The fun ones at least." She lifted her drink. "I was sorry to hear about your mother. She was a fine lady."

"Thank you. She was indeed."

"Nan has known the Lis for decades," Meredith said, giving Patricia a look over her glass.

"Ken Li's death is such a loss for Savannah," Patricia softly said.

"It really is." Nan took a sip from her martini glass. "He was such a lovely man. Upstanding. Family oriented. And I don't have to tell you, any man who pays his accounts on time, every time, no matter the size, is a man you can depend on." Nan brought the martini back to her mouth.

"Did you ever hear the story of how he got started?" Patricia asked, feigning ignorance. "I've always wondered."

Nan stepped closer. "Well, it's quite the story. A sweet deal for all involved. Which, of course, included my family's bank, the Savannah Mercantile Bank. We funded his first venture, a machine shop."

Patricia leveled her eyes on Nan's, recalling Meredith's disparaging remark about the bank. "A machine shop?"

She nodded. "Yes. Ken Li didn't know the first thing about running one, but he had a partner in Hong Kong who wanted to move his tooling business to the US before the colony reverted to China. Since Ken Li had legally migrated here, he became the front man for the business. The Hong Kong partner provided a letter of credit, which my father used to bankroll the equipment purchase. Once the equipment was in place, the Hong Kong partner started sending Ken Li highly experienced operators from Hong Kong. The Savannah business prospered and paid off the equipment loan in a year."

"Amazing," Patricia said.

Nan nodded. "It was family talk around the dinner table for sure. As Daddy always said, we could all learn a thing or two from Mr. Li on how to efficiently get a business up and running."

"I heard Ken had Hong Kong financial backing as well," Patricia said.

Nan collected her thoughts for a moment. "I seem to recall something like that, but I don't remember any details. I don't know why he would have needed additional backing, what with a deep-pocket partner like the one he had on the machine shop." Nan looked around like she'd grown tired of the conversation. They said their goodbyes, and Nan turned away to mingle.

Just as the band switched to a familiar, slow song, Trey came back to Patricia and held out a hand. "Would you like to dance?"

She excused herself from Meredith, took his hand, and walked with him to the crowded dance floor. Once on the floor, she melted into him, rested her head on his shoulder, and inhaled his signature pine scent. She couldn't remember the last time she had slow danced with Trey. It was heavenly to be so close to her man. And the song ended far too soon.

As they walked off the floor, Patricia found herself wondering if Randall Wentworth, the former director of the Savannah Chamber of Commerce, would know anything about Ken's history. Randall always attended the ball. She scanned the room for him, spotting his fluffy gray hair just a few tables away. She excused herself from Trey and headed to Randall's table.

He stood as she approached and they embraced.

She stepped back from the hug. "How have you been, Randy?"

"Fine as a boll weevil in high cotton. And you?"

"Mighty troubled by Ken Li's death," she replied.

"An exceptional man." He studied her and then shook his head and grinned. "Are you working tonight?"

A warmth rose in her cheeks. "Nothing gets by you, Randy." She nodded. "Did you ever do any business with him?"

He paused in thought. "I can't say that I have."

Not what she wanted to hear. She offered a weak smile. "Did the Chamber have any dealings with Hong Kong when it was still a British colony?"

"Periodically," he said. "But everyone we spoke to over there felt they could make more money in Hong Kong than in Savannah. That is until reunification with China became imminent. Then it seemed everyone wanted to move their operations to the US."

A tingle ran up her spine. Progress. Finally. "Were there any Hong Kong government programs to assist the companies that wanted to move to the US?"

He shook his head. "Heavens no. The government wanted to retain jobs in Hong Kong." He took a long sip of his whiskey. "But a surprisingly large number of government officials started transferring their assets to US banks. I think they feared their personal fortunes would be taken by the Chinese."

"Oh. How interesting. I'm sure some of *that* money came to Savannah," Patricia said.

He nodded. "What's your interest?"

Patricia's pulse spiked as it always did when she finally felt as if she had some threads to hold on to within a nebulous mystery. "Simply a conversation I was having with Trey. Oh, I see him now. Lovely to talk with you, Randy." She patted his shoulder and headed determinedly back to her table.

Trey saw her and stood, pulling out her chair.

She pressed her mouth toward his ear and whispered, "It's possible that at some point Ken was laundering money for Hong Kong government officials."

Trey remained silent. They sat and soon dinner was served.

Following dinner, the band switched to throbbing seventies and eighties rock tunes. Patricia and Trey hit the dance floor for a while, then needing to catch a breath, grabbed some drinks and circulated. Ken's death continued to weigh heavily on Patricia's thoughts. He had been a big donor to local charities and attended most of the big galas. His presence tonight was sorely missed. Her investigation of his death percolated at the back of her mind as she and Trey move from one couple to another.

Trey spotted Isabel in line at one of the bars at the back of the ballroom. "I see Isabel is here. I'm going to go see her and ask her to integrate your investigation of Ken's murder into the Cotton Coalition's. Do you want to join me?"

"It might go better if you discuss it one on one with her."

"Okay." He excused himself and headed toward the bar.

Isabel wore a black-sequined formal gown with rhinestone accessories. She stiffened when she noticed Trey approaching, realizing he had something important to talk to her about as their Cotton Coalition protocol was to strictly limit public contact with her. Once she got her drink, she veered off to a corner with no guests.

He followed. "Evening, Isabel," he said on reaching her.

She frowned. "This better be good."

"We have a problem," Trey whispered to her. "I spoke with Patricia. Apparently, she has linked Ken's murder to the Chinese spy camp the Coalition has been concerned about."

Isabel's eyes widened. "How did she make the link?"

"The day after her discovery of Ken's body, she was followed. She got a picture of the man who was tailing her. The next day, the same man showed up at a neighborhood florist and was asking about her. The conversation was captured on the florist's video security system. Voice recognition linked his phonics to specific phonic traits taught at the Savannah, China, camp. Subsequently, Li's daughter identified the man as one of the men who visited Li at his salon in the week before his death."

"That's a solid link. But tell me this, who gave Patricia the phonics link?"

"Timnit Araya."

"So she got a voice match to the Savannah, China phonics. But who told Mrs. Araya the facility was training spies?"

"She's ex-military. I'm sure she has friends at Cyber Command."

"Makes sense."

"Patricia isn't going to stop investigating who killed Ken. And now that she's linked his killer to the camp, I suggest we bring her into our work. I think she's on the right track and will find information we miss. You know we can trust her. What do you say?"

"Bringing her in could be dangerous for her."

"Believe me, I know that. But involving her is no more dangerous than what she's doing right now. She's going after the killer with or without us, and she could find the killer faster if we work together. Then, once the killer is identified, her involvement with us would be over."

"Are you sure you want to do this?"

Trey nodded. "I don't think we have a choice."

"Okay. Bring her up to speed."

As Patricia walked by the silent auction tables, she noticed Doctor Yuliam Rojas, who Patricia hadn't seen since the doctor left Savannah a few years ago to take a position in Atlanta at the Centers for Disease Control. When the doctor had been in Savannah, she and Patricia had become close since both had children in Savannah Country Day School. The tall, striking doctor was dressed in beige silk, and her gray hair was pulled up into a bun.

"Yuliam," Patricia greeted.

The doctor looked up and smiled. "Patricia. So good to see you. It's been so long."

Patricia gave her a warm hug and stepped back. "How have you been?"

"Busy as usual, and you?"

"The same. What brings you to Savannah?"

Yuliam gestured to the ballroom. "Nothing like a Saint Patrick's Day gala to take your mind off work." They chatted about Hayley and also Yuliam's grown daughter, commiserating about how time flew.

"What are you doing nowadays?" Patricia asked.

"I'm chief of CDC's Epidemic Intelligence Service." The doctor handed Patricia her business card.

Patricia raised her eyebrows. "That sounds like an intriguing position."

"It's not nearly as glamourous as all that. Mostly routine

stuff making sure we don't get blindsided again like we were on Covid-19."

Patricia winced. "That must have been rough."

"It was, but our early warning systems are much more robust now."

"Anything out there we need to worry about?"

"Not yet." She paused, then closed her mouth before opening it again. "We're keeping a close eye on the Savannah Sparrow population in Coastal Georgia."

"Why?"

"I'm sure it's nothing. It normally turns out to be nothing. We're simply overly cautious nowadays. But we recently found a sparrow with a bird flu variant. That's all we know. We're testing it for a certain amino acid known to be important for the virus to replicate in humans." She stopped talking, looking uncomfortable, as if she'd said too much. "Gosh, Patricia, you're always so easy to talk to. Now don't go splashing that round. It's probably nothing, and the last thing we need is hysteria."

Patricia felt a hand on her lower back. She turned to see Trey. "Yuliam, this is my husband, Trey. Trey, please meet my friend Yuliam. She works at the CDC."

"Lovely to meet you, Yuliam."

PATRICIA, TREY, AND SIMON GOT HOME FROM THE GALA AT eleven.

"Do you want to head up to bed?" Trey asked.

The sound of his made-in-the-South voice was music to her ears. The strung-out vowels. The unhurried delivery. The soft tones.

"Let's watch a bit of television before turning in." Patricia picked up the remote and turned on the family room TV. The eleven o'clock news appeared on the screen.

Trey ran his hand down his face. "I don't think I can take the news tonight."

"What would you like?"

"Let's just talk."

He'd been so busy lately, they hardly spoke more than a sentence or two. A pang of nostalgia for simpler times struck Patricia. Days long gone when they had time to talk as long as they liked. *Inconsequential days,* she reminded herself. Now, they mostly texted to communicate. And they kept their messages brief. So she had no problem appreciating a real conversation with her husband. She gave him a smile, clicked off the TV, and sat in one of the upholstered chairs. She reached down, removed her heels, and stretched her toes.

Trey sat in the chair next to her. "I spoke to Isabel about your interest in Savannah, China."

"That was quick. Thank you."

Trey nodded. "She asked me to brief you on everything the Cotton Coalition knows about the Chinese spy camp."

"I'm all ears," she said, shocked but pleased things had moved so fast.

"Back in the nineties, the CIA became aware of a couple of remote Chinese spy schools modeled after parts of US cities. The CIA put them under surveillance as much as possible, but the schools were so self-contained, the CIA could only observe them from high altitude overflights. Over time, more schools were added, including Savannah, China. Because of the Cotton Coalition's close collaboration with our government, Coalition leadership was eventually informed about the existence of the Savannah school. The CIA couldn't tell us who the spies were, when they were heading our way, or why. We were just told there were hundreds being trained and that they would eventually be coming our way. Since then, the Coalition has tried to vet every Chinese person we could identify who moved to

Savannah. We've even used birthplace data from individual census files."

"So the Coalition knew Franklin Chow was here?"

"No. Identifying new Chinese residents is extremely imprecise. If a person sneaks into the US and avoids all contact with government entities, we wouldn't know about them."

"What about the voice analysis technique Timnit used?"

"A couple of years ago, the Department of Defense Cyber Command managed to get a drone into the Chinese Savannah camp for a week and recorded a number of people, presumably spies, in conversation before the drone was discovered and destroyed. No information of substance was recorded, but they did get solid voiceprints of some individuals. And from those voice prints they realized all the spies recorded had been taught English by a single individual, and the students shared several unique phonic traits. US Customs, the National Security Agency, and the Cotton Coalition are now on the watch for those traits. They're even using artificial intelligence on recorded conversations to identify people. These are the same traits Timnit found Franklin Chow possesses. So far, Chow is the only person we know of in Savannah with those traits."

"But there were two people in that car."

"Yeah. That troubles us. We'd love to know who that woman is."

"She rented their car with a Georgia driver's license under the name of Emma Zhang. Algenon is checking her name and photo out."

"I hope he comes up with something solid," Trey said.

"Me too." Patricia let out a breath. "Do you think, perhaps, Ken's death was made to look like a triad murder when it was actually the Chinese government?"

"We don't think there would be any reason to have a triad

member at a government-run spy school. So we think Chow is simply a spy and think the triad knife was a clever plan to kill Ken without revealing the presence of a spy."

"So why did Chow, the spy, kill Ken?"

Trey shook his head. "No idea."

"And why was Chow carrying authentic-looking FBI credentials?"

"He had no way of knowing you'd confront him, so we're speculating he used or planned to use the FBI credentials for some other purpose."

"Do you think he was targeting the local FBI?"

"Algenon says they'd cross-check an unfamiliar agent before giving him access to their office, so the fake ID wouldn't be of much help there. However, elsewhere the ID would probably be taken at face value. For example, at the Hyatt the night of Ken's murder, the fake ID could have been used to pass through any perimeter security set up."

"We need to review the crime scene entry/exit logs and interrogation reports to see if an FBI agent was passed through," Patricia said. "I'll contact Rodriquez for them."

"Good idea. Now that you're partnered with the Coalition, you need to continue to investigate Ken's murder and keep me informed."

"You're out of touch too much. How much longer will your depositions go?"

"I know I've been unavailable. Just text me updates so I don't worry about you."

"Will do. And what is the Cotton Coalition doing now about this spy threat? And what are the Chinese spying on? We don't have anything worth spying on in Savannah, do we?"

"First of all, we're highly interested in finding Franklin Chow," Trey said. "We have people checking Chinese restaurants, bars, and grocery stores to see if anyone has seen him.

And since Chow got here undetected, we're now operating on the assumption there could be more operatives already here. Isabel is putting together an investigation team to better identify new Chinese arrivals."

"Franklin was trained in Savannah, China for a reason," she said. "In all likelihood, he's more comfortable eating our food, enjoying our entertainment, and reading our newspapers. To pass as American Chinese, he has probably been thoroughly conditioned to abandon his ethnicity. It's likely the only thing Chinese about him is his appearance."

Trey's eyes widened. "You're probably right. And that makes finding him all the more difficult."

"Maybe. Maybe not. Does the Coalition know what part of Savannah the Chinese duplicated for their school?"

"Yes."

"Then I'd concentrate the Coalition search for Chow on those sectors. That's where he's going to be most comfortable. In fact, it's possible that's where he lives."

"Makes sense, Patsy. I told Isabel she wouldn't regret bringing you aboard."

Patricia's phone announced an incoming text message. She picked up her phone and read.

Unknown Number: Tell your banking friend to stop asking questions about Ken Li, or she will die.

Stunned, Patricia almost dropped her phone.

"Patsy, what's up?"

Raw panic mixed with nausea swept through her. The words branded on her brain, she handed the phone to Trey.

CHAPTER 17

The person threatening Meredith had to be well-positioned in Chinese banking to know Meredith had been looking into Ken's finances. The Chinese government?

She had promised herself she wouldn't put Meredith into harm's way again and now she had, big time. A painful memory surfaced of Meredith taking a near-fatal head shot when Patricia had involved her in the investigation of the murder of Patricia's mother. Meredith had come very close to dying. All for Patricia. She would not-could not-risk her friend's life again. She would have to find another way to investigate the financial side of Ken's murder.

She watched Trey read the disturbing message. He blew out a breath and handed the phone back to her. "This is serious. The fact that someone knows what bank records she's accessing puts us all in danger. We don't know how high this thing goes, but it has to be significant. You need to completely dissociate Meredith from your investigation. We have people who can do what she does."

She rose on weak legs. "I know. And we need to get

Meredith to safety. She doesn't have the kind of resources you have to deal with this kind of threat."

"We can put her in a safe house if that's what she wants."

"I'll check."

"Assume her phone is bugged."

Patricia stepped speed-dialed Meredith.

"Hello, Meredith. I was thinking about that quilt pattern you sent me."

"What?"

Darn. She had hoped Meredith would recall their alert code. "You remember when we first got together, we talked about quilt patterns."

"Oh yes!"

"I was thinking about the red fabric." She prayed Meredith realized she was activating the quilt code for 'code red'. "Can I send a sample over?"

"Sure," her voice wavered. "I'll look for it. Thank you, Patricia."

Once Patricia had completed the call, she turned to Trey. "She wants to go to the safe house."

"I'll have a team pick her up and transport her," he said resolutely. "She'll be safe. I just need to make the call. I don't think I have Meredith's address."

Patricia checked her contacts app and gave Trey the information.

Trey paced the family room as he placed a call that started with the words 'security clearance' and a password she'd never heard before. "Immediate extraction requested for friendly female Meredith Stanwick." He gave Meredith's address. "No hostiles believed to be at address, but the friendly may be under surveillance. Transport code black to alpha nineteen. Confirm both contact and placement." A short, authoritative message that no doubt sent special operatives scrambling to Meredith's home.

Trey put his phone in his tux pants pocket, returned to her and took her trembling hands. His hands were ice-cold. "They'll let us know as soon as they make contact."

"How long?"

"About an hour."

She didn't like the sound of that. Anything could happen in an hour. "Why so long?"

"They're coming from either Pooler or Richmond Hill."

"Can I let Meredith know?"

He smiled. "Of course. But since someone might be listening in, keep it circumspect."

She called Meredith. "The red quilt sample should be over in about an hour."

"Thank you again, Patricia." She disconnected the call.

As pleased as she was for the planned pickup, she remained fearful and knew she would remain so until Meredith was secure within the safe house. Doubt surged. "What if—"

He held his index finger to his lips. "Believe."

"Believe in what?" she asked, her voice stronger than she felt. "That everything will go right? You know better than that. You of all people know the best situations can turn bad instantly."

"Our teams are highly trained for every contingency. It's what they do. Please, Patsy, have faith."

She couldn't help it. The investigator in her constantly considered alternatives. Constantly looked beyond the obvious. It had always served her well. And right now, Trey was telling her to *not* do that. Her chest squeezed.

"I can't, Trey, it's how I'm wired. Meredith is my best friend. I'm going to worry something bad could happen. Something your team can't handle."

He tilted her chin up. His intense, deep-set, dark eyes drilled on hers. "I understand, Patsy." His palm caressed her cheek. "I really do. And for what it's worth, I worry too." His hands returned to hers. "There is no alternative, so let's give them a chance. We should know soon enough if they got her out safely."

"There is an alternative," she insisted. "We could go over and sit with Meredith until the pickup arrives."

"No, Patsy. This is a potential tactical situation. We would only be in the way if the pickup turns bad. We stay here and let the team do what they're trained for."

Patricia knew the wait for news on Meredith's pickup would be intolerable. She needed to keep busy. Anything. "Would you like something to drink?" she asked. "Maybe a cup of chamomile tea."

He nodded.

She went to the kitchen, and while the water heated, she searched the cabinet for the herbal tea. She found the box at the back of the cupboard. As she retrieved the box, she dropped it on the counter, popping the lid and spilling some of the loose tea. Her hands trembled as she cleaned up the mess.

"Let me do that for you," Trey said from behind her, giving her a startle.

She stepped aside while Trey swept the remaining tea from the floor, then she crossed the kitchen and took down two china cups and saucers, dropping and almost shattering one.

Dustpan in hand, Trey came over to her. "I know you're nervous about this operation. Why don't you go back to the family room, and I'll finish up here?"

Knowing she was too frazzled to even make the tea, she gladly accepted his suggestion and returned to the family room. Soon enough, Trey returned with two steaming cups of tea, placed them on the coffee table, and sat next to her.

She took a sip, then another. Though her nerves subsided a bit, her mind continued to stew. She stood and paced.

"Why threaten Meredith rather than me?" she wondered aloud.

"A threat to Meredith *is* a threat to you. We can't underestimate them. We must assume they knew she'd call you immediately. The fact they threatened Meredith about accessing bank records is likely them letting you know how powerful they are."

"You're right. But what if their threat had the opposite effect on us? We're bullheaded. It's possible they know that. What if the threat happened to embolden us to look more closely at Ken's finances?" As she paced the room, she let her mind roll ideas around, but nothing important surfaced. Then it struck her. "Trey, the text to Meredith could be a diversion. If so, we must be getting close to what is actually going on, and they want us to drop what we're doing and focus more on Ken's finances. Whoever sent that note is assuming that's what I'll do. I'm sure of it."

She picked up her phone and read the note again. "Notice they used the word *enquiry* with an E not an I. That's British spelling. This message probably came from someone with a British education. Hong Kong Chinese. Someone old enough to have gone to school when Hong Kong was still a British colony. I'm guessing someone in Hong Kong is sending these messages and possibly running this show."

"I hope you're right about the text being a diversion, but we can't categorically dismiss the threat. We can't take chances with Meredith's life."

"Of course. She still needs to get to that safe house." She felt good to have seen through the diversion, but her mind kept stewing. "Why do you suppose they picked Savannah?" she wondered aloud. "What's so special about Savannah for the Chinese plan? We're not a key economic center for the

United States." She looked at him. "Do you know what cities the other Chinese camps are training operators for?"

He nodded. "Five on the West Coast. Five on the East Coast."

"None in the central US?"

"Just coastal."

She mulled his answer. "Major seaports?"

"Some are major ports, but most are secondary."

"So why is controlling those particular coastal cities important to the Chinese?" She pondered her rhetorical question for a moment. Then her heart rate spiked. "I guess smaller cities are easier to gain control of, and that's what the Chinese Communist Party wants-world domination by 2049, the hundred year anniversary of their victory in China."

"Economic domination," Trey said. "Not military occupation."

"What's the difference?"

"The difference between dependency and slavery." Trey leveled eyes on her. "I know it's in your DNA to look beyond the obvious, but the Coalition, doesn't believe the Chinese plan is to subjugate us."

"So the purpose of the camps is economic domination. But how?"

"Well, they either assimilate into an economy and then slowly work their way into owning it, which explains the model cities or ..."

Patricia took another sip of tea. "Or?"

"Or they somehow cause an economic instability that allows them to dominate the targeted cities faster. Fill the void if you will."

Patricia shook her head. "I haven't the slightest idea how they might accomplish that. But discovering the plan will be the first step to possibly stopping them. If we prevent the initial wreckage and keep our economy intact, they will fail."

"If undermining our economy is their objective, they're going to push hard to win, Patsy. Stopping a few hundred operatives won't be enough. They'll simply regroup and try again, and again. According to our information, they established those first camps back in the early nineties. And they have until 2049 to pull this off. They have plenty of time to deal with contingencies."

She sat on the sofa and exhaled. "My gut feel is that they're close to beginning to establish their foundation here."

"I've learned to trust your instincts. You need to make the FBI aware of your thinking."

Trey's phone rang.

CHAPTER 18

Patricia's heart thudded as Trey took his ringing phone from his tux pants packet. It had been just half an hour since Trey had ordered the Meredith pickup. She closely watched his expressionless face for any clue as he listened to the caller.

"Thank you." Trey put his phone away. "They picked up Meredith without incident and are transporting her to the safe house."

Patricia blew out a gusty breath of relief, then drummed her fingertips on the sofa cushion. She wouldn't be settled until Meredith was totally safe, if there was such a thing. "How long until the next call?"

"Could be a while," he said. "Might be as much as an hour."

She frowned. "Where are they taking her?"

He shook his head. "I don't know, and I won't know. And neither will you."

She nodded her understanding. "I think we should beef up Hayley's security."

"Are you thinking a safe house for her too?"

"Not yet," she said. "But definitely establish a round-the-clock security detail."

"I'll get on it." Trey rose from the sofa and made another call from across the room, then returned and sat. "Done."

"Thank you, Trey."

He dropped an arm around her. "What do you think about doubling up your security?"

"You don't think Simon's enough?"

"Simon's more than enough, but four eyes are always better than two."

"Who do you have in mind?"

"Timnit."

"I don't know if Timnit's available for fulltime security. You know she's married?"

"Why don't you call her and find out. If she's not available, I can get someone else, but it probably won't be a woman."

Patricia picked up her secure phone.

"Assume Timnit's line is bugged," Trey said for the second time that evening, underscoring how serious things had gotten in such a short time.

"It's Timnit, Trey. Her lines are always secure."

Patricia called her friend.

Timnit answered promptly.

"Hello, Timnit. I hope I didn't wake you."

"No. We were watching a movie."

"Could you come over tomorrow morning? I have some business I'd like to discuss with you."

"Sure. What kind of business?"

"It's best we discuss it face-to-face."

"Okay. What time?"

"How about ten?"

"Sounds great. See you then."

Patricia completed her call. "She's coming over tomorrow morning."

"Good. If she's willing to join your security team, we'll want her on the job 24/7 until the threat is removed. That means she'll have to live here."

Just as Patricia nodded her understanding, Trey's cell rang again. He removed his phone and placed it against his ear. She so hoped this was the notification Meredith was safe.

"Well done, sergeant," Trey said, then pocketed his phone. "Meredith is tucked away at a safe house."

Sweet relief blossomed. "Great!"

"Well, there was one problem. The unit leader felt they may have been followed, so they took her to Fort Stewart and asked the gate guards to deny entry to the car following them. They weren't followed into the base, nor were they followed when they left the base by another gate."

"Very professional."

He smiled. "Yes indeed."

"We need to check traffic cameras in the vicinity of Fort Stewart to see if the vehicle was the same one that followed me the day after Ken was murdered."

The following morning, Patricia woke with Trey and went downstairs while he showered to start the coffee and feed the cats. She was happy Meredith was in a safe house and hoped it was a nice place.

As the coffee brewed, she filled the cats' water bowl and went to the back door, surprised to see the two cats circling in the middle of the patio rather than sitting at the door gazing inside as usual. Alerted by the cats' behavior, she slowly opened the door, only to find a small dead bird on the doorstep.

Poor bird. She figured it was the cats' idea of a gift but *eww*. At least it was a more catlike gift. The last time either cat had left a *gift* at the back door, it was a cigarette butt with DNA that helped solve a case. And before that, it was a long-lost necklace, which she gratefully accepted. If only we could let cats know that dead birds, toads, and snakes weren't quite the gift for us humans they intended. She winced as she stepped over it, though she was touched they felt the need to bring her something, and placed the water bowl in the middle of the patio, then returned to the kitchen.

As she shoveled kibble into the feed bowl, she quickly concluded she couldn't leave the dead bird on the doorstep. Once she put the food out, she'd get a shovel from the garage and put the bird corpse in the trash bin.

She took the food bowl out to the patio. When she placed it next to the water bowl, the cats didn't pounce on the food. It was like they were rejecting the food, something they'd never done before. They just sat there staring at her. She offered the grey cat her hand. Normally, he would inch forward and sniff her fingertips, but not today.

"Thank you so much for the gift," she said to the cat, hoping she sounded grateful. Her curiosity piqued about the bird, she went back to the kitchen.

She wondered what kind of bird it was, hoping it wasn't a mommy bird that was expected back in the nest. She did a quick Google search on small brown birds in Savannah. The first result was "Savannah Sparrows" complete with two photos of males that looked remarkably like the bird on her doorstep. She read the brief narrative. There was nothing remarkable about this species. In fact, it was quite common.

Her mind swirled with questions, and she recalled Yuliam mentioning wanting to secure dead Savannah Sparrows to analyze for a unique strain of bird flu. She might want this specimen. Patricia opened the camera app on her phone and took a closeup photo of the sparrow.

She returned to the kitchen, removed Yuliam's card from her purse, and texted the photo and a message to the CDC doctor.

PF: This is probably not a naturally dead bird because my cats brought it to me, but you said last night you were interested in sparrows found in Savannah. Let me know if you want me to send it to you. Great to see you last night.

Moments later, the doctor called. "This is Yuliam."

"Hello, Yuliam."

"Thank you for the message and photo. It's definitely a sparrow. I'm going to need that bird. But whatever you do, don't touch it."

A chill went through Patricia.

Trey came down, poured a cup of coffee, and mouthed, "What's going on?"

"Sorry," she mouthed back.

He dropped an English muffin in the toaster and sat at the table.

"How do I get it to you, Yuliam?"

"You don't. I'll have a technician come to you. What's your address?"

Patricia gave Yuliam the information. "How long?"

"An hour or two."

Trey finished his coffee, poured a travel mug of coffee, wrapped the English muffin in a napkin, and gave her a kiss on the forehead. "Call me when you're done."

She nodded, sad she couldn't chat before he left, and blew him a kiss.

"Do I need to do anything else, Yuliam?"

"It would be helpful if you could protect the specimen from predators," Yuliam said.

"How do I do that?"

"First off, you need to regard the carcass as though it could kill you."

Patricia's heart thudded. "What?"

"If the bird has the specific avian flu variant we're looking for, you could become infected. And an infection could be fatal."

Patricia's throat tightened. "Can I just put a cardboard box over the corpse?"

"Yes. But, and this is the second matter of importance, it would be better for analysis if you refrigerated the specimen."

"I'll put it in a paper bag with some ice."

"Paper is good for biological specimens like the bird but put the ice in a plastic bag first so it doesn't contaminate the specimen."

"Sure."

"Good. Someone from the Savannah office of the Georgia Department of Public Health will contact you today to arrange pickup of the sample. And thank you, Patricia, for being such a conscientious citizen."

"You're welcome. And thanks for the bird flu update last night. Who would have guessed it would come in handy this soon?"

"I hope it's nothing, but one never knows."

Patricia completed the call and packaged the specimen.

Less than a half hour after speaking with Yuliam, Patricia's phone rang. "Patricia Falcon."

"Hello, Mrs. Falcon. This is Grace McKennon from the Georgia Department of Public Health. I understand you have a specimen for us."

"Yes."

"Could you be available at ten?"

"Yes."

"We'll be over then."

Once the call with Grace wrapped up, Patricia called Trey.

He answered on the first ring. "Hello, Patsy. I'm sorry I had to leave this morning before you finished your call. I'm back to a tight schedule of depositions today and tonight."

Her heart sank. With the threat to Meredith, the dead sparrow, and meeting with Timnit, she would have liked to have him around for moral support.

"What were you discussing for so long this morning?" he asked. "It sounded serious."

She knew all his and her phones were secure, so she could be open with him. "The cats left a dead sparrow on our back doorstep. Doctor Yuliam Rojas at the CDC-you met her last night-wants to test it for bird flu. Apparently, there could be a deadly mutation circulating."

There was a pause, and Patricia heard Trey's intake of breath at the potential of her statement. She knew he would alert the Coalition, just in case. "Well, I hope you didn't handle the sparrow," he said.

"Yuliam told me how to stay protected."

"Good. Has Timnit showed up?"

"She should be here at ten."

"What do you plan for today?"

"The Department of Health is picking up the bird, then I'm hoping to spend some time with Cora to get more information on how Ken operated."

"Phone?"

"In person."

"I prefer otherwise, but please take your security team."

"Of course," she replied.

"I know this is redundant, but I fell the need to say it again-be very careful. These people are deadlier than any bird flu. You are my world, lady."

"Thanks for the advice, and good luck with your depositions. I'll miss you."

"I'll miss you as well. Stay safe. Love you."

"Love you too."

AT TEN, THE FRONT DOOR CHIMES WENT OFF.

Simon came into the kitchen where Patricia was closing her laptop. "It's Timnit," he said.

"Thank you," she said, standing. "I'll get it. Also, I'm expecting someone named Grace from the Department of Public Health." She went to the entrance foyer, released the deadbolts, and swung the heavy door open. "Good morning, Timnit."

Timnit, dressed in faded jeans and white tee, gave a smile. "Good morning to you as well."

They hugged, then Patricia led Timnit to the kitchen. "Would you like some coffee?"

"No, thank you. I'm already over-caffeinated. But I'd appreciate some water."

Patricia pulled a bottle of water from the fridge, grabbed a glass from the cupboard, and placed both in front of Timnit as they sat at the kitchen table.

Timnit twisted the top off the bottle and poured water into the glass. "So, what's up?"

"I got a text last night with a death threat if Meredith continued to investigate Ken's finances."

Timnit scowled. "That's terrible. What's she going to do?"

"Trey arranged a safe house for her."

"Good. And you?"

"No direct threat to me yet, but we figure everyone's a target now. We're increasing Hayley's security, and we'd like to increase my security as well."

"Simon's not enough?"

"Trey says four eyes are better than two. And, well, Simon can't go everywhere I go."

"Smart man."

"Would you consider helping out with my security?"

"Hmm. My husband just took an overseas contract. He'll be gone a month or two. I was wondering what I could do in his absence. What would it entail?"

They discussed hours and compensation. Long hours. Lucrative compensation. Well-deserved compensation considering Timnit would be putting her life on the line as well as on hold. "So what do you think?"

"When do I start?"

"Right away. This morning or tomorrow."

"He's leaving this afternoon, and I need to pack, so tomorrow morning would be perfect for me."

The front door chimes pealed.

Simon came into the kitchen. "Hi, Timnit."

"Hello, Simon. How's it going?"

"Going well."

The front door chimed pealed again.

"It's someone I don't recognize," Simon said to Patricia.

"Could you get it, Simon? It's probably Grace McKennon from the Department of Health or someone from her office. If it is, I'm expecting them."

As Simon left, Timnit asked, "Who's Grace McKennon?"

CHAPTER 19

Simon returned to the kitchen followed by two women in white biohazard suits. "They're here for a bird," he said with a raised eyebrow. "I ran their IDs. They're legit."

Timnit straightened in her chair. "What the—"

"I'll explain later," Patricia said as she pointed toward the cardboard box with paper bag on the floor by the back door. "Thanks for coming so soon."

"No problem, ma'am," one of the women said. She placed a red insulated container next to the box and flipped up the hinged lid. The other woman crouched, placed the box in the container, and sprayed something, presumably disinfectant, over her gloved hands. The first woman closed the lid, then also decontaminated her gloves and the floor where the box had been.

"Is the cat that brought you the bird a pet?"

"No. They're a pair of feral cats we look out for. I don't know which one left the bird. I put out food and water on the patio each morning and replenish both during the day."

"Have you had any physical contact with the cats in the past week?"

"No. None at all."

The woman stepped to the back door. "I don't see any cats."

"They come and go all day. I think they sleep in the bushes beside the patio."

"Good to know."

One of the two left with the bird container. Moments later, she returned with two cages and opened the door to the patio.

"What are those for?" Patricia asked, taken aback.

"We want to catch, health check, and quarantine the cats."

"How long will that take?"

"A week if they aren't carrying the bird flu. If they're carriers, we'll have to euthanize them."

Patricia gasped.

"I'm sorry, but as carriers they could spread the disease to other animals and humans. The only way to stop the spread is to stamp out the disease at its source. Hopefully, your cats haven't been infected."

Patricia looked away, blinked, and then turned back to the person doing the talking. "Why are you doing all this now before you know if the sparrow has the flu?"

"The faster and more thoroughly we act, the better chance we have of preventing a pandemic if the sparrow tests positive for bird flu."

Based on what Yuliam had told Patricia the night before, she assumed the precautions were appropriate. But nevertheless, she felt sorry for the cats and said a silent prayer for their safety.

It didn't take more than a minute or two for the tech to place the traps and return to the kitchen.

The doorbell chimed again.

Simon poked his head in the doorway. "Are you expecting anyone else?"

"No," Patricia said.

"It's probably our boss, Grace McKennon," one of the women said. "She'd like to interview Mrs. Falcon."

Simon looked at Patricia. "I'll check her out."

Patricia nodded.

He and the tech left, then Simon returned with a gray-haired woman in a dark-blue pants suit. He motioned toward Patricia. "This is Mrs. Falcon."

The woman stepped forward, gloved hand extended. "Hello, Mrs. Falcon. I'm Grace McKennon. We spoke earlier."

Patricia rose and gave Grace a handshake. "Please call me Patricia. Would you care for some coffee?"

"No, thank you," the woman said in a soft Southern voice.

Patricia indicated for Grace to sit.

Timnit stood. "I should be going."

"Please sit," Grace said. "I want to speak with you both, plus this gentleman." She indicated Simon. "It won't take long, but it's important to our intake procedure."

Timnit settled back into her chair.

Simon grabbed a mug of coffee and took a seat at the kitchen table with the three women.

"As I understand it, you found the bird, Mrs. Falcon?" Grace asked.

"Yes. Right outside the back door. Just after six thirty."

Grace made a note on a pad she'd taken from her canvas carryall. "Was anyone with you when you discovered the bird?"

"No."

"Does anyone else live here?"

"Yes. My husband."

"Where was he when you found the bird?"

"Upstairs getting ready for work."

"And he never had *any* contact with the sparrow?"

"Correct."

Grace made another note. "Are you the person who put the bird in the bag?"

"Yes."

"Please tell me exactly how you put the specimen in the bag."

"With a shovel."

"We'll need to decontaminate the shovel. Where is it?"

"Outside on the patio. Next to the door."

Grace removed an e-tablet from her carryall, booted it up, and handed the device to Patricia. "Would you enter your full name and contact in the spaces provided?"

"What's the purpose of collecting this information?"

"Contact tracing."

While Patricia put her information in, Grace called a tech and asked her to come back in and disinfect the shovel.

Patricia handed the tablet back to Grace.

Grace turned to Timnit and Simon. "Did either of you handle the sparrow or the bag?"

"I think you need to explain what's going on," Simon said.

"Sorry," Grace said. "I thought you knew. Mrs. Falcon reported a dead Savannah Sparrow this morning, a species we're sampling for bird flu."

"Why all the precautions?" Simon asked.

"The flu could be contagious to humans. So, did either of you handle the bird or the bag?"

"No," Timnit and Simon said in unison.

Grace scrolled down the tablet and handed it to Timnit. "Please enter you contact information, and then give it to the gentleman to do the same."

Both Timnit and Simon did as requested.

Grace returned the tablet to her carryall. "Do any of you have *any* respiratory symptoms? Cough? Drainage? Fever?"

All three said no.

"That's good." Grace gave each of them one of her business cards. "If you or anyone in your immediate family develop *any* respiratory symptoms, however mild, in the next ten days, please call me immediately. Day or night."

"How worried should we be? Is this like a cold, or is it something more serious?" Simon asked.

"We don't know. We just don't want you to catch it."

"I can imagine," Simon said.

"Now. This is important," Grace said as firmly as her soft voice would allow. "Do not mention this situation to anyone. We want to avoid misunderstandings. So if anyone communicates about this, it will be us. Understood?"

They nodded.

"That's all I have," Grace said, taking the tablet from Patricia and putting it back in her bag. "Do you have any questions?"

"When do we get results?" Patricia asked.

"I'm sorry, but you won't get results. We keep that kind of information to ourselves to avoid misunderstandings."

Disappointed, Patricia gestured to the backyard. "What do we do about the cages?"

"If you see one or both of your cats in the cages, call me. Whatever you do, do not make contact with the cats, or their water bowls or food bowls."

"Their bowls are on the patio," Patricia said.

"Our tech texted me that they have already taken them when they cleaned the shovel. As for the cats, just let them be. A technician will come by once a day to check on the traps and put out water. Any other questions?"

Patricia frowned. The cats had become dependent on her. What would they do?

When no one said anything, Grace rose. "Thank you for your cooperation."

Patricia escorted Grace to the front door and thanked her for getting on top of the situation.

As soon as Patricia returned to the kitchen, Timnit came over to her. "What's really going on?"

She filled them both in as best she could on everything she knew about the bird. "I didn't realize everything was quite so serious. I was just trying to be conscientious since it was on my mind after seeing Yuliam last night."

When Patricia was done, Simon picked up his mug, refilled it, and headed back to the dining room.

"I should be going." Timnit grabbed her big purse and slung the strap over her shoulder. "I wish I could start today, but I have to get my affairs in order, say goodbye to my husband, and pack. Is tomorrow morning at eight okay?"

Patricia inclined her head in agreement, then led Timnit to the front of the house, where they exchanged hugs before Timnit left.

On her way back to the kitchen, Patricia stopped in the dining room to speak with Simon, who was already absorbed in work on one of his computers.

She cleared her throat.

Startled, he looked up.

"Sorry to interrupt," she said. "Do you have a minute?"

He closed the lid of his laptop. "Sure."

She sat in a chair next to him. "Are you aware I got a threatening text message last night?"

He nodded. "Yeah. Trey filled me in."

"So you know Meredith was taken to a safe house."

"That's my understanding."

Patricia folded her hands on the table. "In view of the

threat, Trey has beefed up Hayley's security, and we want to increase my security as well."

Simon sat back in his chair.

"Timnit has agreed to join my security detail."

"I figured you'd get to that sooner or later. It's a good tactical move. And I don't think you could have a better person for the detail."

Patricia smiled. "You set a high standard, Simon."

"Thank you."

"She starts tomorrow morning," Patricia said. "For the time being, our plan is to have both of you with me whenever I go out."

"Smart move, considering the threat level. She can go places with you I can't."

Patricia nodded. "One more thing. When the unit picked up Meredith last night, the unit leader felt they were followed."

Simon's brow furrowed. "That's interesting. I'm sure the unit was able to shake the following vehicle."

"They were. The pickup unit went to Fort Stewart instead of going directly to the safe house and asked the front gate guards to deny entry to the tail car. It worked. So Meredith is safely tucked away, but I want to get more information on the vehicle that followed the pickup team."

"Traffic cams?"

She nodded. "If you have time."

"Of course I have time," he said. "It was a night pickup, so vehicle identification could be difficult with normal traffic cams or license plate monitors. However, my understanding is that the access roads to Fort Stewart are extremely well monitored with high-res cameras and are well-lit at night. National security, you know."

"Can you access them?"

"I'll talk with the unit leader to get the pertinent details and then get right on the cameras."

"Thank you." Just as she was turning away to go back to the kitchen, her phone signaled an incoming text.

Unknown Number: Red quilt. Really? Hiding the banker won't lessen the consequence if you, she, or anyone else continues to investigate Ken Li's finances.

CHAPTER 20

Patricia whipped up an egg white omelet for lunch, then she spent the early part of the afternoon entering new information, including copies of both threatening texts, into her case file. The heightened threat level from those texts upset Patricia but didn't deter her determination to find justice for the Li family.

She called Detective Rodriquez to see if he had made any progress on the investigation. "We got two threatening texts that suggest a big, technically savvy organization," she told him.

"We're still focusing on parade security for a few more days, then we can get back to the Li case." He went on to tell her if a foreign government was behind the murder, the FBI would have to become involved. She said she intended to discuss the subject further with Algenon.

Patricia phoned Algenon and discussed her current theory that Ken's murder was somehow connected with an imminent takedown and takeover of Savannah's economy by operatives from the Chinese spy school. He listened politely but didn't seem moved by what she shared. He probably had plenty of well-meaning citizens bringing him outlandish suspicions without evidence.

That was the problem. Lack of evidence. She had presented Algenon suspicions of a fertile imagination and nothing more. She felt foolish for even bringing the subject up with him. Yet as disappointing as his lack of interest was, she was still convinced she was on the track of something significant. What else would explain the threatening text messages targeted at Meredith's investigation?

Around three, Simon came into the family room and handed her a folder, then sat in the chair next to her. "Our friend Franklin Chow was driving the car that followed the pickup unit from Meredith's home."

"Another Chow sighting. Great work, Simon." Her mind immediately went to work on the news. If Chow was staking out Meredith's house, that was one explanation for why he wasn't showing up at local Chinese hangouts. And doing such a time consuming, mundane thing like a stakeout indicated he didn't have much help. It also indicated the importance to him of controlling Meredith's investigation. "Was he driving the same car as before?"

"He sure was. Same car. Same plate. The Department of Defense traffic cameras did their job. Unfortunately, once Chow left the immediate base area and got back on Chatham Country traffic cams and plate identifiers, I lost track of his vehicle."

"How do you know he was driving the car?"

"We lucked out. He tried to follow the pickup unit onto the base. The gate guards have their own security cameras. I reviewed the recordings. It's definitely Chow. And get this, he and his passenger produced Georgia driver's licenses."

"His female passenger?"

"No. Male passenger. Anyway, both licenses passed the guards' Georgia License Verification System, but Chow's failed the Department of Defense Watchlist System because the FBI had put out a government-wide detainer on him. Once Chow realized they were taking too long and one guard pulled the other over, he backed his car up and left. The sentries put up a tactical drone to track his car but lost the car in the thick tree canopy a few miles from the base."

"What about the addresses on the driver's licenses?"

"Fake. The guardhouse video also included audio. Timnit's voice recognition file again suggests Chow learned English in Savannah, China."

Patricia shuffled through the folder Simon had given her, stopping at copies of the confiscated licenses. "Any idea how these fake licenses passed the Georgia License Verification System?"

Simon raised his eyebrows. "I looked into that. Apparently, someone hacked the system and inserted the information."

"Hmm. Maybe they inserted more than these two," Patricia said. "The issue dates on these licenses are recent, and they're not the same. Can you recheck the system for the dates these two were inserted and see if any other fake Savannah-based licenses were inserted? I realize that could be hundreds of licenses, but we need to get a handle on how many potential spies we're dealing with."

"Sure."

Patricia closed the folder. "What do you have on Chow's male passenger?"

"No audio on him, but we have a sharp picture and a name. Probably a fake name."

"Did you run facial recognition on the passenger?"

"It's running right now."

"Chow's car is a stakeout vehicle," Patricia said. "Did you

notice any food wrappers or beverage cups that might suggest where he and his passenger were getting food?"

"Good thinking, Patricia. I didn't even think to look for that kind of clue, but I will and will let you know if I find anything."

"Fast food places have security videos. Plus, we might find out what Chow's food preferences are. If it's a major chain, we can check all their Savannah locations and see if any employees recognize his picture."

"I'll follow up as soon as we're finished here."

"Thank you, Simon." There was a moment of silence as Patricia registered another thought. "If Chow is Ken's killer and grew up in Savannah, China, I'm questioning if Chow is actually associated with a triad. I'm thinking the triad connection might be a ruse being used to intimidate local Chinese ... and it worked." Patricia paused to further focus her thinking. "If Chow isn't a triad gangster, I'm wondering what his role is in the Chinese government's plan to take over our economy." She rolled that idea around for a while. "Do you suppose he's a recruiter?"

Simon shrugged.

"If I wanted to establish a beachhead in Savannah, I would probably first send a small delegation to recruit select, disaffected local Chinese, particularly those with relatives still in China, to be a part of the takeover and possibly even become a part of the new leadership."

Simon nodded his agreement.

"Then I'd start to move key personnel from my training camp to Savannah. Considering the scope of a full takeover, that second phase would have to involve quite a few people. All this would occur before the actual takeover. According to Trey, we haven't yet seen a mass influx of Chinese immigrants, so I'd guess they're still in the recruitment process."

"Do you think Chow was recruiting Ken?"

"Perhaps. To tell the truth, I'm considering the possibility that Ken might have been part of the takeover plan, including that he might have been trained in one of those spy schools. After all, he did get funds from a source in China to set up a business here. If he was a product of an early version of the Savannah, China, camp, he might have the distinct voice traits of the others. If you have time, I'd like you to find a good sample of his voice, maybe from voicemail, and run it for unusual traits."

"This runs deep, doesn't it?" Simon said.

Patricia mulled that for a moment. "You know, we've been focusing on an economic takeover. What if the plan included a political takeover as well?"

"You should ask Cora if Ken ever mentioned running for a local council seat. That would lend support to that theory."

"But if Ken was non-compliant, maybe he said no to a political appointment from the onset."

Simon tilted his head. "Maybe Ken's rival has political ambitions. Maybe Ken's murder was a message to his business rival that he should play ball or suffer the same fate."

"I'll ask Cora if any of the Fengs have put their names forward for a council position."

Simon nodded, went into the kitchen to grab a new cup of coffee, then headed back to his control center in the dining room.

Patricia opened her laptop and entered the folder information into her case file.

A couple of hours later, Simon returned carrying another file folder. "I haven't been able to find a recording of Ken Li's voice. I'll keep looking, but could you check with Cora Li to see if she has something with his voice?"

Patricia nodded.

"I reviewed the guardhouse video. I didn't see any fast-food wrappers, but there were two jumbo cups in the console with B and D Burgers logo. I'll send someone over to the downtown location with Chow's photo to see if they recognize him and to ask for their recent security videos."

"I know it's a long shot."

"It is, but it's how we work." Simon smiled. "Your idea to check Savannah-based licenses inserted into the Georgia License Verification system was brilliant. Turns out a total of nine fake licenses were inserted within a month on either side of those two dates. All the drivers appear to be of Asian race. Two families of three people each, plus three others. Franklin, his male passenger, and this woman." Simon handed Patricia a photo.

Pleased with the progress they had made, Patricia took the photo and studied it. "Raylee Peng. Hmm. I'm pretty certain this is the female passenger who was with Chow on the day after the murder."

"I thought Emma Zhang rented the car that followed you."

"Seems like Emma has more than one identity." Patricia put the photo of Raylee on the end table. "I assume you have photos of all nine."

"Yes." He handed her the folder.

She took the folder and opened it. Her pulse accelerated at having photos of the spy cell. This could be concrete evidence to give to Algenon. She should have waited until this afternoon to call him. "If Emma Zhang was willing to use her fake license to rent a car, some of the others may have rented as well. They need transportation. Would you check the local rental agencies to see if they rented vehicles to any of these people?"

"Will do," Simon said. "One other thing, I got a facial recognition hit on Chow's passenger. He's a local criminal named as Alex Feng. He has a long rap sheet, and I found a recent address for him."

"Why would they use a local when they have all those trained spies?"

"As trained as those spies are, nothing can substitute for in-depth local knowledge."

CHAPTER 21

It was midmorning when Patricia leaned back in her chair at the kitchen table. She'd just wasted a tedious hour chasing dead-end leads and unproductive hunches. Swiveling in her chair, Patricia looked out the bay window at the two empty cages on the patio. Part of her wished the cages would remain empty.

Just as she closed her tired eyes, her secure phone pealed. She checked the screen. Cora Li. Patricia had been meaning to check in on her. Concern rose.

"Are you okay, Cora?"

"It's hard, Patricia." Cora let out a sigh, and Patricia's heart squeezed in response. She could only, and never wanted to, imagine. "Anyhow, that's not why I called. I was wondering if you were free for lunch today?"

Patricia glanced at her watch, surprised. But she hadn't yet eaten. "Sure. Where were you thinking?"

"How about my son's place downstairs?"

"Sounds great. Shall we meet at noon?"

"Could you make it earlier? It gets crowded with the noon rush. How about eleven or eleven-thirty?"

Patricia glanced at the time on her phone. No way could she make eleven. "How about eleven-thirty. And, Cora, I know it's rude, but do you mind if I bring a work colleague with me? She'd like to meet you."

"I'd rather just the two of us meet. Who is she?"

"She's helping me with my investigation." Patricia paused as she waited for Cora's decision, then decided to add, "She can be trusted."

"All right then."

Patricia smiled as they said their goodbyes. It would be good for Cora to know she could count on Patricia and her team.

CORA, DRESSED IN A SIMPLE WHITE CHEONGSAM, WAS ALREADY seated in a dim corner when Patricia and Timnit arrived. Patricia observed each guest, quickly cataloging their faces, mannerisms, and manner of dress. All useful data should any of them attempt to follow her when she left the restaurant.

Simon came in and took a seat beside the entrance and Patricia and Timnit went to Cora's table in the back.

Cora rose, and Patricia noted the telltale signs of crying and not sleeping under her friend's dull eyes. Grief was a physical mantle Cora wore, Patricia thought as she embraced her friend.

"Cora, this is my friend Timnit. Timnit, please meet Cora."

Timnit, wearing loose black pants and a matching shirt, stepped forward. They exchanged greetings.

"Timnit is helping me investigate. We've worked together previously. She's an excellent resource for us."

"That's wonderful," Cora said. "Thank you," she added to Timnit.

Timnit gave a small nod.

Cora's eyes returned to Patricia's. "I'm so glad to see you, Patricia. Thanks to my family and good friends like you, I'm getting through each day. I know life goes on, but I miss Ken so very much." Cora gestured for Patricia and Timnit to sit.

Patricia sat with her back to the wall, then straightened her pink Lilly Pulitzer shift. Maybe Timnit had the right idea-dress so you blend in. "Is there anything you need, Cora?"

Cora gave a weak smile as she sat. "Time with you is such a gift. It always is, my dear friend. But even more so now."

"Thank you. I feel the same way about you."

A waiter arrived once Patricia and Timnit were seated, and they ordered tea and shrimp dumplings. The waiter left and promptly returned with an ornate jade-green porcelain teapot.

Cora poured for Timnit and Patricia, then for herself.

Cora lifted her cup and sipped her tea. Long gray tendrils framed her flawless, pale face. Her teacup trembled slightly when she returned it to the saucer. She brushed invisible crumbs from the table, then locked eyes on Patricia's. "Thank you for seeing me on such short notice," Cora said solemnly. "I have a favor to ask of you."

Patricia leveled her eyes on Cora. "And what would that be?"

Cora inhaled deeply. "I'd like you to stop investigating Ken's death." Her voice was tight.

The words shocked Patricia who, in turn, just stared at Cora. "Why?"

Cora's lower lip trembled. "Reprisals."

A knot formed in Patricia's stomach as her brain whirled trying to make sense of Cora's request. "Did someone threaten you?"

Cora looked conflicted. "It's just that … that knife. That triad knife. The triad responsible for Ken's murder is very powerful," she said in a quiet voice as she leaned forward. "They're one of China's deadliest gangs, well-known to be relentless. I'm scared."

"But Ken's murder cannot remain unsolved."

"It is solved," Cora said firmly. "And I have to think of my family now."

"But surely you don't want Ken's murder to have been in vain."

She shook her head. "Of course, I don't. But I have my children to worry about. And you will be a target. I couldn't forgive myself if I put you in harm's way."

"Cora, you must see that if everything you're saying is true, then Ken won't be the last. There are things I've uncovered. I think I may have the advantage of surprise. Plus, we have powerful resources the triad doesn't know about." She thought about Meredith stuck in a safe house. "And I'm in too deep to stop now. There's something afoot. Something I'm missing. I fear if I don't put my finger on it, the Savannah we know will change for the worse."

Cora gasped and looked away. "Oh my." She gathered herself and, with eyebrows arched, returned her focus to Patricia. "For my family's protection, I withheld some important information from you. Now, I feel I must share it. Maybe then you'll understand why you must stop." Cora did a quick scan of the establishment. "A couple of months ago, a Chinese government official called Ken and set up a meeting. Very strange. To my knowledge, Ken never had any dealings with the Chinese government before. The official told Ken the Communist Party wanted his help in establishing a much greater Chinese presence in Savannah."

Patricia drew a sharp breath. "What kind of presence?"

Cora's eyes kept looking left and right. "Commercial."

"Why Savannah?"

"That was what Ken asked. And he didn't get a meaningful answer." She shook her head, her expression troubled. "Just double-talk. So Ken told the official Savannah wasn't a good place for foreign investment and that he didn't care to help. It was unlike Ken, but he said something about the official's inquiry seemed off to him." Cora paused, squeezing her eyes shut and dropping her head, as though the conversation was too much for her.

Patricia remained silent. To get confirmation that Ken had been approached by a Chinese government official was gratifying, but the two-month distance in time from approach to death was a mystery. He'd probably been approached several times since the initial encounter. Patricia tried to quiet her streaming thoughts and concentrate on Cora's readily offered information.

Cora raised her head and opened her eyes. "The official told Ken the request wasn't optional. That's when the official mentioned the Forty-four Brothers triad. They're well-known to do muscle-for-hire work for the Chinese government. Ken still said no, but he told me he understood the threat from the official was real. Very real. But what could he do about it? He hoped they would not take such a risk to physical harm us, maybe just some business intimidation." She paused. "But now Ken's dead." Cora's voice broke on the word, and her eyes filled. Quickly, she lifted her teacup with a shaking hand.

"Did he know the official? Had they met before?"

"He said he'd never seen the man before."

"Did you meet the official?"

"No."

Patricia sat back. Suddenly, she felt vulnerable sitting out in the open in this establishment she didn't know well. Even with a loaded gun in her purse, Timnit at her side, and Simon by the front door. She tucked a strand of hair behind her ear and did a surreptitious head turn. None of the twenty or so customers seemed to be looking at them.

"Was Ken visited again after the initial contact?"

"I don't know."

"Have you or your family been contacted by any Chinese official since?"

Cora stared down at her plate. "Not as far as I know. To tell the truth, I've been so grief-stricken I haven't asked my family."

"Do you know where the initial meeting occurred?"

"Not for sure, but Ken usually conducted business here."

"And the meeting occurred a couple of months ago?"

"That's when he told me about it."

"Does the restaurant have security cameras inside?"

"Yes."

Patricia glanced at Timnit, who gave a subtle nod to let her know she'd look into it.

"Did you tell the police about the threat?"

"No. I was too scared. Me talking to the police would do nothing but provoke reprisals against my family. And what could the local police do to stop the Chinese government?"

"There are several federal agencies that deal with external threats to our country. You've seen them at play in how our country deals with terrorism. This situation may not yet be terrorism, but it is clearly a serious threat to you and, I suspect, to Savannah, if not the entire nation." Patricia let out a long breath. "To get the government involved, I have to gather abundant hard evidence, like what you just told me, to take to the local FBI. And, Cora, the FBI *must* be involved to stop this threat. I realize you're concerned for your family, and so am I. The good news is the FBI can provide protection, even new identities for y'all while we investigate." She took Cora's hand and pressed it between her palms. "I think we should go to the FBI."

"I must protect my family."

"The only way to do that is to bring the federal government in."

Cora looked up, her face grim. "I don't know. I don't have proof or even the name of the official."

"Doesn't matter."

Cora nodded. "I guess so. You know, Patricia, I haven't been thinking clearly lately. But I know enough to know that this is a real danger. Are you sure going to the FBI will keep me safe?"

"If what you're saying is true, you are not safe now. Your son could be approached next, if he hasn't been already. At least with FBI involvement, you'll be safer."

Cora squeezed Patricia's hand. "You're such a friend."

"Thank you." Patricia pulled her phone from her purse, brought up the picture of Franklin Chow and showed it to Cora. "Do you know this guy?"

"No. Why?"

"He followed my car the day after Ken's murder."

Cora's gaze sharpened as she peered at the picture. "Do you think he did it?"

"Hard to tell, but it's possible." Patricia brought up the photo from Emma Zhang's driver's license. "How about this woman?"

Cora shook her head. "I don't. I'm sorry."

"I know you mentioned the Feng family previously. Do you happen to know Alex Feng?"

Cora's face turned sour. "Not personally. But Ken told me he's a very bad person." Cora signaled the waiter to clear the dishes and bring fresh tea. Perhaps it was her way of stopping the conversation, Patricia thought. Cora poured when the tea arrived, and they sat in silence for a long moment.

Timnit took a sip of ginseng tea. "Cora, I was wondering, how did Ken get into hairdressing?"

Cora stared into space for a while gathering her thoughts. "Ken's family made high-end wigs in Hong Kong, so I suppose hair designing was in his DNA, but he never liked the manufacturing part of the family business. While still in Hong Kong, Ken decided to help a family friend start a tooling shop in Savannah. Ken wanted to leave Hong Kong before the Chinese took over, so we immigrated here, and he started the shop. Despite it being very successful, Ken didn't like the work. He went to night school to study hair dressing, got his license, then sold his share of the tooling shop to his partner and opened a small beauty salon. It, too, was very successful, and more importantly, Ken enjoyed the work. He loved Savannah and never regretted leaving Hong Kong, though he missed his parents."

"Ken never mentioned his parents," Patricia said. "Are they still alive?"

"After Hong Kong reunified with China, his father moved his Hong Kong wig business back to the mainland where, due to government interference, it faltered and failed. Ken tried to get his parents to move to Savannah, but they wanted to stay in China. His father died fifteen years ago, but his mother is still in China living with her family." Cora trailed off, a shadow passing over her face. She frowned. "You know, Ken always thought his father got crosswise with the regional government and was murdered. That was one of the main reasons he avoided politics here." Cora sniffled. "And it may have killed him anyway."

Patricia reached across the table and again took Cora's hand. "I'm going to do my best to try to keep your family safe and to get the FBI involved. Though it won't bring Ken back." Patricia smiled sadly at Cora.

Patricia's mind whirled. She had to get Algenon to prioritize protecting Cora and her family. Patricia sent Simon a text to let him know they were done, then waited as he paid his check and left.

CHAPTER 22

*P*atricia and Timnit stepped out of the restaurant into a warm, sunny spring day. Cora had left a few minutes earlier, going upstairs to her residence with her security chief.

Patricia methodically looked over the surroundings for possible threats, noting the Saint Patrick's Day decorations on the storefronts. Timnit was scanning as well. When their gazes met, they smiled.

Simon pulled the Navigator to the curb. Patricia slipped into the passenger seat, and Timnit climbed into the back.

"Anyone have any ideas on how we can keep Cora safe?" Patricia asked.

Timnit spoke up first. "We tried unsuccessfully to penetrate the Li building back when you were looking into the Ponzi scheme. That place is built like a fortress, and it has top-tier electronic security. I think Cora's already unreachable by the triad. She just needs to remain there until the FBI gets their arms around this."

Patricia nodded. "Plus, she has onsite personal security."

"I don't see how we could improve on that," Timnit said from the back.

"Any ideas about protection for her extended family?" Patricia asked. "I checked with the FBI yesterday, and they're still reluctant to get involved."

Simon started up the Navigator. "We have no idea what's on the second and third floors of the building. If it's warehouse space, she could bring in cots for the rest of the families."

"I'll check with her to find out if that's practical." Patricia picked up her phone, punched in Cora's speed dial, and clicked on the speaker phone. "Hello, Cora. I was wondering what is on the second and third floors of your building?"

"Several apartments that are empty and some storage areas. Why?"

Aware Cora's line could be compromised, Patricia said, "Just working on an idea. If I can put all the pieces together, I'll get back to you." Once the call was completed, Patricia turned to Simon. "What do you think of putting everyone up at the Li Building?"

Simon frowned. "How do we maintain security with daily reprovisioning? Not to mention school for the children and, God forbid, any medical needs? We would need a lot more than secure guest rooms."

Patricia nodded and sat in silence for a moment. "I need to get FBI protection for them."

"It's too early," Simon said. "We need to get our facts worked out. And we need a contingency plan in case the FBI doesn't want to protect the family."

LATER THAT DAY, PATRICIA AND TIMNIT MET LILY LI AT THE Gryphon Tea Room for a follow-up interview.

After introducing Timnit, they spoke of Lily's plans to reopen the salon. "Father would like that," Lily said, moisture glistening her large, luminous eyes. Her hair hung in a straight dark sheet on one side of her face and was tucked behind her ear on the other. She was petite like her mother, but Patricia could see so much of her dear friend Ken in Lily's face.

"Your father had a great impact on my life and will be greatly missed by so many of us. To be able to visit his salon, to hear the familiar music and to smell the unique Asian fragrances would be a nice way to remember him. But I think it would be too dangerous at this time. Like your mother is doing, I think it best if you sequester yourself until the FBI tells us it's safe to return to normal."

"It's probably premature right now, but we need to plan for the future." Her shoulders drooped and she paused. "I've been training under my father to run the business, and, when it's time, I'll step up to honor his legacy."

"I was wondering, Lily, if anyone from the Chinese government has approached you since your father's death?" Timnit asked.

She cocked her head to the side. "No. However, many people have wished us condolences. Some I don't know, but I don't think any of them were what you said."

Timnit nodded. "You weren't working the night your father passed."

Lily looked into the distance with an empty stare. "Father told me I could take the evening off. He said he'd take care of everything."

"You were always there for my evening appointments," Patricia said.

"Yes," Lily said in a flat monotone voice. "At the time I wondered why he gave me the evening off, but I didn't ask."

"Was I the only appointment for the salon that night?"

"You were his very last appointment. We usually had a full salon until sunset, but Father sent the stylists home at five and rescheduled their appointments. I thought it was strange, but we never questioned Father."

"So he cancelled everyone but me?"

"I assumed whatever he had planned for the early evening would be done in time for your appointment. Or perhaps he planned to cancel you too but couldn't reach you in time."

"Have you spoken with the police?" Timnit asked.

Lily nodded.

"Have you told them about rescheduling the appointments?"

"No." Lily bit her lip. "They just wanted to know where I was that night. I told them I was home with Mother."

"I think you should tell the police about your father sending everyone home," Patricia said.

Lily blinked. "Do you think it might have something to do with his death?"

"Hard to tell. But it might."

As the conversation began to wrap up, Patricia texted Simon, who got his check and left the tearoom as soon as he received the text. Patricia, Lily, and Timnit left five minutes later.

Cynthia Kwok, aka Emma Zhang and a host of other aliases, watched Miss Li, Mrs. Falcon, and a third woman from a dark corner table well beyond Li's circle of protection in the Gryphon Tea Room. She had been shadowing the Lily since killing the woman's father, learning Lily's security routines as well as her public habits. Unlike her catlike father, Lily seemed to be situationally naïve. So typical of privileged children. She guessed Lily's father had trained her to succeed in business but had failed to school her in how to survive in the brutal jungle Cynthia knew as life.

As an enforcer, Cynthia had been trained from her

earliest years to survive and thrive in the most severe of situations. She took no pride in the fact she had excelled. Her father had beaten pride out of her years ago.

Cynthia turned the page of her fashion design textbook, shoved the fake glasses up her nose, and pretended to continue to read. She hadn't liked formal education back home. Unlike her life, school in China was so predictable. Boring. Rules. Lots of them.

It was different at the Savannah Design Academy. Here she was being taught rules, then encouraged to break them. Nothing was forbidden in the name of creativity. It was so liberating. Of course, like her martial arts training, she had to survive and excel, but she had no trouble with that. Like her glorious ancestors, she was meant to defeat, to dominate, to rule.

Cynthia looked up as she turned the page again. The three were still deep in conversation. To avoid staring, she immediately looked down again, her eyes focusing on the text for a moment. She would actually study the chapter when she returned to her apartment. Her mind filled with what-ifs. Part of her hoped Lily would be as stubborn as her father so she could kill again, so she could once again feel the raw power of taking a life. But she'd been told the woman was the key to a much larger plan and that it would be best for China if Lily cooperated. And Cynthia wanted above all else what was best for China.

She watched as Miss Li, Mrs. Falcon, and the third woman concluded their business and one of Lily's security team went outside and looked around. When he returned to the door, the three women left the coffee house. Only one of Lily's security detail followed them out, the big one who had been seated, as always, closest to Lily. The one Cynthia would certainly have to go through if she was called upon to kill Lily.

Unlike Lily, her chief security man was clearly strong. But what made him even more formidable was his situational awareness. His eyes never left the people in the room. Cynthia knew he was cataloguing each person, making note of those who had showed up at previous engagements. Something she had dealt with by using a wide variety of cleaver disguises. Hats. Wigs. Makeup. Clothing. His eyes slid right past her as she had expected.

Plus, the number one security guy was always properly positioned to intercept a close-in attack and seemed to anticipate all movement toward his boss. Every waiter, every guest was screened away from Lily Li.

The remaining members of Lily's security team left after she was completely out of the building. Cynthia had seen the same maneuver from the same men over and over in the past few days. A major weakness by Lily's security team-repetitive security procedures. Procedures she had learned and would exploit if needed.

Cynthia knew better, however, than to assume she had a total fix on Lily's security. It was that 'checking her pride' thing again. Thank you, Father. So she sat patiently taking in everything, waiting for someone she'd overlooked to reveal themselves. *Always question your assumptions,* her father had told her over and over.

A fit younger white man seated on the other side of the shop stood and followed the security team out. Cynthia hadn't noticed him before, but her intuition screamed that one or both could be part of Lily's security team. She decided to follow the white male.

It didn't take long for Simon to realized he was being shadowed by an Asian woman. Twice he'd abruptly changed direction at an intersection, and each time, she had eventually changed her direction as well. Simon realized his classic countersurveillance tactic could tip off the woman that he was onto her, but it was a calculated risk he had to take to confirm she was indeed following him.

As easy as Simon had identified the tail, he also quickly established she was well-schooled in surveillance tradecraft. She kept well back from him and, with the exception of the intersection blunders, moved at her own pace. And she had stayed on the other side of the street for more than half of the time she was following him. But what really convinced Simon she was a professional was that she kept altering her appearance.

When she left the coffeehouse, her long black hair was down. Then it was up in a ponytail, and now it was tucked into a Savannah Bananas baseball cap. Simple, but clever. Even more clever was putting on a black hoodie after leaving the tearoom, then five minutes later putting it back in her backpack.

So who was this woman? And why was she following him?

Simon stopped at a storefront, turned sideways to the woman, and pulled his phone from his cargo pants. He put his camera on full zoom, then as if making a phone call, he brought the phone to his ear and started taking photos of the woman in the distance. Once he had sufficient photos, he returned the phone to his pocket and headed directly toward the stalker. The best way to put a tail into panic was to approach them.

Sure enough, the woman immediately turned down a side street. When Simon got to the side street, there was no trace of her. He knew better than to think that was the last time he'd see her, but with any luck, he'd know much more about her when she reappeared.

Catching up with Timnit and Patricia was his next priority. He speed-dialed Timnit. "Simon here, Timnit. What's your location?"

"Where'd you go?" she asked, irritation in her tone.

"I'll tell you about it when we meet up. Where are you?"

"I'm in the lobby of Hotel Bardo. Patricia is meeting with the catering director."

"Copy that. By the way, can you check the Gryphon Tea Room's security video of our visit?"

"Sure. What are you looking for?"

"An Asian woman followed us out, then tailed me. From her surveillance technique, I can tell she's well-trained. I took some smartphone photos but want to see what the security video can tell us about the woman as well. Did you notice her?"

"No," Timnit said. "She must be good at what she does. I'll check the security videos."

By the time Simon sat down with Timnit in the lobby, she'd already isolated two videos of the Asian woman. One showed her sitting alone in the tearoom facing Patricia, reading a fashion design textbook. A student? No way. Not with that kind of surveillance training. But the agent could be enrolled at the Design Academy for cover. If so, the school would have a photo, a corresponding name and, quite possibly, a dorm address. And someone had to be paying her sizable tuition.

The second video Timnit had isolated was of the woman leaving the shop. The quality was good. They would be able to get an excellent image to submit for facial recognition. If the woman had a driver's license, criminal record, or a passport, he'd get another fix on her. Maybe a real name. Or at least a current alias.

"Pretty good counterintelligence work, Timnit," Simon

said. "But we still don't know why she was following me." BAM. He snapped his fingers. "This person was studying Patricia's security. But why? Could she be planning on killing Patricia?"

er home delivery meals settled upon, Patricia walked from the catering director's office back into the hotel lobby. With everything that had happened since Ken's death, including meeting Lily this morning, Patricia found she'd neglected the running of her household with Trey. It had felt good to reestablish some normalcy. And with the long hours he was working, she wanted to make sure there were always healthy and delicious meals available.

She was surprised to see Timnit and Simon seated at a table in the corner with their laptops open. Only Timnit had come to the hotel with her. She had expected Simon would be long gone after her meeting with Lily. "What's up?" she asked, sitting.

"I was followed by a pro when I left the Gryphon," Simon said. "She was Asian, probably Chinese. Apparently, she was seated inside the shop during your meeting with Lily."

"Any idea why she was following you?" Patricia asked.

"That's what we're trying to figure out. Our best guess is that she thought I was a new member of Lily's security unit and was looking for vulnerabilities."

"Or she thought Simon was part of your security," Timnit added. "It's not as though you haven't been stalked recently." Timnit turned to Simon. "Show Patricia the woman's photo."

Patricia gasped when Simon turned his screen toward her. "That's one of the two people posing as FBI agents who followed me the day after Ken's murder."

"Are you sure?" he asked.

"I am. She was the passenger and kept making fun of the driver and laughing." Patricia opened her email from Algenon and showed them both the photo of the driver's license used to rent the car. "The car was rented by this person, under the name of Emma Zhang."

"I'm willing to bet the name on the license is an alias," Simon said.

Patricia's phone chimed. She checked the screen. *Algenon.* "I need to take this."

"Can you talk?" he asked.

"For a moment. What's up?"

"We couldn't get a facial match on either of the individuals who were following you."

She bit her lower lip. It was too much to expect a match, but they had to try. "The woman used a fake driver's license to rent the car. I thought it was impossible to make fake licenses."

"It is for most people. Whoever produced her license had access to some high-end technology. Probably a government intelligence service or a major gang that traffics in phony ID documents."

"Chinese?"

"It could be."

"Forty-four Brothers triad?"

"Why did you mention them?" Algenon asked.

Patricia could practically hear the wheels spinning in

Algenon's head. "Both Cora and Luke Li think the Forty-four Brothers triad is behind Ken's murder."

She heard him let out a low whistle. "Do they have proof?"

"No."

"Okay," Algenon said. "I'll get right on this. I need to inform Homeland Security. And, Patricia, watch your flanks."

"Speaking of which, the woman known as Emma Zhang followed Simon today."

"That's not a good sign. Be careful."

"I will," she said. "We found her on the surveillance video from the Gryphon Tea Room. I'll forward it to you."

"That's okay," Algenon said. "We'll get the video ourselves. Thanks for the heads-up. Also, the credit card used to rent the car was issued by the Hong Kong and Macau Bank. They're not cooperating with our request for more information on the account."

Patricia tensed. "That adds credibility to our assumption about the Chinese government being involved."

"Which makes her all the more dangerous," he said. "I'll give this top priority."

She loved his concern, as well as his upbeat attitude. "Thank you, Algenon."

She disconnected. "Algenon says no match on the photos."

Simon frowned. "It was a long shot at best. What else do you know about this woman?"

"Physically, her photo is exactly what I recall. That's it."

"Other than the car, have you seen her elsewhere?"

Patricia reflected for a moment. "No. What did you see?"

"She was dressed in dark clothing and sitting well away from the entrance, studying a textbook."

Patricia sat up straighter, shocked the woman was able to be there without anyone noticing. "A student?"

"Based on her surveillance technique, I'd say she was

anything but a student. However, she might be using a local college as a cover."

Patricia's phone signaled an incoming text. She checked the screen. *Chief Patrick.* "Let me check this text."

CP: Ken Li's autopsy in. Sending you a copy by email.

PF: Key finding?

CP: COD: toxic level of gelsemine. Highly rare substance. Quick acting.

PF: How administered?

CP: On blade of knife, directly into his heart.

Patricia grimaced at the awful news of just how determined the killer was to murder her friend. If she didn't know it before, she did now. It hadn't been a meeting or disagreement that went bad. It was a cold, calculated assassination. Thank the Lord for the small mercy that his death had obviously been quick. Too quick to be painful.

PF: Thank you.

Patricia put her phone on the table. "Autopsy indicates Ken was poisoned."

"I thought he was stabbed," Timnit said.

"He was," Patricia replied. "But the actual cause of death was a quick-acting poison on the blade."

"What kind of poison?" Timnit asked.

"Gelsemine. And Ken had no obvious defensive wounds so he must have known his attacker or simply didn't consider them a threat."

Timnit tapped her cellphone. "Gelsemine. A highly toxic compound related to strychnine," she said. "One of the active ingredients in *Gelsemium Elegans*, the most poisonous indigenous plant in China. Used in the 2011 poisoning of Long Liyuan, a Chinese timber baron. Also a favorite poison of the Forty-four Brothers triad."

Patricia nodded. "All roads keep leading back to the triad."

"It's just a hunch, but based on their sudden interest in

you, my guess is that your stalkers are the murderers," Simon said.

The hairs stood up on her arm. "Makes sense. But since I was face-to-face with them the day after Ken's death, why didn't they kill me?"

"Who knows? Maybe at the time they didn't think you were important. But with the success of your investigation, you've become an obstacle to them," Timnit said. "That's why we have you covered now."

"And remember, that woman was able to get close to you without being detected," Simon said. "We need to find and neutralize those two killers. We've got nothing to go on with the driver other than his photo and phony FBI credential. On the other hand, we have much more, relatively speaking, on the woman going by Emma Zhang. Timnit, can you get into local college records?"

"I don't know why not."

"Start with the Design Academy."

Timnit tapped her keyboard and stared at the screen. "I'm into the Savannah Design Academy. Lame security."

"And some well-developed skills," Simon added. "See if they have an Emma Zhang registered."

"There is no Emma Zhang at the Academy," Timnit said. "Maybe she's at another school."

"Wait," Patricia said. "Before that, let's take a look at their freshman photos."

Timnit pulled up the photos, and the three of them scanned the pages of images for a few minutes.

"There she is," Patricia said. "She has a different name, Pat Wo, and she has glasses and different hair, but those eyes—that's definitely her. Check that student's profile, Timnit."

"Okay, here she is," Timnit said. "At twenty-seven, she's older than a typical student, but she's registered as a first year. Home is shown as Hong Kong. She's taking a full load and maintaining a decent GPA. What is the number on the credit card she used to rent the car?"

Patricia read off the number.

"Nope. That's not the account paying for her school costs."

"Is she in a dorm?" Patricia asked, her pulse quickening. Could it really be this easy to trace the woman?

Timnit tapped a couple of keys. "Nope. But there's a local address for her." Timnit rekeyed her laptop. "Just as I suspected. It's an empty lot. She obviously doesn't want it to be easy for us to find her."

Simon stroked his stubbled chin. "Do you have access to her class schedule?"

Timnit wiggled her fingers. "Of course."

Simon scowled. "Easy, tiger. When is her next class?"

"This afternoon," Timnit said proudly. "One o'clock."

"What are you thinking?" Patricia asked Simon.

"I'm thinking we drop a nano-drone on Emma's backpack and have her carry it to wherever she sleeps." Simon looked at Timnit.

"Why not just follow her?" Patricia asked.

"She's too skilled to be followed. The nano-drone is the only way."

After Timnit left, Patricia and Simon took an Uber home. While Simon did yet another sweep of the house, Patricia called Trey from the front entryway to brief him on the Chinese threat, but he was in a trial. She left a message, then as soon as she was given the all-clear by Simon went to the office and added today's new information to her Ken Li case file. Once all was in place, she called Algenon and Chief Patrick to bring each up to date.

She supposed the FBI had already done a review of Ken's

digital footprint in the days leading up to his murder, as combing through that information might reveal the identity of the killer.

Maybe she could save the bureaucratic organization some time. She had Ken's phone number and email address. Though she didn't have access to his phone or his computers, maybe Timnit could still work her magic.

Patricia called her.

"Can you identify who Ken contacted with his cellphone in the days before his murder?"

"Sure, but don't you think the FBI has already done that?"

"Yes, but I'm looking for someone specific. I want to identify any non-local Chinese who spoke with Ken just prior to his murder."

"No problem," Timnit said. "I'll go ahead and isolate the calls during the week before his murder, then we'll eliminate all the numbers you, Cora, and Luke can identify. That will leave a much smaller number of contacts for us to get names for. If the killer and Ken spoke in that week, we'll soon know who it is. Anything else?"

"Same question on Ken's emails."

"Just give me his email address."

Patricia provided the information.

"His email history should be in the cloud. It shouldn't be hard to get to."

Optimism that she'd soon get the name of the killer filled Patricia. She checked the time. It was well after Emma Zhang's class. "Did you get the nano-drone on Ms. Zhang?"

"Sure did. It rode her backpack back to an apartment building. We're getting a strong signal from it."

"What's the location?"

"A building on Jones Street."

"Are we sure it's her room?"

"No. It's just where she went after class."

"How long is the drone battery good for?"

"Twelve more hours."

"Then what?" Patricia asked.

"Then we send in another drone."

"Thanks, Timnit. Let me know when you have the phone and email info."

"Sure will." Timnit swore.

"What?"

"We just lost the drone signal."

CHAPTER 24

The home chef service dropped off barbequed ribs, collards, and coleslaw on schedule at five. As much as Patricia loved to cook, between her odd hours of sleuthing and Trey's extended work schedule, they'd become dependent on precooked dinners during the week.

Once she got the food stowed in the fridge, she went into the dining room where Simon had set up his command center. "I know I can't call Cora because there's no doubt whoever is behind Ken's murder has tapped her phone and maybe even ours," Patricia said. "But I need to talk to her, so I'd like to visit."

"Visiting Cora is too dangerous."

"I understand the danger, but not knowing absolutely *everything* she knows about the Chinese threat right now is more dangerous."

He frowned. "I could send Timnit over there with one of our secure satellite phones."

"Thank you. That'd be great. Let me know when secure communication is established."

"Give me a half hour."

"Okay," Patricia said. "I'll let Cora know to expect Timnit."

Patricia called Cora on the secure phone Simon had assigned her. "How are you doing, Cora?"

"Oh, Patricia. I still can't believe he's gone."

Patricia's throat thickened at the anguish in her friend's voice. "I know. I'm so sorry. Is there anything I can do for you?"

"The kids have been wonderful. We have been strong for each other, as well as weak for each other when needed. We're just getting through each day one at a time."

"That's good."

"So, what can I do for you, Patricia?"

"Could Timnit pop by in the next hour? She has a small gift for you."

"That's very kind of her."

A HALF HOUR LATER, AN UNKNOWN NUMBER APPEARED ON Patricia's phone. She answered the call.

"Nice phone," Cora said. "Thank you, Patricia."

"We felt secure communication for all of us would be advisable. No point in letting the Chinese government listen in on our conversation."

"Very thoughtful."

Patricia grabbed a pen and pad from the kitchen table and headed for the family room. "First off, can you recall when the Chinese official first contacted your husband?"

"Hmm. Let's see. As far as I remember, last week was the first time Ken mentioned a meeting with the man, but it's possible they conversed before then."

Patricia sat, jotted the answer on the pad and stared at it. That answer should help Timnit set the range on the phone and email data. "Were there multiple contacts after that? And what were they, phone, email, or physical meetings?"

"There were multiple meetings. And I believe there were some calls to set up those meetings. I'm not sure about emails."

"How many meetings?"

"I don't know. Ken said he met with the official a few times during the week, and each time they met, the official was more demanding."

Patricia put her phone on speaker and placed it on the table beside her so she could take notes easier. "Okay. Remind me what was it exactly this guy was demanding from your husband?"

"Ken said the official wanted him to buy selected local businesses and later resell them to offshore Chinese investors."

"Why would they need Ken for that? Couldn't they just buy them directly?"

"They didn't want people knowing they were behind the purchases."

"Why would Ken object to buying businesses for them? Savannah has always encouraged foreign investment."

Cora paused. "He told me he feared that on the scale the official suggested, it would ultimately lead to Chinese control of much of Savannah's economy. China has a long-range goal of world trade dominance, and Ken didn't want any part of that."

"I see," Patricia said. "When did the official actually move to threatening Ken?"

"The day ... the day before they ... they killed him," Cora replied in a shaky voice.

"I'm so sorry, Cora. I didn't want to upset you further."

Cora sniffled. "No. No, I want to go on."

Knowing the *when* and *where* of those meetings could

reveal the *who*. "Okay. Let's break this down. Were those meetings face-to-face?"

"I believe so." Cora paused as if in thought. "Now that I think of it, I'm sure they were."

"Where did the meetings occur?"

"I believe they met at Ken's Barnard Street office. He didn't like discussing business in public or other people's offices."

Thankful that Cora was so forthcoming, Patricia made a note of her answer. "Did Ken ever mention any specific calls?"

"I know of one for sure. Ken was terribly upset after that call."

"A cellphone call?"

"Yes. He didn't use a landline."

"When was that call?"

Cora paused for a moment. "I'm pretty sure it was a couple of days before his death."

"Morning? Evening?"

"Evening. About seven. We had just finished dinner."

"Do you have access to the Barnard Street building security videos?"

"Yes."

Patricia's heart sped. "Could you provide me with the security videos for the week prior to his death?"

"Luke has already given a set to the police," Cora said.

"That's good, but I need a copy of my own to get a fix on those who saw Ken and when they met."

"Sure. I'll ask Luke to send you video and audio copies tomorrow," Cora replied.

"Audio?"

"Why yes," Cora said. "Ken always recorded everyone he met with in his office. It's why he preferred having meetings there. He said someone's word was their bond, so he would always make certain to record all business dealings."

What luck thought Patricia. She hoped she would be able to identify the people involved in Ken's murder and have all of them brought to justice.

Shortly after Patricia wrapped up her conversation with Cora, Trey arrived home. His face was uncharacteristically somber. He walked to her and gave her a perfunctory hug, then stepped back.

Patricia saw the pain in his red-rimmed, bloodshot eyes. "Hard day?"

He nodded.

"The trial?"

"We lost a big one."

"Would you care for a drink?" Patricia asked.

"Yes please. Scotch."

Patricia poured a glass of sparkling wine for herself and a scotch on the rocks for Trey, then handed the drink to him. "Trey, honey, I hate to add to your misery, but I need to share some disturbing information with you."

His eyes widened. "Are you okay?"

"It's not me."

Trey sat back in his chair. "Thank God." He took a sip of scotch. "Okay, what's the bad news?"

A flicker of doubt paused Patricia. No. The Chinese threat was too real. Too big. It was time to involve Trey. "Broad brushstroke first."

He dipped his chin in understanding.

She met his eyes and held the gaze for a moment, then let out a long breath. "A Chinese government economic takeover of Savannah."

Trey's mouth tightened. He looked toward the front of the house, then glanced at her out of the corner of his eye. "Are you sure?"

"Pretty much."

He turned to her and cocked an eyebrow.

Patricia swallowed hard. "If I'm to believe Cora, and I do, her husband was killed because he wouldn't agree to buy local businesses for offshore Chinese investors."

"Buying up some local businesses is hardly a takeover," Trey said quietly.

"Apparently, Ken had reason to believe the purchases would be on a much larger scale."

Trey's jaw muscles twitched. "I didn't know Ken that well."

"I did. For twenty years. He wasn't one to overreact. I believe him. In my opinion, the threat is real, and we need to figure out how to stop it."

Trey rubbed his brow. "Okay. What evidence do you have?"

"Ken was directly threatened by a Chinese government official. Tomorrow, I expect to receive a recording of the Chinese official threatening Ken, as well as videos of the official entering and leaving Ken's office building. According to Chief Patrick, Ken was killed by a decorative knife frequently used by the Forty-four Brothers triad, which was coated with poison from a plant indigenous to China. A poison, coincidently, that is favored by the Forty-four Brothers triad assassins."

"I thought the Forty-four Brothers triad started off as opposition to the Chinese government."

"According to Cora, they've morphed into mercenaries for hire," Patricia said.

Trey's eyes narrowed. "Do you have names?"

Her fingers tightened on the stem of her wineglass. "Simon, Timnit, and I are working on identifying the Chinese government official. As for Ken's killer, we've narrowed our suspects to a Chinese man known as Franklin

Chow and—"

Trey's eyes widened. "Isn't Chow the guy who followed you the day after Ken's murder?"

"That's him. He appears to be working with a Chinese woman going by Emma Zhang. We believe all the names are aliases. We have photos of both. Algenon ran name and facial traces on our suspects and came up empty. Earlier today, the woman followed Simon. He said her surveillance techniques were professional. She's registered as a student at the Savannah Design Academy."

The foyer clock chimed six. Their normal dinner time but, of course, neither of them made a move. The information was too staggering.

Trey pursed his lips, his expression was distant. She could almost see his mind whirling, shuffling and reshuffling what she had just told him. "I'd say that was reasonably compelling evidence," he said at length. "And utterly alarming. If what you've uncovered is true, then *you* aren't safe."

"If?"

He glanced up, a flicker of a question in his eyes, then looked down without voicing the question. Why the hesitation? He swallowed, exhaled hard and looked up. "If it's actually a Chinese government plan to consume Savannah economically, it's dangerous for you, and frankly, it's well beyond the scope of even the Coalition. More like something Homeland Security should handle." He considered her silently for a moment. "But it's an assault on Savannah, and that's what the Cotton Coalition was created for."

Patricia drummed her fingers on the armrest. "Either way, we have to make sure the threat gets on the radar of whoever should be tasked with something like this."

"It's not that easy. There are limited resources. Well established, pre-existing priorities. Politics. We can talk to Homeland Security or the State Department, but this will get much more traction if a prominent figure brings it forward to them rather than us."

"Algenon?"

"This could get mucked up in FBI politics."

"If not Algenon, who?"

Trey was silent for a moment. "The governor. I can talk with him tomorrow after you get the recording of the threat. If the governor buys into combating this plot, he'll be much more successful getting federal resources on it than us."

"What do you need from me?"

"Every piece of information you have. Names. Incidents. Sources. Witnesses. Phone and bank records. Security video."

"Everything we have so far is in my case file." Patricia went to the kitchen, found a thumb drive with the case file, returned, and handed it to him.

He put the thumb drive on the table between them. "I wish I knew why they choose Savannah."

"It's a major shipping port," Patricia said. "As such, it's a key link in international trade."

Trey's lips pinched. "There are larger ports close by. Jacksonville to the south, Charleston to the north. Why are they targeting Savannah over those two?"

A sense of foreboding settled over Patricia. "Why indeed?"

CHAPTER 25

*P*atricia awoke the following morning surprised to see Trey still in bed, scanning his phone. She turned on her side. "Not going in today?"

Trey put down the phone. "Mining the Ken Li recordings as soon as possible is my top priority today. That and meeting with the governor." He leaned over and pecked her lips.

"I spoke with Timnit last night after you went to sleep." Patricia stretched her stiff body. "She has key word software that should accelerate our search."

Trey sat up. "Which words will you search for?"

"*Peoples Republic, Chinese consulate,* and *failing businesses* to start with." Patricia sat up as well, then followed Trey into the bathroom, where she turned on the shower. "Summer is coming over at nine to help analyze the recordings."

Trey looked at his watch. "When do you expect to receive them?"

"Cora said this morning. I'll call her after eight to get a more precise time." Patricia tossed her sleep shirt in the hamper and stepped into the shower.

An hour later, she and Trey were sitting in the kitchen drinking coffee when Patricia's secure phone rang with Cora's number.

"It's Luke," Cora's son said when Patricia answered. "I'm using mother's phone. Could I drop off the recordings you requested in the next half hour?"

"Morning, Luke. And sure. We'll be here."

"See you then. And, Patricia, thank you for setting up secure communications for mother. It means a lot to her, and to me."

"No problem." Patricia glanced at the kitchen clock. "See you at eight thirty."

True to his word, Luke was at the door a half hour later with the recordings, plus a dozen Krispy Kreme doughnuts and three security men.

"Do y'all have time for coffee and doughnuts?" Luke asked.

She nodded and stepped aside as his entourage entered, then led them to the kitchen. His security men took their coffee and doughnuts to the dining room to talk with Simon. Luke greeted Trey, then sat at the table.

Trey buried his face in his hands, massaged his temple, then parted his hands and looked up. "I keep asking myself, 'Why Savannah?'"

"Me too." Luke gestured palms up. "And I keep coming up empty."

"I know what you mean. It's so frustrating." Trey leaned forward a tad. "Have the Chinese contacted you since your father's death?"

"No. Why?"

Trey stroked his chin as he stared off into space. "If they contact you and ask you for help, I think you should say yes."

"My father wouldn't cooperate, why should I?"

"They killed him." Trey raised his palms. "Sorry, but the only way we're going to find out what's really going on with them is to have someone on the inside."

Patricia's mouth dropped open. "That's too dangerous."

"Wait. I think Trey's onto something here." Luke's eyes narrowed. "For some reason, the people who approached my father felt they needed his involvement to make their plan successful. Since he wouldn't cooperate, they killed him. Which means he personally wasn't critical to their plan, just buying property for them. I could do that."

"But why haven't they approached you?" Patricia asked.

"I don't know," Luke said. "Maybe they found someone else."

His security team came into the kitchen. Luke took a sip of coffee. "We should be going."

Patricia and Trey accompanied them to the front door. "Thank you for the security video," Patricia said. "And the doughnuts."

Luke and his team left.

"Found it," Simon shouted from the hallway.

"Found what?" Patricia asked.

"The Chinese official, a Kenneth Kwok, threatening Ken Li."

"That was fast," Patricia said.

"Just a matter of using the right key word," Simon said.

"Which was?" she asked.

"'You will die.'"

The two of them followed Simon back into the dining room.

"I'll bring up the relevant section on that monitor." Simon pointed to a fifty-inch screen at the end of the table. They all moved to the screen, which showed four views simultaneously-front and back, as well as left and right. The well-lit images were surprisingly sharp. "At this point, Mr. Kwok hasn't arrived."

"They met several times. What's the time frame on this section?" Patricia asked.

"Two days before his murder," Simon said.

A buzz sounded on the screen. Ken reached forward, hit a button, and said, "Yes."

"Mr. Kwok is here for you," said a female voice.

"Bring him in," Ken said, standing.

An Asian man with black, slicked-back hair and dressed in a black suit entered the scene from the left.

They bowed to each other.

"The visitor has a ring on," Patricia said. "Zoom in on it please."

She narrowed her eyes as the video zoomed in on a gold dragon head ring on Mr. Kwok's hand. He also wore a vintage gold Rolex and diamond cufflinks. Clearly a man accustomed to wealth. Yet this person was said to be a Chinese government official.

They exchanged greetings in what Patricia assumed to be Mandarin. "We should have asked Luke to stay so he could translate," Patricia said.

"It's okay. I can do that." Simon stopped the video. "I speak Mandarin as well as Cantonese."

She gave Simon a smile. "You continue to surprise me, Simon. Can you do simultaneous translation?"

"Sure." The video resumed. "Mr. Li is inviting Mr. Kwok to take a seat," Simon said as he froze the video. "You'll notice here that Kwok has his hand under the front lip of Ken's desk. At this point, we don't know if he's placing or removing a listening device." Simon restarted the video. "Kwok says, 'Have you made a decision regarding our request?' and Ken replies, 'No. I need another day.' As you can see, this surprises Kwok." Simon froze the video again. "I think it's important to note that no tea or coffee has been served. I believe that indicates hostility between these two." Simon restarted the video. "Kwok says, 'As you wish, Mr. Li. One more day. But if you fail to agree to the Peoples' request tomorrow, you will die."

Patricia watched as Kwok stood and bowed ever so slightly to Ken, then Ken accompanied Kwok off frame to the left.

Simon stopped the video. "Okay. We have a name and several high quality screen-grabs of Kwok."

"Good work, Simon," Trey said.

"I agree," Patricia added.

"I'll need a copy of this scene and a written translation for presentation to the governor," Trey said.

"Of course," Simon said. "Right away. Then we'll get back to work on the audio to find out how many meetings are documented and what exactly was discussed. With any luck, we can coax more information out of these recordings."

Patricia's phone chimed an incoming text. She checked the screen. *Willie May.* He never texted unless it was impor-tant. She read his message.

WM: Check local TV. Breaking news on bird flu in Savannah.

Patricia wondered why Willie would think she'd be inter-ested in the bird flu. Well, the man sometimes worked in mysterious ways, so she'd just go with it.

PF: Will do. Thanks for the heads-up.

Patricia went into the family room and turned on the television.

"This just in," the female newscaster said with urgency in her voice. "The Centers for Disease Control have just confirmed the existence of a highly pathogenic bird flu variety in Savannah that could infect humans."

Patricia recalled the Chinese government involvement

with COVID in the past and wondered if this strain was from the Chinese as well.

"Trey," Patricia shouted. "You have to see this."

Trey rushed into family room just as the newscaster said, "So far, the flu variety discovered in a single bird in Savannah does not appear to have actually infected a human. However, local medical facilities have been alerted to be vigilant." A photo of a poultry farm appeared on the screen. "The bird flu, also known as H5N1, has killed hundreds of millions of animals in Asia, Europe, the Near East, and Africa since it first appeared in 1997, and it has infected hundreds of people worldwide, killing about half of them."

Patricia looked at Trey and shook her head. "Bird flu *here* in Savannah. I wonder if that was the bird I turned in."

"Bird flu isn't good in a densely populated place like a city," he said.

"This new, highly pathogenic flu strain has been identified as a Type A influenza virus, which constantly changes as it replicates," the newscaster said. "According to the World Health Organization, H5N1 has a documented ability to cause life threatening infection in humans. CDC is working closely with the Georgia Department of Health to minimize any human health risk posed by this new strain. They advise the public to take the following steps to reduce possible risk: first, avoid wild birds and observe them only from a distance. Second, avoid contact with domestic birds that appear ill or have died. And third, avoid contact with surfaces that appear contaminated with feces from wild or domestic birds. The CDC will provide updates as new information becomes available. In other news, police are investigating a shooting at—"

Patricia turned off the television. "What do you know about bird flu?"

"Next to nothing," Trey said. "Just that Tamiflu is the only effective treatment for bird flu in humans. It doesn't prevent the flu, just reduces the effects."

"Should we get the pills?" she asked.

"It's just one bird."

"It's one bird found. Who knows how many other infected birds haven't been found?" Patricia scrubbed her face with her hand. "Remember COVID? I have the feeling this is just the tip of the iceberg."

* * *

CENTERS FOR DISEASE CONTROL

Atlanta, Georgia

"There's no way this bird flu strain could have picked up these human flu traits while in the bird population," said Doctor Yuliam Rojas, chief of CDC's Epidemic Intelligence Service. "As such, we must assume it's a manmade strain." She looked around the conference room table.

"Do you think this could be the big one?" Cybil Bowen, Homeland Security liaison to CDC, leaned forward, pen in hand.

"It could be," Dr. Rojas said. "It's highly pathogenic, manmade, and resilient."

"One bird isn't an epidemic," said Arlene McGuire, representing the Georgia Bureau of Investigation's Counterterrorism Task Force.

"It's highly probable the sparrow passed the pathogen to several others before dying," Dr. Rojas said. "And it's also probable those carriers have infected many others."

"We have no evidence of that, nor do we have any evidence this strain has crossed species and infected humans," Arlene said.

"True," Dr. Rojas said. "But the mere existence of this pathogen in the wild is problematic. In my opinion, it's not a question of 'if' humans will be infected. They will be. And when they are, we could have an influenza pandemic on our hands."

CHAPTER 26

On the walk to the Liberty Street parking garage, Patricia mulled the limited options to protect Cora and her large extended family. Other than putting everyone up in the highly secure Li building, there didn't appear to be a simple, easy answer. When Patricia and Timnit paused at a stoplight, Patricia turned to her friend.

"Do you have any additional thoughts on how we can protect Cora and her family? Cora and Ken have fourteen children. Half are married. I've been to their weddings. And there are at least ten grandkids. And many of them have staff. There should be at least fifteen households."

"Okay. Let's go with that number," Timnit said as they started walking again. "I suppose they could take an extended vacation to a private island, but I don't see how we could provide reliable security for a place like that."

Patricia nodded. "Finding that many *secure* beds anywhere is a serious issue."

"Yeah. We need someplace impregnable like the presidential retreat at Camp David."

"That's it!" Patricia stopped mid-block. "Fort Stewart.

They prevented Franklin Chow from following Meredith onto the base, and I bet they have high-end perimeter security. If we could get the Li family moved to the base, it would be extremely hard for the triad to get to them."

Timnit beamed. "Great idea, Patricia. Fort Stewart has plenty of on-base rental family homes, grocery stores, a hospital, and an on-base school system. It's totally self-contained."

"Okay," Patricia said. "I'll check to see if we can get the FBI to secure a dozen or so homes located close together on Fort Stewart."

On the way home, Patricia arranged to meet with Algenon the next day. She figured she could assemble enough data that evening to make a convincing evidential argument for the FBI to pick up the case, to grant her request to move the family to safety, and to possibly provide additional protection for them.

As soon as Patricia arrived home, she, Simon, and Timnit gathered at the kitchen table and brainstormed the best evidence to present to the FBI. It quickly became clear they had no idea when the Chinese government intrusion of Savannah had actually begun. They had a time frame for Chow's initial contact with Ken, but was that meeting really the first incursion by the Chinese?

Patricia suddenly recalled the huge land deal when she was investigating her mother's death. She felt a tingling at the back of her neck. She called Sonny Carothers, her deceased mother's former accountant. "Good afternoon, Sonny."

"Hello, Patricia. How are you doing today?"

"I'm doing well, thank you. Do you mind if I put you on speaker phone? Simon and Timnit are here with me."

"No problem. Hi, Simon. Hi, Timnit."

After both responded, Patricia continued. "I'm investigating a case involving some Chinese suspects."

"Sounds interesting. How can I help?"

"Have you ever heard of a guy named Franklin Chow?"

"Hmmm. Let's see." The sound of a keyboard clicking filtered through the silence. "Yes. He was involved in the land transactions I did for your mother shortly before her death."

Timnit's and Simon's eyes widened.

Patricia took a calming breath. "What role did he play?"

"He was the registered agent for the Chinese high rollers buying the properties. A total of 30,000 acres. Roughly the size of Disney World in Florida."

"Did they buy through a front company?"

"Yes. Long Street Investment Partners."

"Where were the properties located that they acquired?"

More clicking registered. "Out I-16, toward Statesboro."

"Statesboro. Oh my." Patricia looked at Timnit, who already had pulled her laptop toward her and was keying it.

"Thanks, Sonny. Much appreciated."

"Anytime, Patricia."

Patricia leveled eyes on Timnit. "We need to find out who bought that Statesboro airport we infiltrated last year."

Timnit's face was grim. "Already on it."

CHAPTER 27

*P*atricia looked at Timnit, who was busily keying her laptop, and Simon, who sat in silence at the kitchen table with them. It was only five, but twilight was already dimming the light coming in the bay window. It was going to be a long night for all of them getting ready for the meeting with Algenon.

"Got it," Timnit said. "The airport property was purchased by Long Street Investment Partners in 2018. Franklin Chow is the registered agent for Long Street Investment."

Patricia's heart pounded.

"And here's an interesting tidbit for you," Timnit added. "Did you know the word 'long' is Mandarin for 'dragon'?"

"How'd you know that?" Simon asked.

"Mandarin is one of my fluencies. I learned it in the military. It helped out a lot in Cyber Command."

Patricia rubbed the gooseflesh that had risen on her arms. "Great job. Let's see what other purchases have been made by Long Street in the region."

Timnit nodded.

"And I'll find out if Chow used any other front companies to conduct business in Georgia." Patricia paused. "And South Carolina while I'm at it."

Patricia brought up the 'corporations' database from the Georgia Secretary of State's website, navigated to a restricted access window, and searched on Franklin Chow's name. Ten entities appeared in the results, including Long Street Investment. Patricia printed off two copies of the list. The South Carolina registry failed to produce a single company. She went to her office and retrieved the Georgia list from the printer.

"Simon," she said on returning to the kitchen. "I have ten Georgia entities dating to 2008 that have Franklin Chow as the registered agent. Timnit is already checking on Long Street Investment's activities. We need to check out what the rest of these companies have been up to. I'll take the first five of the remaining entities. Can you take the last four? Let's find out if any of these have been active in the region."

He nodded as she handed him the list.

"Wow," Timnit said in a sharp voice. "Long Street Investment bought some homes in Savannah in 2010. Wait. There are more. There has to be at least twenty homes purchased by them in a ten-day period."

Patricia's heart raced. Those purchases were well before the massive land purchases near Statesboro. "Anything earlier?"

"Not by Long Street Investment."

Patricia keyed the search bar on her laptop. "Well, look at this. A different Franklin Chow company also bought some homes in Savannah in 2011. Expensive ones in the Historic District."

Over the course of the next two hours, the three of them identified forty-eight homes in Savannah's Historic District purchased by Chow's companies. Nearly a hundred million dollars of transactions. And the properties for the Statesboro amusement park project were hundreds of millions of dollars more. Chow and his backers certainly had deep pockets.

"Good gracious," Patricia whispered in shock sometime later when the three of them had compiled the numerous properties each had located.

THE DOORBELL AWOKE PATRICIA, AND SHE BLINKED AT THE morning sun. She'd overslept and missed Trey again. She sighed and sat up, wishing she hadn't tossed and turned half the night worrying about how the Algenon meeting would go. It was imperative the meeting be successful, or she'd never get Meredith back home, nor keep Cora's family truly safe. The doorbell rang again. Shoot. Who would be here so early? She quickly opened the doorbell app on her phone and used the microphone. "Who is this?"

"Mrs. Falcon? Sorry to disturb you. We're here collecting the cats for evaluation."

"Oh. Sure. I apologize for the delay. I'll be down in a moment." In all the craziness of discovering Franklin Chow's real estate ties yesterday, she'd completely forgotten Doctor Rojas and the dead birds. And she'd miss those cats, darn it.

Pushing aside a swell of sadness, she hurriedly got dressed, wishing she could lean on Trey. She had sorely missed his presence and support the last few days.

Downstairs, the cats were both nestled together in one cage just off the patio and gave mournful yowls as the techs efficiently locked them in and carried the cage around the home and out the side gate. Her aching heart told her she'd probably never see her little friends again. Blinking away tears, Patricia took a deep breath and headed back into the house. She needed to keep focused today.

· · ·

Patricia and Timnit met Algenon at the Savannah FBI office at ten. After some small talk, Algenon leaned back and steepled his fingers. "What can I do for you, Patricia?"

"I know you have your hands full right now with the Saint Patrick's Day parade, but that's why this is so urgent. What I've discovered may well be specifically engineered to take advantage of your stretched resources."

"Go on."

"Are you aware Meredith Stanwick is currently in a safe house?"

Algenon's eyebrows shifted together. He stood, picked up his coffee mug, came around his desk, and sat in a chair next to her. "Whose safe house? Which agency?"

"It's off books, but I'll get to that. Let me start at the beginning."

"The murder you're investigating?"

She shook her head. "No. It starts in 2010 when a group of Chinese investors led by a person called Franklin Chow came to Savannah and, over the course of ten days, bought twenty historical homes at bargain basement prices. They returned a few months later and bought a dozen more. This continued off and on until Savannah home prices started to recover."

They sat for a moment. Algenon drummed his fingers on the armrest. "How many homes in total?"

"I can document forty-eight homes in the historic district acquired by various investor groups all headed by Franklin Chow."

"I'll need that documentation."

Patricia handed him a thumb drive. "My case file and all my documentation."

He took the drive. "And remind me again who Franklin Chow is?"

"He's the Chinese national who followed me from Cora

Li's home the day after Ken Li was murdered. But I'm getting ahead of myself."

"Sorry for interrupting. Go ahead."

"A few years ago, Franklin Chow was the registered agent for a consortium of Chinese investors who bought approximately 30,000 acres off I-16 for what they described as a huge Disney World style amusement complex. And a couple of years ago, another company Chow was part of bought additional acreage close to the original 30,000 acres."

"This is documented?"

She nodded. "The homes appear to have been rented out since their acquisition and, as far as I can tell, nothing has been applied for or developed on the first 30,000 acres. However, the second acreage I mentioned was involved in a Ponzi scheme I investigated a couple of years ago."

"Yes. I remember. Chinese reproductions of vintage cars passed off as authentic. Impressive investigative work, Patricia."

"Thank you. And if you remember, that acreage had a very large private airport on it."

"I remember."

"Two months ago, a Chinese official met with Ken Li, the murder victim, to discuss what has been described by Ken's wife as a *commercial* proposal. I'm sorry I don't have anything further on the nature of the proposal. I do know that it was of great concern to Ken, and he shared his feelings with his wife. He felt it was a threat. Maybe a warning."

Algenon reached over his desk, pulled the tablet to him, and tapped out a message. Moments later, he looked up. "Franklin Chow doesn't exist."

"I know. But if you check the Georgia driver's license database, you'll find him there associated with a fictitious address. And he's in the Georgia Secretary of State's database of registered agents and associated with various post office boxes in Atlanta."

"Are you telling me that not a civilian, but an agent for the Chinese government, is currently one of the largest property owners in the area and also owns an airfield?" Algenon stood and paced.

"Yes. And he and a female associate followed me the day after Ken's murder."

"So also potentially involved in that murder?"

"Yes. And this week he and a male associate followed the crew who transported Meredith to a safe house."

Algenon squeezed the back of his neck. Patricia understood the tension all too well. And if she knew Algenon, which she did, she'd bet he'd heard chatter, and his whip-smart brain was now putting puzzle pieces together. "Tell me about Meredith Stanwick. How does she fit in?"

Patricia briefly filled him in on the financial investigating she'd asked Meredith to do, and the subsequent threatening texts. "We felt it was prudent, especially factoring in what happened to Ken, to take her out of play. But I still didn't have enough to come to you for help."

"I dismissed your theory so easily last time. I'm not surprised you hesitated to come back for help. I'm sorry, Patricia. I'm not saying all you've told me adds up to an imminent threat, but—"

"Wait," Patricia said. "There's more. Analysis of Franklin Chow's voice indicates he probably learned English at a training facility in Savannah, China."

Algenon stiffened, his face flushed, and she knew she'd been right. He must have seen reports or intelligence chatter about the place.

"Patricia, are you sure Chow came from Savannah, China?"

Patricia nodded to Timnit.

"The Department of Defense has voice recordings of several residents of Savannah, China. They all speak with the same distinct accent. I accessed that database and got a ninety percent match on Chow."

Algenon's eyes widened as he sat. "Do you routinely access DOD databases?"

Timnit glanced at Patricia, who nodded again.

Timnit returned her attention to Algenon. "Yes, sir."

"You're a civilian."

"Yes, sir."

"Who gave you that clearance?"

"The Cotton Coalition gave her the clearance," Patricia said.

"Is this voice analysis documented?"

Patricia nodded. "It's all on the thumb drive."

Algenon moved to the edge of his seat. "This Franklin Chow situation is serious."

"I know. And this goes beyond him. At least a dozen Chinese named people had data inserted in the Georgia driver's license database around the time Chow's information was inserted. We suspect they could be accomplices. Possibly members of a Chinese triad. And a local guy named Alex Feng has joined Chow's crew."

"Is that everything?" Algenon asked.

The quiet hum of the office felt like the aftermath of an explosion. Patricia figured it kind of had been. "No more facts. That's all I know for sure."

"And since your earlier theories have proved to hold water, I must ask, what do you think their agenda is?"

"I think it all stems back to the reason for the establishment of Savannah, China, and, more recently, to China's Belt and Road initiative to achieve world economic domination by 2049. I think they're planning to take over Savannah economically."

"Why Savannah?"

She chewed her lower lip. "I don't know for sure. It's a

major port with transportation connections throughout the Southeast. But whatever the reason is, they're coming, and they're coming now. Knowing how stretched thin the city resources currently are, I'm concerned they'll make some sort of a move soon. One that we won't be prepared for."

His eyes were full of concern. "It certainly seems they have all their pieces laid out well on the board. Who else have you talked to regarding this?"

"I'll make you a list."

"No more discussions with others at this time. I'm going to get a task force on this immediately." He reached for his phone.

"I'd like to help in any way I can."

He put his phone down. "With the parade imminent, we *do* have a serious staffing issue that will impede our investigation. I suppose we could work something out." He made a call and told someone to get her and Timnit clearance badges. "As of this moment, you are both civilian consultants to my office."

Patricia glanced at Timnit, who cracked a smile.

CHAPTER 28

Patricia's shoulders loosened, and she gave Algenon a smile of appreciation. "I won't make you regret that decision."

"Nor I," Timnit said.

"Being a civilian consultant comes with a condition that your team only works on what I assign you, and that you get my permission before you go beyond your assignment. I don't want us duplicating each other's work. We don't have the staff to afford any of that. We work focused or not at all. Can you live with that for the time being?"

She mashed her lips together to temper her happiness. "I suppose we'll have to."

It was his time to smile. "Good."

Curiosity stewed. "What's our first assignment?"

He pursed his lips, then picked up the tablet and tapped the screen. Did he already have a case file on Franklin Chow? Algenon looked up and rested his eyes on her, hesitating before speaking, as if weighing his words. "I want you and your team to dig deeper on Franklin Chow. Go as deep as you possibly can. No detail is insignificant. I want you to document *every* transaction Chow or his businesses have made in the region. Do nothing more than that for now. Understand?"

"Understood." Everything in her screamed to get moving on the task, but decorum kept her rooted.

"I want a written progress report every day at noon."

"Noon. Yes, sir." She paused. "About the Li family?"

"What about them?"

"Cora Li, Ken's wife, thinks they'll eventually be targeted."

"She's probably right. As we turn the heat up on Chow and his crew, they're bound to react. And killing people seems to be on their menu of options." He paused. "Once we verify your information, we could put Mrs. Li in a safe house if—"

"Algenon. Sorry to interrupt. The threat is real, and it's urgent. Plus, it's not just Cora who is vulnerable. It's her entire family. Adult children. Spouses. Grandchildren. Every one of them is a potential target."

He stared into space for a moment. "We can arrange housing for them at Fort Stewart. I know the base has plenty of empty housing. We're pretty good at doing that on short notice."

"Can I offer that to Cora?"

He sat back in his chair. "Sure."

Feeling better about Cora's future security, she smiled. "Thank you, Algenon. If there's nothing else, I have an assignment I'm eager to get to work on."

He nodded, stood, and walked Patricia and Timnit to the lobby. "I appreciate your thoroughness, Patricia. And I look forward to your progress report tomorrow. And it's my pleasure to have finally met you, Timnit." He shook her and Timnit's hands. "Y'all be safe."

Timnit led Patricia outside to Simon's car.

"How'd it go?" Simon asked as Patricia and Timnit climbed in.

"Algenon is onboard, but we have a lot of work to do for him this afternoon."

Just as Simon pulled from the parking lot, a shot rang out, shattering the glass of the FBI's front door into fragments.

Shock coursed through Patricia, heightening her senses. She ducked down behind the dash, pulled her gun from her purse, and released the safety.

Simon accelerated, swerving left and right. Her seat belt dug deeply into her shoulder with each sharp evasive maneuver. She took deep breaths to settle herself. "Everyone okay?" she asked, fearing a negative answer.

"No damage here," Simon replied.

"Armed and ready," Timnit shouted from the backseat. "How about you?"

Patricia's phone signaled an incoming text. She sat up, put her gun in her lap and, with her heart pounding in her chest, pulled out her phone.

Annon: Stay away from the FBI or next time it won't be a door.

Patricia, rattled to the core, turned to Simon. "We need to get Cora and her family to safety right away."

Reaching the main road, Simon accelerated. "I don't see anyone following us. Do you, Timnit?"

"No one," Timnit said.

"What if Cora hesitates about taking her family to the base?" Patricia asked.

"We just *have* to convince her," Simon said.

Patricia swallowed her concern, picked up her secure phone, and punched in Cora's speed dial.

"Hello, Patricia. I was just thinking about you," Cora said cheerfully.

"And I of you," Patricia replied, wishing she could be as

cheerful. "Could Timnit and I come over? I have something important I'd like to discuss with you."

"Of course. How about in a half hour or so? And I'll have Luke send up some of those steamed shrimp dumplings you're so found of."

"Sure. See you then." Patricia ended the call, her shoulders relaxing a bit. "Cora's place in half an hour?" she said to Simon.

"That's cutting it tight, but I believe we can make it."

"If Cora agrees to relocate her family, how are we going to move that many people?" Timnit asked.

"They will have to transport themselves," Patricia said. "They'll need their cars on base."

"Timnit, check again to see if anyone is following us," Simon said.

Timnit twisted and looked out the back window. "Not that I can see."

Simon eased out of the high-speed lane to get around a slow-moving sedan.

Patricia's phone rang. She checked the screen. Algenon.

"Hello, Patricia. Are you okay?"

"We're fine," Patricia said. "Still wondering how they knew we were at your office. We used Simon's car to prevent being tracked."

"Maybe they're tracking your phones."

"They're secure."

"Even secure phones emit signals," Algenon said. "Some can be tracked."

"Gawd." Patricia shook her head. "By the way, right after the shooting, I got a threatening text warning me to stay away from the FBI."

"I think you should ditch those phones and sequester at home."

"Do you have any idea who might be behind this?"

Algenon didn't answer right away. "It certainly looks like a Chinese triad, but I have no idea who might be directing them. It could be an off-the-books cabal of Chinese autocrats, or a rogue fraction of the Chinese Communist Party. But then, it's the stated goal of the CCP to achieve world economic dominance by 2049. It's anyone's guess."

"Thank you, Algenon."

She disconnected. "Algenon says the Chinese government can track our secure phones."

Simon shook his head. "Not these phones."

"Then how did they track us to the FBI office?"

"I'm guessing we have an undetectable tail, or they're using drones."

Chan Xian pushed back from the array of computer monitors in front of him, then swiveled his chair to look out on the Hong Kong cityscape and harbor far below his office tower. It was a city and an economy he and his fellow officials dominated. And it was just a small piece, a grain of rice, compared to what was soon to come.

Putting the many elements into play over the past thirty years had been easy, but keeping the plan running smoothly in these final days was proving to be exhausting. The AI software was excellent at solving most problems but required human interventions from time to time.

And as much as he needed to recharge, there was no time for that. There would be an abundance of time for relaxation once they had taken economic control of the targeted American port cities. Until then, he'd rely on ginseng tablets and *wu wei zi* tea to keep fully alert.

Xian ran his palm over the leather arm of his chair. He should have trusted the AI program, ignored Ken Li's refusal, and moved on. It had been a big mistake to authorize the kill;

a kill that had attracted attention to the plan. Too much attention. And the AI programing was an utter failure at finding a solution to the problem he'd created. Fortunately, he had the triad in place to neutralize those pesky investigators. Kidnappings, not killings, this time. The sooner the better.

He returned to his computer and placed another short order on General Dynamics stock.

As the Simon's car entered the Historic District, Patricia noticed the Saint Patrick's Day bunting, banners and flags hanging from light poles as the city wrapped up preparations for the parade. A joyful city completely oblivious to the threat she'd just discussed with Algenon.

Dressed in a baggy, long-sleeved shirt that concealed his muscular build, Chen Ming met Patricia and Timnit in the parking garage, led them up to the penthouse, then through a warren of hallways to a small yet ornate sitting room with no windows.

Cora stood as they entered. "Patricia. Timnit. I'm glad to see you both. I hope you each are well, considering the circumstances."

"We're well, Cora," Patricia said, intentionally avoiding any mention of the gunshot at the FBI office. "It's been quite the morning. We had an excellent visit with the FBI resident agent in charge, and he's agreed to take on your case. In fact, the reason I wanted to see you so urgently is to propose a plan for the safety of your family. Everyone, including your grandchildren."

"Since your proposal covers all my family, do you mind if I invite Luke to join us?"

Patricia nodded. "Of course."

Cora phoned Luke and spoke in Chinese, then disconnected and turned to Patricia. "He said he'd be right up." She gestured to the sofa which was covered in emerald brocade. "Please be seated. Would you care for some tea while we wait?"

"No. Thank you." As Patricia sat, she noticed Chen had remained in the room by the door, only sitting once Cora had. Patricia took in small details about the room that others might miss. Cameras imbedded in picture frames. The double locks on the door. More air vents than typical. While they were waiting for Luke, Patricia asked Cora about what safety precautions the rest of her family were taking.

"They're not doing anything other than staying home and severely restricting any outside trips."

"Some of your children have businesses, don't they? Are they able to manage their businesses from home?"

"Yes. All but Luke. He feels it's important to be in the restaurant greeting guests and making sure they are well served."

At the mention of Luke's name, there was a knock on the door. Chen stood and opened the door. Luke walked in, greeted his mother, and turned to Patricia and Timnit, both of whom stood. Patricia was again struck by how much he looked like a tall, younger version of his father.

After some small talk, they all sat.

"Patricia has a proposal to discuss with us regarding our safety," Cora said to Luke.

Luke pushed thick glasses up his nose, nodded, and looked to Patricia.

"Before going into the proposal, I'd like to recap for Luke why we all feel it is important to protect your family. And, Cora, you'll notice we have additional information regarding the threat."

Patricia then went over the information she had shared with Algenon earlier. When Patricia got to the part about Savannah, China, Cora gasped.

"Yes, Cora. It's much more serious than either you or I imagined." Patricia paused. "I spoke with the FBI this morning, and they're picking up the case. I'll be working with them on a limited basis."

"And what about the proposal?" Cora asked.

"The FBI has located a cluster of newly built, furnished family homes on a well-protected military base that can accommodate your extended family. The base has everything you need inside the fences including schools, grocery stores and a hospital."

"Would we be free to leave if we wanted?" Luke asked.

"Of course," Patricia said. "But I wouldn't recommend it if you're trying to stay safe and protected."

"Very interesting." Cora said. "What do you think, Chen?"

He nodded slowly. "It's better than anything we currently have or could arrange."

"Do you think the others would go for it?" Cora asked Luke.

"If they hear what you and I just heard, I'm sure they'll move immediately," Luke said.

"We need to keep those specific details to ourselves," Patricia injected.

Cora nodded. "I understand. We can tell them we're acting on confidential information. When can we move?"

"Tomorrow," Patricia replied.

"Sounds like a plan." Cora turned to Luke. "Assemble the elders this afternoon, and we'll go over the plan with them."

"Yes, Mother."

· · ·

On Patricia's way back home, Meredith called. "How's the investigation going?"

"Fine."

"Do you have any idea when I can get out of this safe house?"

"I'm working on it, but right now, I don't know when."

"I've been thinking about how best to collapse a city's economy," Meredith said. "And the quickest way I could think of was to kill a lot of the workers or to destroy the biggest workplaces. Either way, the economy collapses."

"That's radical," Patricia said.

"Sometimes you have to go big. Anyway, I asked myself, how do the Chinese benefit from something like that. And I came up with shorting stock or buying put options. Both are ways you benefit when the stock price goes down. With that in mind, I checked the short interest ratio on General Dynamics stock."

"How does this affect the takeover of infrastructure in Savannah?" Patricia asked.

"It's in addition to infrastructure," Meredith said. "Let me fill you in on what I know. Gulfstream, a major Savannah employer, accounts for roughly twenty-five percent of General Dynamics' profits. I found the short interest ratio has recently jumped from under 1% to just over 10%. Someone is betting against General Dynamics. I checked with a friend at the Security & Exchange Commission and found several Chinese banks are the ones shorting the stock. Patricia, whatever is going to happen to Savannah is going to happen soon."

According to Meredith, the catastrophe could happen in mere days. And Patricia didn't have a clue what the threat was. It had to be huge in order to topple Savannah's economy. Possibly mass destruction. But what weapon of mass destruction would they use? Part of her wondered if they'd use an existing weapon, but maybe it was something new. But how could her team stop it if they didn't know what *it* was?

At least the FBI, and who knew what other agencies, was now on the case.

Because she couldn't be certain Algenon had the stock shorting information Meredith had just shared, Patricia called him. He answered right away. "Hello, Algenon. How are thing going today?"

"Well, your discoveries have opened a hornet's nest over here. We've formed a multi-agency task force, and we're uncovering a ton of supporting facts. Now that we're focused, new evidence is coming in hourly. Quite frankly, the scale of the threat is scary." The tension in his voice was distinct.

"Speaking of new evidence, Meredith called me with a big heads-up. Has anyone on your task force been checking the New York Stock Exchange?"

"No. Why?"

"Chinese banks are shorting General Dynamics."

"Oh my."

His obvious concern elevated her stress. "She told me that shorting a stock is something usually done in a tight time frame."

"Correct. Do you have any additional details?"

"Short interest on General Dynamics recently jumped from under one percent to over ten percent."

"Which Chinese banks?"

"She didn't say. I'll check with her."

"That's okay. I'll have someone contact the Securities & Exchange Commission." He exhaled. "It's becoming increasingly clear to me the threat is imminent."

"What have you seen to draw that conclusion?"

"There are an abundance of indicators but more importantly, yesterday the Chinese repositioned one of their spy satellites over Savannah. The Chinese government controls those satellites, so we're now certain this is a Chinese government plan. And as to immediacy, you don't reposition satellite unless you're about to do something."

"Can our Space Force neutralize the satellite?"

"That would be above my pay grade."

"Do you have any idea what kind of threat we're looking for?"

"We don't have a clue."

The whole quagmire weighed heavily on her mind, threating to bog her down. "What's our best move?"

"We keep doing what we've been doing. We put every resource we can on looking for the nature of the threat."

"What if we don't find out in time?"

"Then we'll have to take the hit and scramble to recover as well as possible. To that end, we're positioning emergency response teams at a safe distance from Savannah. Much the same as we do when a major hurricane hit is imminent."

"Let's hope we don't need them, but it's reassuring they will be there."

"Precisely," Algenon said firmly. "Well, if you don't have anything else, I have another task force meeting coming up. Thanks for the heads-up on the shorting."

Following the call, Patricia added the satellite information to her case file, then texted the information to her team, who were working in another room tracking Franklin Chow's business dealings.

The doorbell chimed. She wasn't expecting anyone. Besides, their protocol was that Simon would answer all doorbells. When he didn't come into the kitchen, she went to the dining room, where he sat going through some security footage. "What's up?" she asked.

Simon eyed her with a serious look that told her he was concerned. "Someone put a small, brown box on our doorstep. No address on the box. No obvious markings. Just a taped cardboard box. Are you expecting a delivery?"

"No."

"Okay. Until I know better, we'll treat it as a bomb."

Goosebumps rose on her arms.

Simon keyed his computer. "I just called in the Savannah bomb guys." His computer dinged. "They're on the way."

"How'd the box get there?" she asked.

"Home security video recorded a hooded individual placing the package, but the person's face was fully hidden."

"What do we do?"

"Wait until the bomb squad arrives. If it is a bomb, it's

probably rigged to detonate when it's moved or opened. So I think it's safe just sitting there until they arrive."

"I'll let Timnit and Summer know about the bomb."

Patricia went to the family room and told them about the situation. When Timnit began to stand, Patricia gestured her to sit. "We're supposed to stay put until the bomb squad is done."

Timnit sat.

Patricia sat across from her. "I feel we're looking in the wrong place, and now there's a Chinese satellite over Savannah. What are we missing?" She bit her lip.

When Simon came into the family room, Patricia looked up.

"The bomb guys opened the box and found it empty."

She nodded her understanding.

"I suspect the box was a ploy to see what our defenses were. And because we called the bomb squad, they didn't learn much. They'll probably do some more poking around."

"If the triggering event is as imminent as we and the FBI think, they don't have much time to figure out our defenses."

"Yeah," he said. "At some point soon, they may just walk away and let us be. But I'm not counting on it. We'll stay locked up and vigilant here."

"They're trying to keep us here." Patricia stroked her chin. "Out of the way. What are we not seeing?"

Simon shrugged. "There's nothing we can do other than what we're doing."

"I need to get my mind off our failures."

Simon stepped forward. "We need you to be researching, Patricia, not worrying."

"I don't know what to research."

"I was about to look up the relationship you found between Long Street and the shipbuilding company," Timnit said. "Why don't you do it instead."

Patricia nodded, stood, returned to the kitchen, where her laptop was set up.

Fifteen minutes later, Patricia discovered a Long Street Investment partnership with the China State Shipbuilding Corporation and Carnival Corporation. CSSC owned sixty percent. Long Street and Carnival each owned twenty percent. The company was formed to build and operate a cruise ship terminal in Savannah. Further research indicated the terminal was recently completed and was simply awaiting final inspections. So far, only one cruise line had been granted permission to dock at the facility, Decade Ocean Cruise Line, a private Chinese-owned corporation.

Running down leads, Patricia found some articles about China's plans to dominate the global cruise industry. But that wouldn't require a collapse of Savannah's economy. Quite the opposite. The cruise industry would bring thousands of new jobs to Savannah. Savannah would need a flourishing economy to absorb those jobs. Clearly something else was at play, and whatever it was, it was imminent.

A loud crash from outside the front of the house erupted. Pushing back her panic, Patricia dashed to the dining room, where Simon was keying his computer and pulling up the front security feed again. Timnit and Summer joined them.

"What was that?" Patricia asked.

"Looks like a car accident." Simon's voice was steady and assured.

"Oh my goodness." Summer looked over his shoulder at the screen.

"It looks bad," Simon said. "Probably injuries."

"I'll call 911," Timnit said.

Patricia headed to the front door.

"Don't go outside," Simon said.

"Why?"

"Too much of a coincidence. First the box, now an accident."

"Another test?" Patricia asked.

"Could be," Simon said. "Perhaps a distraction." He brought up the backyard security cameras on his second monitor. He scanned several views, then looked up. "All clear in the back."

Patricia's nerves settled a bit. "Being a target is a nightmare."

"Hold it," Simon said a little too loud. He was hunched over the backyard security video and zooming it in on the black mat outside the back door. A red rectangle was on the mat. He zoomed further. An envelope … addressed to her. He looked up at her. "Don't even think of retrieving that note. I'll get it."

Simon went to the corner where he kept his protective gear, put on his armored vest, and grabbed a rifle. Then, crouched low, he went to the back door, avoiding windows and the door itself, which was filled with small bulletproof windows. From the crouch, he unlatched the deadbolt and inched the door open a bit. Then he quickly reached out and snatched the red envelop. A silenced bullet slammed into the heavy steel doorjamb next to his arm but failed to penetrate. He swung the door shut and flipped the deadbolt.

Timnit charged into the kitchen, rifle in hand.

"Get down!" Simon shouted.

Timnit went down in a crouch. "Are you okay?"

"I'm fine. Clearly there's at least one shooter out there. Now they know we have reinforced the house."

Timnit nodded. "If they're serious, they'll switch to more powerful rounds."

"Yep," Simon said. "We need to close all the curtains and avoid windows without curtains." Simon looked at Patricia, who was crouching in the kitchen doorway. "That means no more sitting at the kitchen table in full view of the outside."

"I'll move my work to an inner room."

Simon made his way back to the dining room, again avoiding the windows. Sweating profusely, he handed the envelope to Patricia.

She opened the envelope, removed the message, and read:

You will die today.

Patricia couldn't move. "I was sitting right here in full view from the backyard. Why didn't they just take a shot at me?"

"They probably assumed the windows were bulletproof," Timnit said.

Patricia reread the note. This wasn't intimidation. It was an outright death sentence. She handed the note to Simon.

He blanched as he read it. "We're officially under siege."

"Trey," she said. "We have to warn Trey. Oh no. What if they target him to get to me?"

"I'll alert Trey," Simon said. "As for Timnit and Summer, it would be best if they stayed here until this was over."

"I think that's what they both were planning on."

"Good," Simon said.

Patricia took a breath. "How does this siege end?"

"They win, or we do," Simon said quietly. "Get your body armor on. And I'm calling in reinforcements."

"If they wanted to send me a message, why didn't they just text me like in the past?"

"It's not about the message," Simon said. "It's about how we handled retrieving the message. Based on the bullet, I'd say they were trying to knock off you or one of your guards. They failed, so now they know we're sharp, and with a single shot, they learned your home is built like a tank. All important information for them to know *before* an assault. Clever people. Hopefully, we're more clever."

"When are the reinforcements coming?" Patricia asked.

Simon looked at his watch. "Soon."

"Retired Rangers?" Timnit asked.

"Yes. An entire team."

"I hope they get here in time."

"If I were going to assault a home, particularly a well-fortified home, I'd do it at night."

"If they can wait—"

"If they can wait," Simon repeated.

"And if they can't wait?"

"You and Summer will be in the safe room, while Timnit and I return fire."

"Can you hold them off?"

"Depends on how many there are. There are only two of us."

Patricia took a deep breath. "I'm not going into the safe room. I want to fight."

"Let's cross that bridge when and if we get there," Simon said. "Right now, I think we all have some urgent research to do."

Crouching low, Patricia gathered her laptop from the kitchen table and went into the curtained family room where Timnit and Summer were already back hard at work. Patricia sat in an upholstered chair in front of the fireplace and resumed her research on the cruise terminal, immediately noticing the newly constructed buildings were well upstream from central Savannah. Suspicion surged. Maybe the so-called terminal was something else as well.

"Timnit, pardon me for interrupting, but can you access architectural plans of newly constructed buildings in Savannah?"

"Sure. Which ones?"

Patricia gave her the information, and a few minutes later Patricia's computer dinged signaling a new email. She clicked on the email and opened the link Timnit provided. Several pages of architectural plans of the terminal came up. She paged through the plans in shock. Not only was it a state-of-the-art cruise terminal, it was also a sizable hotel, a massive multilevel parking garage, and a huge subterranean hurricane shelter.

CHAPTER 30

*P*atricia hurried through the house to her ringing cell and snatched it up.

"Patsy?"

"Trey. Did Simon tell yo—"

"Yes. Are you safe? Unhurt? Simon said you were okay."

"I'm fine. But we're under some kind of siege, I guess. They've come to the front door and the back. You're probably being watched too. You shouldn't come home."

"I can use the tunnels, Patsy. That's what they're there for. I need to see that you're alright with my own eyes. I'm finishing up here and will be out in a couple of minutes."

"Okay. Be careful. I love you."

"I will," he said. "And I love you too."

Next, she called Algenon. "We had a shot fired here. Simon says we're under some sort of a siege. He called in reinforcements."

"What do you mean?"

Patricia gave Algenon the details.

"How can I help?"

"Shut down these guys as soon as possible," she replied.

"We have all our resources on it."

"So do we. By the way, did you know that a cruise line terminal was being built just west of Savannah?"

"I recall hearing something about that. Why?"

"It's a Chinese joint venture, and it's just recently completed. And get this, it includes a huge subterranean hurricane shelter. Maybe it's just a coincidence, but I'm suspicious at it being completed right before a possible collapse of the Savannah economy."

"Maybe the terminal is part of the Chinese government plans following the collapse of our economy," Algenon said. "We've had reports that a Chinese cruise line, Decade Ocean, has received permits to dock their vessels in Jacksonville and Charleston. Their first vessel is scheduled to arrive in Jacksonville next week."

Stunned, Patricia jotted a note about the two docking permits. "That's interesting, because Decade Ocean is the first and only cruise line to have a permit to dock at the new Savannah terminal."

Algenon groaned. "This isn't looking good. You can put several thousand people on a cruise ship. That's a flood of people hitting those ports. And, in the aftermath of a disaster, it could be a much-needed new workforce."

"Wouldn't they need work permits?"

"They would. And guess what? In the past year, there's been a significant surge in applications for work permits at our consulates in China, and because the applicants typically had

substantial assets and important job skills, we've been granting many of the requests."

Patricia's mind swirled. This was such a massive, complex plan, with each element coordinated to come together at a specific time. A time that loomed large. Guilt that she had yet to discover the triggering event rose. Research called. "That's all I have, Algenon."

"The Savannah terminal is quite a revelation. You're doing great work. Keep at it."

"Thank you. So are you. We make a good team."

"I appreciate that, Patricia. And please send me that cruise terminal information in a written report as fast as you can. I don't want anyone questioning that we didn't account for every aspect of what's starting to look like a significant economic destabilization operation."

"I'm finishing it up now."

Patricia disconnected the call, quickly completed the report, and sent it to Algenon.

A short time later, Trey called. "I'm at Sheila's flower shop. About to enter the tunnel."

Relief filled Patricia. Trey would be safer, and the two of them together could do anything. "Where's your car?"

"I left it at work. Took an Uber over. The traffic was terrible with all the tourists in town for the parade. Just a couple more days, and we'll get our town back."

"Good. I'll meet you in the basement." She disconnected the call, told Simon Trey was inbound, and headed downstairs eager to have Trey by her side.

At the bottom of the stairs, Patricia took a sharp inhale. The air was stale. And she wasn't prepared for the utter silence. Her hearing seemed intensified. She could actually hear her heart pounding.

Upstairs, there had been a steady buzz of action. One discovery after another. Endless discussions of what to do next. The basement was another world. Another planet. She went to the east wall, unlocked the door to the historic tunnel that connected her home with so many others, and swung the heavy door open. The faint sound of Trey's shoes on the cobblestone floor accentuated her anticipation. A prickly sensation ran down her arms right to her fingertips.

She stepped into the cool, damp tunnel, looked down the dimly lit expanse, and made out an approaching silhouette. *Trey.* His silver hair shone under the lamps. Her heart sped. Coming face-to-face, she noticed the worry that lined his handsome face. He drew her into a warm embrace.

"Are you okay?" he murmured into her hair.

"Yes," she whispered. This man, this relationship, this feeling were the central parts of her being. "Especially since you're here."

He gave her a squeeze, melting away her fears, bringing her the comfort she so needed, then stepped back. "I'm sorry you've been facing this alone the last week. Let's head upstairs. We need to talk with Simon."

She closed and locked the door to the ancient tunnel, her thoughts still troubled by the threats, and the unknown. "He said he called in the reserves."

"They'll give us plenty of protection, but we need to go on the offensive."

"How do we do that?" she asked as she crossed the basement to the stairs.

"That's what we need to figure out. Fast."

Simon met them at the top of the stairs. The men shook hands, hugged, and slapped each other's backs. Simon led them into the dining room command center.

"What else do you need, Simon?" Trey asked.

"Answers," Simon said.

Trey smiled. "Besides that?"

"You've given us everything we've asked for."

"What's the status of the reinforcements?" Trey asked.

"They're in the neighborhood. Half have set up a perimeter and are deploying anti-intrusion devices. The other half are canvassing neighbors to warn them to stay inside and to solicit security videos that might give us a clue where the shot came from. So far, we're coming up blank."

Summer came into the dining room with Timnit. After they greeted Trey, Summer approached Patricia. "We've exhausted all possible company connections with Franklin Chow. His local holdings are massive but offer no clue to as to a triggering event. However, I went back over our original information-his acquisition of all those historic homes-and I noticed that in the last two days six of the homes transferred to new Chinese owners." Summer gestured to Timnit.

"I checked out the new owners," Timnit said. "Each is a legal immigrant with a work permit or green card. And all are currently living in the Southeast, primarily in Atlanta. No police records."

"Do any of those homes have connecting tunnels?" Patricia asked.

"Yes," Timnit said. "All are on the same tunnel system."

"Good work," Patricia said. "Would y'all check to see if our new owners have made any other property purchases?"

"Already have," Summer said. "Nothing. Just the homes. And before you ask, I checked incorporations and none of the newcomers have any Georgia companies registered in their names."

Algenon called. Patricia put him on speakerphone and briefed him on the title transfers.

"That's an interesting development," Algenon said. "Because I called to let you know the people of Savannah, China, are on the move. A large convoy of twenty buses left the compound an hour ago. We're keeping an eye on the convoy from a satellite. The buses seem to be heading toward Hong Kong. We have assets in Hong Kong that will track the buses once they enter the city."

"Where exactly in Hong Kong are they headed?" Trey asked.

"Don't know yet," Algenon said. "Could be the airport or the ship docks."

"Can we stop the buses?" Trey asked.

"It's too late to set that up," Algenon said. "But we've asked our Hong Kong assets to get as many photos of the individuals as possible, and we'll provide those images to immigration. We may not be able to stop the buses, but we'll try to stop the individuals if they try to come here legally."

Once the call was completed, Summer spoke up. "We're out of leads to check. What do you want us to do?"

Patricia shrugged. "I don't know, and we're running out of time. Simon? Trey? Do either of you have any ideas?"

Both shook their heads.

"The woman with Chow?" Patricia asked.

"Fake name. Fake address," Timnit said.

"The people with phony Georgia licenses?"

"Same," Timnit said.

Patricia turned to Simon. "The woman who followed you?"

"She dropped out of sight. Total dead end."

"Who are we missing?" Patricia's mind whirled. "Wait! Alex Feng. Chow recruited him for some reason. Let's check out any property acquisitions or corporate fillings in Feng's name."

"We're on it," Summer said as she turned to follow Timnit into the family room.

CHAPTER 31

Patricia paced the family room, frequently looking over to Summer and Timnit, who were working feverishly to find everything possible about Alex Feng. Summer was scouring local databases, while Timnit was searching federal databases.

Alex Feng. Patricia's instincts told her Alex was likely the key to what the Chinese government had planned for Savannah. And her instincts were rarely wrong. But how exactly was Alex, a convicted criminal and son of a local patriarch, involved?

If the triggering event had anything to do with the Saint Patrick's Day parade, just seventeen hours away, they didn't have much time to identify and stop whatever was planned. Patricia let out a long breath. So close. Yet so far.

"I found something." Summer's excited voice carried through the otherwise silent room. She looked up from her laptop.

Timnit, sitting on the other end of the sofa from Summer, scooted closer to her teammate.

Trey and Simon came in from the dining room.

"A couple of weeks ago, Alex Feng bought a small, local warehouse," Summer said, her voice tight with excitement. "He doesn't appear to have purchased any other property, before or after. Bank records indicate Alex doesn't have sufficient assets or credit to buy anything substantial. Remember that Franklin Chow wanted Ken Li to make property purchases for him. Assuming Alex was brought on to fulfill this role that Ken refused, then we could say the warehouse purchase was likely on behalf of Chow, who appears to have deep pockets. Not that this purchase was expensive."

"Yes," Patricia said. "Franklin bought expensive homes, an airport, and tens of thousands of acres of undeveloped property. A cheap warehouse is a first. Something unique."

Timnit nodded. "Possibly something strategic."

"Why does he need a small warehouse when he has an empty hanger at his airport?" Patricia wondered aloud.

"Maybe the hanger isn't empty anymore. I can have someone check it out." Trey brought his phone to his ear.

"When we were at the hanger last year, they had exceptionally tight security," Timnit said. "State-of-the-art anti-intrusion electronics. We got in and out undetected, but we had to use stealth technology, and it was pretty hair-raising."

Patricia turned back to Summer. "What do we know about the warehouse?"

"It's old," Summer said. "Constructed in the fifties. Small. Just over three thousand square feet. It's located in a blighted neighborhood. Google Maps photo shows a general state of disrepair."

"What's the address?" Patricia asked.

Summer gave her the information.

Patricia keyed the information into her laptop, then straightened in shock. "It's just a block from the parade route. We need to find out what, if anything, is in that facility."

Timnit frowned. "If what's in the warehouse is important to their plan, the terrorists are certain to have heavy duty security. At least the level we saw at the hanger, possibly more."

"You got around it last year," Simon added.

"Can the FBI get a search warrant?" Summer asked.

"Not without probable cause," Patricia responded.

"This is national security," Summer said. "What more probable cause would they need?"

Patricia closed her laptop. "Good point. I think we should give the FBI a chance to handle this."

Trey ended his call and put his phone in his pocket. "The FBI bureaucracy will slow this to a crawl."

"Algenon knows how to cut red tape," Patricia said. "I've seen him in action. He's mobilizing. He formed a task force. And, heaven knows, the FBI has the local manpower, assets, and training to quickly handle a raid like this."

Patricia placed the call.

"You have an update?" Algenon said by way of greeting. Patricia was grateful they worked together so well.

"I do. We believe we've found something important that needs further investigation that's beyond our authority and means."

"I'm all ears," Algenon said.

Patricia explained the situation to him, gave him the address, and sent him the evidence.

"We'll definitely look into that right away."

"Will you let me know what you find?"

"Better yet," Algenon said. "Once we get the warrant, I'll text you a link, and you can watch as we check it out. It's the least I can do for you and your team."

Patricia's heart surged. "Much appreciated, Algenon."

Patricia disconnected the call and shared the news with her team.

A HALF HOUR LATER, PATRICIA RECEIVED A TEXT FROM Algenon with a URL and a message that transmissions were about to start. Apparently, Algenon had no problem getting a search warrant.

Simon brought the FBI channel up on a large monitor in the dining room. The five of them sat around one end of the dining room table in front of the monitor. The current shaky view was from a hovering drone, showing the front of the warehouse in full color. A shiver went through Patricia at seeing the suspect building live.

The warehouse was a small, shabby, one-story building with no windows, a loading bay to the left and a door to the right. The mildewed exterior was run-down, the roof sagged, and the driveway needed repairs.

The screen flickered, and a more stable overhead view came on. Patricia scanned the screen. Two people, each tagged with a number, approached the building from the front. One by one, their bodycam videos took over the top of the screen like a Zoom meeting, only this was an FBI raid.

The main view shifted to a bodycam at the front door. There was a loud, extended knock on the door. Nobody appeared. "FBI. FBI. FBI," someone shouted moments later. "We're coming in."

There was a loud crash as a ram shattered the door lock. Patricia stiffened in shock. The door swung open. As the two bodycams went through the doorway and entered the darkness, anticipation filled Patricia.

Overhead lights flashed on, revealing a small, grungy office with a dusty steel desk, a five-drawer file cabinet, and two dilapidated office chairs. One by one, the bodycams left the office for the warehouse proper.

One bodycam cleared a restroom by the office, then joined the other entering the rest of the warehouse. A bodycam with night vision found a light switch panel. A gloved hand flipped the switches. Patricia steeled her nerves.

Lights came on in the larger room. The sight intrigued Patricia. Dozens of large cardboard boxes with Chinese markings on pallets. One box per pallet. Each looked to be three or four feet cubed. Big boxes. From China. Patricia's heart hammered.

"Can you read those markings, Simon?" Patricia asked, realizing her mouth was dry.

"Long Novelty Company. Gwang Cho. China. One thousand pieces," Simon said.

One of the bodycams showed a box being opened. The inside was stuffed with long, green stadium horns. Musical novelties, of all things. The kind vendors sold at sports events and parades. Quite innocent. The agent dug down through the box, discovering even more horns, but nothing else. Another box was opened revealing the same contents.

"It's just tacky stuff to sell to tourists at the parade," one of the agents said. "I see them sell this stuff every year."

A different bodycam went to the left side of the warehouse, where a dozen pushcarts were parked. Again, vendors selling Chinese-sourced trinkets from pushcarts was quite normal at the parade.

Another bodycam veered to the right, where a huge fabric covered dragon head was placed along with a pile of brightly colored fabric. Patricia guessed it was a dragon dance outfit. She recalled it from the previous year's parade. Two people operated the head. Ten people made up the massive body.

Patricia felt embarrassed that the warehouse had been a

wild-goose chase. This was her shot with the FBI, and she had blown it.

As the FBI agents left the warehouse, the failure to find anything suspicious hung in the air unchallenged.

But concern rose within her. Concern that the agents had overlooked something. After all, they hadn't opened all the boxes. They hadn't searched every nook and cranny. As what-ifs spun in Patricia's mind, she became more sure they'd missed something important. She paced the room.

As dangerous as it might be, she wanted desperately to go to the warehouse and have a look for herself. Perhaps, with her eagle eyes, she'd find something the agents had over-looked. But she couldn't legally enter the building without permission. She stopped pacing.

If they were wrong, and hadn't looked properly, the whole fate of Savannah could be in her hands. Hers and her team. Which, she glanced over at her dear husband, also included Trey. Whose work with the Cotton Coalition meant he would understand how she was feeling.

Trey caught her eye. "What is it, Patsy?"

She chewed her lip.

"You think they missed something, don't you?"

"I do. I need to take a closer look at that building."

Trey frowned. "That's too dangerous."

"The FBI says the warehouse doesn't have anything suspicious, so there should be no danger in me taking a look."

"But—"

"There was no one at the warehouse when the FBI went there," Patricia said. "Do you think the terrorists would leave the key to their plan unprotected? No. Going to the ware-house is only dangerous if there's something there the terrorists want to protect. Something the FBI didn't find. And the agents are probably right. But maybe there's a clue in that warehouse, one that only I would recognize. Those agents haven't been sleeping and breathing this threat for weeks. They don't have a best friend locked away in a safe house. Heck, they probably don't even know that the whole fate of Savannah might rest in their hands. Who knows if the stakes have been shared with them. It has to be me that goes in next." Patricia paused, her heart pounding.

Timnit stood. "I'll go with you."

Trey let out a defeated sigh, then nodded. "Use the tunnel to leave here. Wear body armor. Use comms to stay in touch with us. I'll alert the Rangers."

After looking over the front of the old warehouse, Patricia and Timnit edged wordlessly around the weed-strewn right side. From there, they saw an alley and a gravel parking lot behind the building. They paused at the back right. Patricia glanced around the corner. Her heart leapt. There was a black, late-model Ford pickup behind the building, backed in next to an open door.

She took a calming breath. "There's someone here," she whispered to Timnit, sure her communications microphone picked up the message.

Timnit nodded, then pointed to her chest, then the truck.

Patricia nodded her understanding that Timnit would check out the truck. Patricia pointed to herself and the back door.

Timnit nodded and mouthed, "But don't go in alone."

As soon as Patricia dipped her chin, they both took off, guns ready.

Unease surged as Patricia approached the back door. She tightened her grip on her pistol.

At the door, she pressed herself against the wall and took a quick glance at Timnit, who was at the truck. Timnit flashed a thumbs-up. "Pickup and open door at rear," she whispered into her comm microphone.

Patricia quickly returned her attention to the open door. Gun up, she peered in. The lights were on. Her vision focused. There were the pallets with the familiar cardboard boxes. Just inside the door were six one-gallon gasoline containers. She reached in and lifted one. Full. She stepped back against the wall. "Six full gasoline containers just inside the open door," she whispered.

Timnit joined her beside the door.

Patricia indicated she'd go in toward the left, and Timnit should go to the right.

They both rechecked their weapons, took a deep breath, and stepped in. Patricia spun left. The huge dragon head loomed ahead of her. Patricia's breath caught. The dragon head was pushed to the side, revealing a large refrigerator with its door open. A refrigerator the FBI hadn't seen. But Patricia didn't have time to feel happiness that her hunch to recheck the warehouse had been correct because a slender, dark-haired woman stood at the refrigerator removing a cardboard box with both hands. No weapon in sight.

Patricia scanned left and right. She didn't see anyone. "There's a person in here," Patricia whispered into her comms.

"Roger. One person," Timnit responded.

Patricia slowly, silently closed the distance until she was twenty feet from the suspect.

The woman shut the refrigerator door and, box in hand, turned for the back door. Her eyes widened on seeing Patricia.

Patricia recognized her as the woman they knew as Raylee Peng. Gooseflesh rose on Patricia's skin. She leveled the gun on the Chinese agent. "Put the box down!" Patricia commanded.

Keeping her eyes on Patricia, Raylee squatted and slowly placed the box on the concrete floor.

"Kneel and put your hands on your head," Patricia directed.

But Raylee's hand left the box, produced a knife, and flung the blade at Patricia.

Patricia spun to avoid the knife but managed to get off three deafening shots. The blade hit her body armor at rib level and fell to the floor. Patricia kicked the dragon knife away, guessing they'd found Ken's killer.

"On the floor, now." Patricia advanced on the assassin, who cradled her wounded right arm. Adrenalin coursed through Patricia's bloodstream. The aftershocks traveled up her arms, making them shake a bit.

Timnit fanned to the side, her gun also trained on the woman.

Raylee groaned as she tried to rise.

"Get down!" Patricia shouted. "And stay down."

Raylee flattened, arms outstretched. Blood spewed from her right biceps.

Timnit came around Patricia and patted the woman down. "No other weapons. No comms. No ID."

The door at the front of the warehouse banged open. Footsteps pounded on the concrete.

Gun up, Patricia spun toward the intruders.

As Trey, Simon and Summer surged into Patricia's view, she lowered her gun. "Thank goodness you're here."

"We came as soon as you mentioned the pickup truck and open door," Trey said. "We figured you might need some backup. But it looks like, as usual, you have everything under control." Trey glanced at the bleeding woman whimpering in pain on the floor. "What's going on there?"

Patricia gestured toward Raylee. "Apparently, she's one of the conspirators. And she may be the assassin who killed Ken. She was removing a box from the refrigerator. As soon as she saw me, she threw that knife at me. Thank goodness for my armored vest."

"So you shot her?"

Patricia nodded. "I didn't know what else she had up her sleeve."

"Okay. Timnit, cover the back," Trey said. "Summer, cover the woman. Simon, take the front. And I'll get us some additional help just in case." Trey made a quick call and pocketed the phone. "Okay, Patsy, where do we start?"

"The cardboard box seemed important to her, so let's see what it contains."

Patricia put the box on a nearby pushcart, lifted the cardboard flaps, and stepped back in shock. It was filled with small bottles with a water-white liquid. *Poison?* The assassin had killed Kenwith poison. "Does anyone have evidence gloves?"

Simon handed her a pair.

She slipped them on, then removed a bottle. "What do the markings on this box say, Simon?"

"Three Dragons Pharmaceutical Company," Simon said. "Keep refrigerated. One hundred units."

She handed the bottle to Simon, who had just put on gloves. "What about the label?"

"Experimental product five, nine, seven, two. Batch seventy-four." He handed the bottle back to her.

"Any idea what's in the bottle?" she asked.

"It looks like a vaccine bottle," Simon said.

Patricia looked closer at the bottle. "But why would they have a vaccine in here?"

"The only reason to have a vaccine is to protect against a virus," Simon said.

"Oh my gosh," Patricia said. "We have the solution, but not the problem. I need to talk with Yuliam to get to the root of this."

Patricia went to Raylee. "Is the virus here?"

She gave Patricia a sly smile. "You won't stop us. You can't stop us."

"If she's triad," Simon said, "she's not going to talk."

Patricia whipped out her phone, photographed the label, and texted the image to Yuliam at the Centers for Disease Control. Then she called the doctor.

"Hello, Patricia. Your cats are okay."

"Thank you, Yuliam. But that's not why I'm calling. We

just discovered a box with bottles of white liquid that might be part of a plot to bring harm to Savannah tomorrow."

"Oh my."

"I just sent you a photo of the label on the off chance it might mean something to you. It's in Chinese."

"Sure. I have several colleagues fluent in Chinese dialects. Okay. I just received the image."

Patricia waited for a response.

Moments later, Yuliam returned to the phone. "It appears to be an experimental vaccine produced by Three Dragons Pharmaceutical Company in China. I'm familiar with the company."

"Hold on," Patricia said. "I'd like to patch the FBI in on this call."

"Okay."

Patricia called Algenon and filled him in. "Okay, Yuliam. I have Algenon Melfive, resident agent in charge for the Savannah FBI office, on this call. Go ahead with what the label says."

"The company on this label does work on biologicals for the Chinese military. The product identification number is in our surveillance database. It purports to be a bird flu vaccine. We know it was tested in humans, but we've never acquired a sample of the vaccine."

"Bird flu?"

"Yes. We know the Chinese military have active research programs to weaponize bird flu, but we haven't heard of any significant successes. If they have succeeded, they'd need to have a vaccine to protect their troops. Mind you, the existence of a vaccine doesn't mean they've succeeded."

"Well, we have the vaccine here. Lots of it. But we haven't got the biological. What does weaponized bird flu look like?"

"Probably a fine white powder."

"How much powder would it take to infect a thousand people?"

"Depends on the strength of the flu strain, but it wouldn't take much. All they would need to do is get it into a person's respiratory system."

"How would they disperse it?"

"It would be ideal to disperse it directly into people's faces."

"So we should be looking for packages of white powder?"

"Yes. And a way of dispersing it."

"Thank you, Yuliam."

"Be safe, Patricia. And hang on to all the vaccine. We'll want to analyze it."

"Okay everyone!" Patricia called, her voice breaking with nervous tension. "These bottles are a vaccine, which means there's a virus about to be unleashed. Doctor Rojas says the best way to disperse the virus would be as a powder. We don't know where it is or how they plan to disperse it. If it's not in this warehouse, we and Savannah are doomed. If it is here, we need to find it. Now!"

Patricia directed Timnit to stay with Raylee, Summer and Simon to search one end of the room, and her and Trey would search the other.

"Since we don't know what we're looking for, be thorough, but careful. We don't want to accidently unleash it."

Each team hurried to the search. Patricia approached the vendor carts, while Trey began feeling along the huge dragon head and its voluminous fabric.

"This dragon will be full of a team wearing it and dancing through the crowd," Trey said. "If I were diabolically minded, I'd choose something like this, but I'm not finding anything." Frustration leeched into his tone.

"Keep looking," Patricia said. "Leave no seam, no corner,

no nook unexamined. And, Trey, how long until we get those reinforcements?"

"I hope soon. We're sitting ducks in this place while we look."

A couple of minutes later, Patricia let out a frustrated sigh. Nothing left but a bunch of novelties. She scooted over to the large cardboard box that had been opened earlier and looked inside. Nothing jumped out at her. Just yard-long, green plastic horns. A ton of them. Toys.

She carefully picked up one of the horns and examined it. No powder. She peered into the large end of the tube but couldn't see through the horn. She put it back down and looked around, her heart pounding and her stomach tying itself into knots. What if they couldn't stop this? Think. A respiratory virus needed… She opened her eyes on the horns again.

"Trey. Do you have your Leatherman knife?"

Trey hurried over, holding it out. "What are you thinking?"

But Patricia was already carefully slicing into the horn a few inches from the small mouthpiece.

And there it was.

A small vial of white powder.

"Oh my goodness." Trey's voice floated through her shock. And then he was yelling. "She found it! You were right, Patsy. Where in devil's name is our backup?"

Simon ran over to corroborate the discovery. "About to enter in seconds."

Patricia gestured to the pallets surrounding them, her voice shaking. "There must be tens of thousands of those lethal horns in this warehouse."

"Yes. But you found them in time, Patsy. You found them." Trey wrapped Patricia in his arms, and she sagged against him.

Two weeks later

The Savannah Saint Patrick's Day parade was long over. It had been a joyous celebration, not the tragedy the Chinese government had planned.

Patricia, Timnit, Meredith and Summer had watched the parade on television in the air-conditioned comfort of Summer's Jones Street home. Trey had hosted his annual parade party on Falcon Square just across the street from his law office. Algenon Melfive and Chief Patrick had attended Trey's party, along with many of Trey's biggest clients. Cora and her entire family had watched the parade on televisions spread throughout Cora's penthouse.

Now Patricia sat on a park bench in Falcon Square, dressed in a pink Lilly Pulitzer shift. It was a beautiful, sunny day without a cloud in the sky, though it was hard to tell in the dense shade cast by the massive oak canopy. The air was mild and there was a slight cooling breeze that ruffled the Spanish moss hanging like grey curtains from the oaks. Huge pink and red azalea bushes, so typical of Savannah's city squares, were still in full bloom.

Algenon, dressed casually in faded jeans and a short-sleeved, white button-down, approached with two takeout cups of coffee. Patricia stood and greeted him. He handed her a coffee and they sat. He took a long draw of coffee, then gestured to the surroundings. "But for you, this could have been much different."

"We were lucky."

His eyebrows raised. "It wasn't luck. You followed your instinct. That's what makes you such a talented investigator."

"Thank you, Algenon. That means a lot. How are the cases going?"

"Chatham Police have charged Raylee Peng with Ken Li's murder. After finding video of her entering and leaving the hotel around the time of the murder, along with all the other evidence, they feel they now have a strong case. Though it's still early."

"Is she getting any legal help from the Chinese government?"

"No. They've disavowed her," he said with a roll of his eyes.

"How about her family?"

"They've also disowned her and, as restitution for her crimes, offered a million-dollar grant to the Savannah Design Academy, which was wisely turned down." Algenon took another drink of coffee. "And three Chinese students suddenly left the academy and returned to China."

She wondered how many others had been in Savannah, how many remained. "What about Franklin Chow?"

Algenon gave a smirk. "We finally apprehended Chow, and Alex Feng, a few days ago in Miami trying to board a flight to Cuba."

She breathed a sigh of relief at the news.

"We've charged them with conspiracy to commit terrorism, and both are being held at ADX Florence awaiting trial.

Feng is talking, and we hope Chow will soon be talking as well. We're processing warrants to seize all of Chow's assets, and the City of Savannah is negotiating with the Chinese government to purchase the recently completed cruise terminal."

"Were you able to locate Kenneth Kwok, the dragon master who threatened Ken Li?"

Algenon let out a long breath. "Not yet. But thanks to the Li's security system, we have excellent photos, audio, biometrics of him. He's now in every wanted database we have."

"How about the six people from Atlanta who purchased local homes from Chow right before the parade?"

"They passed through TSA security at the Detroit Airport enroute to Toronto late the same day we apprehended Raylee Peng. Canadian immigration has records of their arrival, but no exit from Canada. The Atlanta six may still be in Canada, or they may have exited under aliases. Their data is now in all our databases in case they ever try to re-enter our country."

"What about the bird flu?"

"The virus and vaccine samples were a treasure trove for the CDC. They now have a much better idea of the current state of Chinese research in both areas and are developing countermeasures."

"Do you think the Chinese government will try again?"

"We think we got their primary weapon. They repositioned their spy satellite away from Savannah, and the bus convoy of people from Savannah, China, has returned to their training base. But we know they think long-term, and I have no question Savannah is still on their radar." He grimaced. "For the time being we don't think there's an imminent threat, but we've notified other port cities of what occurred here."

"That's reassuring. I'm so relieved." Patricia's fingers

smoothed the already perfectly pressed hem of her dress. "So, ah, does this mean I have to return my FBI credentials?" She held her breath.

Algenon assessed her with a twinkle in his eye, then shook his head. "No. I think it's in our best interest to keep a civilian investigator with your impressive talent on retainer. If you wish?"

"I do," she said softly.

He tilted his head. "By the way, Patricia, how are your cats?"

"Safe and sound. Just like Savannah on this beautiful day."

The End

SAVANNAH

Med

VIGILANTES FOR JUSTICE — BOOK FIVE

ALAN CHAPUT

SAVANNAH MED

Vigilantes For Justice Book Four

Alan Chaput

ONE

Patricia Falcon was rearranging the heirloom Thanksgiving swag on her mantel when her cell chimed. *Isabel Alton.* Patricia paused, trying to recall if she had any unfinished legal business with her attorney. But none came to mind.

Suddenly, Patricia's breath caught. Had something happened to Isabel's father? Lucius had been battling stage-four cancer for almost a year. "Hello, Isabel," Patricia said. "How are you?"

"Not well." Isabel's voice sounded strained.

Patricia stiffened. "Oh. I'm *so* sorry. Is … is Lucius okay?"

"He's … well." Isabel sniffed. "I'd rather talk in person, Patricia. I know it's early in the morning and short notice, but … but could you come over?"

"Of course."

"My house. Not my office."

Except for social events, Isabel, a very private person, never saw anyone at home. And the urgency in Isabel's voice spoke volumes. This was not to be a social visit. "I'll be right over."

It was raining when Patricia parked her Navigator in front of Isabel's home, one of the many meticulously restored houses in Savannah's acclaimed historic district. Patricia stepped out of her SUV, popped an umbrella, and dashed to Isabel's immense wrap-around front porch. Just as she closed the umbrella, one of the etched glass doors opened to reveal a somber-faced Isabel. Her grey hair was mostly pulled back, and she was dressed in tattered jeans and a loose white t-shirt. Her face was void of makeup. Despite knowing Isabel for years, Patricia had never seen her dressed so casually or looking so disheveled.

Patricia's heart sank as she leaned the umbrella against the doorframe. She embraced Isabel, feeling tiny as she was enveloped by Isabel's tall and large-boned body.

"Thank you for coming over," Isabel said, sustaining the hug.

"Anytime." Patricia stroked her friend's back.

Isabel led Patricia to a Victorian sitting room just off the large foyer. A beautiful Tiffany chandelier provided illumination. Rain pounded on the floral-chintz-covered windows.

Elizabeth, Isabel's housekeeper, appeared.

"Would you care for some tea?" Isabel asked.

"Yes. Please."

"My guest will have some PG Tips tea, Elizabeth."

Elizabeth left to fetch the tea.

Patricia gave Isabel a heart-felt smile. "Thank you for remembering my favorite brand."

"That's what friends do." Isabel gestured toward an antique settee.

Isabel and Patricia sat facing each other.

Elizabeth returned with tea and placed the silver service tray on an antique mahogany coffee table in front of them. Once Elizabeth left, Isabel served. The process seemed to bring Isabel some comfort.

Patricia took the offered cup. "Thank you." Patricia sipped tea and returned her cup to the saucer more or less in tandem with Isabel. Then Patricia raised her eyebrows to encourage conversation.

Isabel took a sheet of paper from the end table beside her. "I think Lucius may have been conned into a shady deal that could kill him."

"Oh no. What kind of deal?"

"Medical fraud." Isabel handed the paper to Patricia. It was a photocopy of an advertisement for Magnum Oncology, a local cancer treatment clinic often featured in glitzy local television ads. The photocopied ad featured a claim for guaranteed, groundbreaking cancer treatments.

"Why do you think there's fraud?"

"Magnum has been giving Lucius daily infusions for a month. And, apparently, they didn't work." Isabel's hazel eyes narrowed. "Totally useless and outrageously expensive."

"Perhaps they take some time to produce results. Are his treatments done?"

"Yes. And because the infusion didn't work at all, they're switching him to another, even more expensive drug."

Patricia felt her eyebrows pinch together. "What about Medicare? Surely Medicare covers cancer treatments."

"His insurance said Magnum's treatments weren't FDA approved, so they wouldn't cover any of his treatments and won't cover the next one. Something about that doesn't seem right. I'd like you to check Magnum out?"

Patricia gnawed her lower lip. "Why don't you use the Cotton Coalition to investigate Magnum? You're the head of the Coalition. They have far more resources and contacts than I do."

Isabel seemed to bow over the weight of her worry. "That's a good question. The Cotton Coalition has great lawyers like your husband and ex-doctors like Beau Simpson, so they could easily investigate Magnum. However, if the Cotton Coalition got involved, my father would certainly to find out," Isabel said in a slightly disapproving voice. "Until I'm absolutely certain Magnum is running a fraud, I don't want my father to know about the investigation. If he found out, he'd go ballistic. He thinks Doctor Gryoti is a medical genius. It's common knowledge that a patient's confidence in his doctor greatly affects his attitude, and a positive attitude has been shown to increase the odds of whipping cancer. Lucius can't know until we're sure. That is why I called you."

"I appreciate your faith in me." Patricia straightened. "What do you have on Magnum?"

"Just suspicions. I'm not certain anything is wrong. In fact, I'd be delighted if you determined Magnum Oncology was totally legitimate. But the information about the clinic on the internet is spotty, my father's treatments didn't work, and I'm suspicious."

"Are you sure you want to do this? If I find Magnum is a fraud, it will take that glimmer of hope from your father."

"He's a reasonable man, and he's dying. He's running out of time. He can't afford to waste a week or a month on ineffective treatments."

"Okay." Patricia took Isabel's hand. "Anything else?"

"Please be discreet in your work, Patricia. I *do not* want this to get back to my father."

"I understand."

"Thank you for rushing right over."

"My pleasure." Patricia leaned in and gave Isabel a hug.

"By the way, would you and Lucius like to join Trey and I for the Thanksgiving buffet at the Hyatt?"

Isabel leaned back, pinched the bridge of her nose, then looked up. "I'd love to, Patricia, but with all the treatments Lucius is highly vulnerable to infection. So we don't go out. Doctor's orders." Isabel stood. "I've arranged for catering. Thank you so much for thinking of us."

Patricia put the photocopy in her purse, stood and walked with Isabel to the front door.

"Thank you for your understanding," Isabel said.

"Twenty years of friendship, Isabel. We'll figure this one out just like we always have."

Patricia sat in her Navigator for a moment before starting the engine. She loved investigation but, even more, she took great pride in turning a solid case over to the authorities. This one was different. Poor Lucius. If he was simply the recipient of bad luck that these last resort treatments didn't work, that would be one thing. But to think Lucius could be the target of some unscrupulous charlatan cashing in on a dying man's last hope, made her blood boil.

She didn't have a clue on how to go about investigating possible medical fraud. Where to start? Well, she'd learned long ago to call in experts when she was out of her element. And the best physician, actually ex-physician, she knew, Isabel had already mentioned, Beau Simpson. Patricia called Beau and arranged to see him on the way home.

Ten minutes later, Patricia parked her SUV in the public garage across the street from Beau's new employer, a printing company. She took the elevator to ground level, crossed the street and entered the stark commercial building where she identified herself to a security guard.

Moments later, a young lady came into the lobby. "Mr. Simpson will see you now."

Patricia followed the woman down a dingy linoleum tiled hall to the entrance to Beau's office.

The girl gestured Patricia to enter.

Patricia stepped into a sparsely furnished, harshly lit office.

Beau, dressed in khakis and a short-sleeved white shirt, stood in front of a simple steel desk that had seen better days. He looked heavier and harder than the last time she'd seen him. No doubt the result of his year in prison. And his dark brown hair was even longer than she remembered. "So nice of you to stop by." Beau extended his hand. After shaking Patricia's hand, he led her to a small conference table and held her chair while she sat. Always the gentleman.

"How have you been, Beau?" Patricia asked.

He nodded slowly. "I'm doing okay. Thanks to Trey and the Cotton Coalition, I landed a well-paying product management job with a pharmaceutical company after prison. It's not a physician position, but it pays the bills while I try to get my medical license back. How are you doing, Patricia?"

"Empty-nesting has been a challenge for us, but we're doing well."

Beau stroked his wide, tapered chin. "So. You're interested in Magnum Oncology?"

"Yes. What do you know about them?"

"Doctor Gryoti is a reputable oncologist. If I had cancer, I wouldn't hesitate to go to him. He has an outstanding traditional medical education and is board certified. Also, he's been at the forefront of several so-called promising non-traditional cancer treatments," Beau said in a steady voice. "And in lieu of traditional treatments, I'm told he offers many of his patients the opportunity to participate in clinical trials of non-FDA approved drugs *he* deems appropriate for them." Beau paused, focusing on his hands now resting on the table. "It's scientifically responsible to conduct carefully controlled human trials of these experimental drugs. But there is no real scientific evidence that those non-approved drugs in his trials are effective or totally safe. That's why companies do clinical trials and why all the subjects have to volunteer."

Patricia showed Beau a recent Magnum Oncology advertisement. "What do you think of this ad?"

Beau's brow furrowed as his dark brown eyes scanned the photocopy. "I wouldn't advertise that way, if I advertised at all. However, I've heard Magnum Oncology has all the business they can handle and are recruiting additional oncologists."

"What specifically don't you like about the ad?"

Beau looked more closely at the copy. "It's retailing medicine. It's claiming to be the best cancer center which is fine if that's what they believe. But it's also falsely claiming to get results others don't get. Guaranteed results. Drug results can't be guaranteed. There are too many variables. I definitely think the ad is misleading."

"But the Magnum ad works."

Beau nodded. "From what I've heard, it definitely works to get more people through the door."

"Why doesn't Medicare cover Magnum's treatments?"

Beau eyes widened. "Insurance companies should cover FDA approved treatments that are medically indicated and prescribed by a licensed doctor. But, typically, people involved in clinical trials are only charged for the doctor's time, if even that, not the drugs. Could there be some confusion on whether they are participating in a clinical trial with an unproven treatment? What's going on, Patricia?"

Patricia wished she could tell Beau everything, but she'd told Isabel she'd keep her investigation discrete to avoid problems with Lucius. "A friend of mine was treated unsuccessfully at Magnum, and his insurance won't cover the infusions nor a proposed additional treatment."

"Insurance companies won't pay if the meds aren't FDA approved or if they don't feel the medication is necessary, even if it's FDA approved."

"That's why I'm looking into his case." Patricia leaned forward. "Do you think this could be classified as medical fraud?"

"I'm not a lawyer so you should talk with Trey about the legal aspects of what constitutes fraud. From a physician's standpoint, I could be guilty of fraud if I knowingly mislead a patient about a treatment or a drug. And I'd certainly be guilty if the patient relied on my false statements, and I charged them for the treatment." Beau took a breath. "Now the courts have held that if I sugar-coat or puff up a treatment that's not fraud if my statements are minor misrepresentations. In addition, to be fraudulent the misrepresentations must have been a significant factor in the patient's decision to participate in the treatment or use the drug."

"This sounds quite technical," Patricia said.

Beau shrugged. "It can be. But it can also be pretty simple. Back in 2019, a California physician was indicted for selling a pineapple extract as a cancer cure despite the lack of any clinical trials proving the claim. Whether or not it worked was moot."

"So, the key point is whether or not the treatment has been FDA approved so everyone knows it may work on most people, not necessarily all?"

Beau nodded. "The only exception to that is for patients participating in clinical trials. In that case the treatment is, by definition, unproven. To protect themselves, after a physician discusses participation in a clinical trial with a patient, they generally have each patient sign an informed consent form that fully describes the risks and benefits of the product and the terms of the patient's participation."

"How can I tell if a cancer treatment has been proven to work?"

"The National Cancer Institute and others publish lists on the internet of the drugs approved by the FDA for specific types of cancer. They're totally searchable."

"Is there anything else I should know?" Patricia asked.

Beau's face tightened. "Just a warning to be careful. Big, successful practices like Magnum Oncology don't take criticism lightly. If you go after them, they're likely to push back hard. And, if they're knowingly engaging in fraud, they'll probably hit you with everything they can. In a word, Patricia, investigating Magnum could get expensive in lawyer fees and might even become *dangerous*."

End of preview of 'Savannah Med'
Coming 2024

Sign up for my new release newsletter at https://www. AlanChaput.com for an email notification when *Savannah Med* becomes available.

ACKNOWLEDGMENTS

First and foremost, I'm grateful to you for reading *Savannah Dragon* and hope you enjoyed it. You are the reason I write.

Thank you to the reviewers and bloggers who've so generously spread the word about *Savannah Dragon*, and who've taken the time to give readers an opinion about it.

Thank you to my wonderful critique partners, Natasha Boyd and Dave McDonald. Their editing, advice, and brainstorming helped me eliminate slow and irrelevant passages and challenged me to further strengthen relevant scenes.

Thank you to my beta reader, Amy Coury, who read a final draft and pointed out several errors.

And finally, thank you to my editor, Elizabeth A. White, who not only improved my writing, grammar, and punctuation, but also fact-checked everything from law details to all things Savannah.

As you can see, it takes a team to produce a book, and I'm very grateful to be on this one.

ABOUT THE AUTHOR

Alan Chaput writes Southern mysteries. His novels have finaled in the Daphne and the Claymore. Al lives with his wife in Coastal South Carolina. When not writing, Al can be found Shag dancing, pursuing genealogy, or interacting on social media.

BOOKS BY ALAN CHAPUT

1. *Savannah Sleuth* (2017)

2. *Savannah Secrets* (2018)

3. *Savannah Justice* (2019)

4. *Savannah Dragon* (2023)

5. *Savannah Med* (coming 2024)

6. *Savannah Christmas* (coming 2025)